I0635693

Whippoorwill Hill

by

Jules Parker

Dedication

This one is for Mr. Wonderful. You lucky devil.

Praise for Jules Parker

"The last place Marcelina wants to go is her only chance at freedom. Can she do what needs to be done, especially when all she wants to do is kiss her sexy lawyer, Walker? Bygones Be Damned is an addictive romantic suspense. The dialogue and romantic tension are reason enough to read Bygones Be Damned. Throw in descriptive narration, dangerous situations, and characters so real, they leap from the page, and you'll start to see why I couldn't put down Bygones Be Damned.

"Let's talk about these characters. Marcelina has her back to the wall. Facing serious jail time, she hires the best lawyer she can. She's instantly attracted to him, but what woman could resist his charm. To save her own skin, she cuts a deal. What happens next is a gripping plot with an eye-opening ending.

"Walker is a sexy-as-sin lawyer who's used to clients keeping secrets. But his latest client has him tied up in knots. Can he get her off while protecting her at the same time?

"This is my first time reading Jules Parker. She impressed me with her writing skills and ability to build romantic tension while amping up the suspense. I look forward to reading more from her."

~ *N.N. Light's Book Heaven, 5 stars for* Bygones Be Damned

Chapter 1

A rumble penetrated Leslie Downing's dreams, forcing her eyes open in the damp, midnight heat. All was dark. Quiet. She twisted around and blinked bleary-eyed at the gauzy drapes flapping against the open window of her bedroom. Distant sounds of heavy construction equipment caught the wind just enough to indicate what had interrupted her sleep. "Assholes," she mumbled before taking a fistful of her sweaty camisole, peeling it away from her skin and rolling over. As her eyes drifted closed once again, another rumble resonated through the walls of her bedroom.

Only this rumble was coming from the front door below her, and it was most certainly a knock.

She picked up her phone and checked the time. 1:52 in the damned morning. Since her sheets were bunched up at the foot of her bed, she rolled off and reached for her silk pajama pants. She slipped them on along with the pair of flip-flops she kept close by to protect her bare feet against the scuffed wood floors.

Another round of knocks came from below. Despite her petite frame, her footsteps banged through the old farmhouse as if she were a three-hundred-pound linebacker. Downstairs, she crossed the living room and approached the front door where she grabbed a sweater from the coatrack. As she slipped her arms through the sleeves, she flipped on the porch light and checked the peephole. A policeman stood on her front porch, his body twisted away as he swept the nearby woods behind him with the wide beam of his flashlight.

Police? The fog began to clear out of Leslie's eyes. She slid the chain aside and unlocked the deadbolt. Opened the door about six inches. "Yes?"

The officer was full-frontal now, his flashlight going back in his utility belt as he gave her a sober nod. "Sorry to bother you, Ma'am. We've been ordered to evacuate the immediate area due to a gas leak. I'm afraid you're going to have to leave the premises."

He had a thin beard and medium brown hair that curled out from beneath a low, POLICE ball cap. Not as groomed as most cops, she thought, but she guessed his age to be in the late thirties or early forties. Probably had some experience behind those serious, hooded eyes of his, enough to give him clout in a small town like Rosemont, Kansas. He certainly wore the uniform as if he'd been born in it.

"Leave?" She cleared the sleep from her throat. "Gas leak?"

"Construction crews ruptured a gas line."

Of course they did. The road going in a couple miles southeast of the house, at the other end of her uncle's new property, seemed to be a round-the-clock operation. No better time for a mistake like that than in the middle of the night. "Is that what caused my house to shake a bit ago?"

He nodded. "Everyone within a two-mile radius is under mandatory evacuation."

"You're kidding me. It's *two* in the morning."

His mouth thinned, an indication that she needed to reprioritize her concerns, and soon so that he could move on to the next property. "Is there someone you can stay with?" he asked.

Leslie closed her eyes, ran a hand through her tousled blonde hair. "No."

"Is it just you here?"

"For now." Until her Uncle Claven arrived in a couple of days to settle into his new home—certainly not enough time for her to make it habitable for him. She wasn't a freaking miracle worker, after all, but she would stay with the outrageous old fart as long as he needed her. What the hell else did she have to do? She was thirty-one years old, unemployed, newly divorced, and unable to obtain the Wi-Fi needed to fill out the many online applications she'd been looking forward to during her down time.

Welcome to rural Kansas.

"I guess I'll get dressed and sit it out in town," she said. "Do you have any idea how long this will take?"

"Crews are working on it as we speak. Should only be a few hours."

Ha! A few hours her ass. Wrapping the edges of her thin sweater tighter around her middle, Leslie gave a dumb nod. "Whatever. Thanks." And she closed the door.

Hell if she was going anywhere. The proudly displayed American flag her uncle had raised and illuminated in the front yard indicated a northerly wind, meaning any escaping gas fumes were being blown south. She was north of the road construction, and far enough to stay clear. If she smelled fumes, she'd put on one of the gas masks she'd stored in the basement, along with the rest of Uncle Claven's survival gear. According to him the Cold War—yes, the one that ended thirty years ago—could still erupt into a nuclear apocalypse, which was primarily why he'd chosen this house. He knew the family who'd built it. Claimed they'd installed a fallout shelter after the Cuban Missile Crisis.

Good one, Uncle C, she thought as a mouse streaked across the floor. *Good one*.

Unfortunately, her mother and sisters couldn't tolerate Claven's bouts of paranoid ramblings for very long. The only reason Leslie had been dumped with the task of settling him back into his hometown was because the old man seemed to favor her. And, of course, she'd drawn the short straw. Again.

Screw it. Screw cops. Screw gas leaks. She was going back to bed.

Before she left the door, though, Leslie spared one last peek through the peephole and confirmed that the policeman was descending the porch steps and heading back toward the highway.

"Nice ass," she murmured appreciatively. Nice biceps. Nice everything, though she couldn't see his face well, almost as if he were hiding it. What she could see was a little too rugged and solemn beneath the dark bill of his cap. The tough-guy swagger came with the blue uniform, she supposed, something they all learned in the academy.

With a sigh, she ambled back up the stairs, closed her bedroom window to keep out any wayward, noxious fumes, and slipped out of her pajama pants. The policeman and his mandatory warning were already forgotten when she aimed for her soft, rumpled sheets for the second time that night.

A few minutes later the pounding returned. With a

tired sigh, Leslie once again got up and repeated her act of getting decent while tripping down the stairs. She flipped the porch light on and opened the door to find Officer Serious propped against the doorjamb, arms crossed, looking none too pleased with her lack of compliance.

She gave him a lame smile. "I guess you meant now?"

Her answer came in the form of a silent, deadpan stare.

Five minutes later, having traded her pajama bottoms for a pair of soft jeans, Leslie pulled out of her driveway with every intention of spending the rest of her morning in town. After a brief argument with the officer that she was not *legally* obligated to leave her home, he'd managed to convince her that it was for the best. Besides, she could use this time in front of the library. They had free Wi-Fi that she could steal from within the confines of her car to fill out a few applications. Maybe Officer Serious was a blessing in disguise, and she would actually have a job waiting for her when she returned to Nebraska. Her ex-husband, Kyle, didn't run the only newspaper in Omaha. There were others, maybe even some online rags that needed a good editor, one with enough experience to negate her need for a degree—a degree she hadn't needed with Kyle's paper.

The next driveway loomed up ahead, hard to miss in the beam of her Toyota Camry's headlights with its glowing blue markers and enormous reflective mailbox. Upon passing the house, she noticed that all the lights were out, and that all the cars were accounted for, still parked in the driveway. Leslie pulled over, watched for a moment, and concluded that her neighbors didn't seem too worried about a little ole' gas leak either.

As if on queue, her stomach growled, reminding her that she'd skipped dinner. There would be no shops or restaurants open at this time of morning. Then an image of the leftover pizza sitting in her fridge blocked out all desire to fill out applications. With a defiant huff, she cranked the wheel… and headed back home.

****

Plastered against the dank concrete wall of his old basement, Dane watched the blonde's silhouette descend the moonlit stairwell, unable to believe his rotten luck. So far he'd only had time to unbar the hidden hatch in the basement floor that would allow him easy access in the future, but he hadn't even begun the search for what had really brought him here. All he needed was an hour in the house. After surveying its new occupant for two whole days, however, it was determined some serious subterfuge would be needed to get her out of it. After all his planning and posturing about gas leaks, she'd decided to ignore his warning, and for some reason felt the need to invade the basement where he was already hiding when she'd returned home. Damn woman couldn't do as she was told. She just had to test the limits, which—he had to admit—he kind of admired.

She'd removed her sweater since they'd parted ways, her raw, slender figure outlined by the thin camisole above her jeans. High, pert nipples pressed against the silky cloth, jiggling slightly with her movements and magnifying the exquisite shape of her breasts, which were just under a handful. A stirring down below prompted a groan, which Dane choked back before the sound came out. Here he was in a highly dangerous situation, on the verge of getting caught in a very real disaster, and all he could focus on was a pair of tits.

Jesus Jones, how long had it been? Almost two years, he supposed. Two, long, miserable years since he'd held a pair of breasts in his hands.

The basement light came on and the new resident of his family's old homestead—who continuously exercised a gross lack of caution—didn't bother turning around as she headed straight for a weather-beaten, wood cabinet. Piled on top of it was a variety of equipment and lots of olive-green paraphernalia from what looked like the Korean War era. She picked up a gas mask and studied its large glass eyes and snout. When that cute, freckled nose of hers wrinkled up, he wondered why. Was it the mask she didn't like, or the pungent smell of wet concrete and mold surrounding them?

Hanging from the low wooden beams of the basement was a dusty layer of cobwebs. When she ran into one, Dane was impressed by her quiet acceptance of it, foregoing the usual squeals of panic most women would emit in such an event. Little seemed to bother her, including the threat of a gas leak—perhaps something that could work in his favor despite the fact she'd blatantly ignored his advice.

Since she was still fixated on the mask in her hands, he was able to move slightly to his right, close enough to the stairs to appear to have just descended them behind her. The scuffle of grit beneath his boots gave him away, and she looked up with a gasp.

"Thought we finally had an understanding," he

drawled.

The woman—Leslie Downing according to her vehicle registration—took a few deep breaths, hand to heart as she recuperated before him. "You scared the hell out of me," she complained, managing to sound like the victim of an unspeakable crime. "Where did you come from, anyway?"

"I followed you down."

Her hazel gaze darted to the stairs behind him, the ones that had made plenty of racket when she'd descended them. His look dared her to question it. He was a cop. She was a pain in the ass, which meant he'd already won this fight before it started.

"Go on," he prodded. "Get on up there. And this time I want you to actually make it to town."

"The neighbors weren't leaving when I passed by their house," she argued. "And we already went over the fact that you can't legally force me to leave."

The problem was he didn't give two shits about what he could or couldn't legally do. Maybe if he was still a real cop. Maybe if he weren't an asshole. "The Watson's home was my next stop," he said smoothly. "The longer I stay here babysitting you, the longer it'll take for me to move on to the other households."

Her eyes narrowed on him, and for a moment Dane was truly worried she was about to figure him out. Before she could, he gave a lazy shrug. "Alright," he said, resigning himself to the idea of coming back, especially now that his way into the house was all but guaranteed. "I'll be moving along. Just do me a favor and keep your windows closed till morning."

When a spark of trust re-entered her eyes, his gut relaxed a bit. Allowing her plenty of clearance, he watched as she shuffled past him and toward the stairs with mask in hand. Her shapely bottom was a thing of beauty, especially when she took the steps one by one. Before reaching for the light's pull cord, Dane paused long enough to curse his dick for *its* sudden shift in priorities.

Then he heard a sharp intake of breath, followed by the slamming of the basement door.

"Oh no!"

"What now?" he asked.

She rattled the handle. "The wind blew the door shut. It feels like it's locked."

Or the handle had frozen again, like numerous times in the past because he hadn't gotten around to fixing it. Dane wanted to laugh. And cry. And shake the living shit out of Leslie Downing. "Let me try it," he said, moving aside once again so they could trade places. Not that he liked having a stranger at his back, but if he didn't get out of there soon, his chances of getting caught would double.

And, of course, the door wouldn't budge, at least without him causing some serious damage to it. He went back down to the ground level, keeping his face in shadows beneath the bill of his ball cap. His gaze darted toward the back of the basement, knowing the way into the house was behind several stacks of iron dining room chairs. But he couldn't afford to reveal his deep knowledge of the place. "I could try and bust through," he suggested.

She barked out a laugh. "Better not. With my luck, it'll all come down on us like popsicle sticks."

It wasn't that bad. He'd only been gone nineteen months, and the place was sturdy when he left it. "Then

I suggest we start looking around for a tool of some kind. Something I can use to pry it open or jimmy the latch."

"Or you could radio one of your colleagues and have them bust us out."

He paused in his search. Threw her a wry smile. "This is Rosemont, Ma'am. My colleagues—all three of them—are busy evacuating homes, same as me. Same as the fire department, which is volunteer by the way."

The lie was growing, spiraling out of control the longer he stayed with this woman.

As if reading his mind, her gaze lowered to the name patch on his uniform and lingered there for a bit. "Well, Officer Kennedy, maybe we'll just have to buckle in and wait this gas leak out together."

The use of his roommate's surname amped up the guilt, and the angst. Not that Caleb Kennedy would catch heat for the theft of his uniform, because Ms. Downing didn't seem to notice that it wasn't a local one. All uniforms looked the same, after all, at least to most people. Lucky for Dane, he and Caleb were close enough in size, only Dane couldn't fit the bulletproof vest beneath the shirt. With endless months of nothing to do but pump iron and watch his back, he'd gained a bit of muscle mass during his hiatus from civilized society.

"I think I can manage a basement door," he replied with bite. "Why don't you have a seat? I'll look around for something to use."

With a heavy sigh, she planted her shapely butt on the second step, watching him with chin in palms and her straight blonde hair brushing her knees. "Can't you use a credit card or something?"

The beam of his flashlight swept over all the nooks and crannies as he moved closer to the stack of chairs. "Not unless you have your purse on you."

"Left it in the car. Don't you have one in your wallet?"

Not presently, but it was on his to-do list, which read: find papers; clear name; get property back; kill Mayor Tosh; apply for credit card. Instead of answering her, though, he touched his beam on the trap door no one knew about. Asked, "What's this?" and proceeded to shimmy his way into the deepest, darkest recess of the basement.

Behind the chairs, past the concrete floor, and onto a mixture of dirt and gravel, Dane fought a mass of stringy cobwebs until he was directly beneath the small, square opening that led into a cubby beneath the stairs of the house—a cubby that could be accessed through the kitchen's pantry. The perfect size for a child or a very small adult. Dane had grown some since he'd last used it, what...thirty years ago? When he was ten or eleven years old?

"What is it?" the woman asked directly behind him, startling Dane out of his ruminations. Hell, there were spiders everywhere, probably even snakes. This chick was right behind him, unafraid and perhaps a little reckless in her un-protective flip-flops. It hit him that this was no ordinary, pretty face. No, Leslie Downing was a woman with balls, someone who could keep up. Take shit from no one.

And he suddenly wanted her number.

But, asshole that he was, even *he* wouldn't use romance as a guise for getting his land back. Besides, that method wouldn't be as much fun as exposing Thurlow Tosh and his crimes. And when that happened, Dane didn't want to be anywhere near Ms. Downing when she and her uncle were forced to sell his land back to him—land that would always, rightfully, belong to him.

****

Leslie counted five cars in the parking lot of Rosemont's only grocery store, which meant it was crowded for a weekday afternoon. Was everyone panicking after last night's gas leak? Would there be any bottled water left? All she needed were a few before the plumbers came to her uncle's house to replace all the seals and gaskets that began leaking upon the first turn of the tap. Though Uncle C would gripe over the expense, she also decided to purchase a filtration system for the kitchen sink. It was a guess, but she bet that even he would hesitate over the amount of white matter floating in his glass of water.

The list of repairs was astonishing. Sagging gutters, wood rot, loose cabinet hinges, outdated wiring, cracked ceilings, peeling paint, and a freaking disaster of a side porch. Though…Leslie supposed the place *did* have its charm. Once she'd peeled up a corner of the rodent-stained carpet, she'd found beautiful hardwood floors beneath it. Then the rest of the woodwork began to stand out, unpainted and in need of a good oiling. Her perception began to shift as the house moved up a notch from lost cause to legit work in progress.

And if the house could be salvaged, maybe there was some hope for her, too.

She pulled into a spot facing a display of outdoor plants that was situated beneath the shade of the overhang. Leslie got out, contemplating the wisdom of buying some for the porch as heat from the asphalt shot right up the skirt of her beach-style sundress. When the store's door slid open, she was greeted with a tired smile from the cashier and an annoyed frown from the sweaty old woman she was taking money from. The frown turned to a tisk of disapproval, probably because of the amount of skin Leslie was showing. Okay, maybe her wardrobe was a little chic for rural Kansas, but Kyle had loved this particular dress on her. Said the electric-blue complimented her slender shape and fair coloring. And it was the last clean article of clothing she had left before her trip to the laundromat.

When she loaded her five gallons of water onto the belt, the cashier eyed her with open curiosity. "You live up at the old Chappell place, don't you?"

Leslie nodded.

"Where you from?"

"Omaha. I'm just visiting until my uncle gets settled into the house. He's the one who bought it." While the register beeped out her purchases, the clerk's mouth hitched with a curious smirk that bespoke of her low opinion of the place. "Yes, it's a dump," Leslie added. "But he was rather insistent."

"Who's your uncle?"

"Claven Gallagher. He's from here, but he's been gone a long time."

They exchanged money. "So he knew the Chappells, then?"

"Probably. He seemed to know the house, anyway." Since he'd sworn her to secrecy about the supposed fallout shelter beneath the house, she refrained from mentioning it as his favorite part.

The cashier gave her another one of those probing looks. "If I were you, I'd tell him to get an alarm system."

Leslie hesitated before taking the receipt. "Why? Isn't this a safe town?"

"It was, before Dane Chappell made parole last week. Now everyone here is keeping an eye out just in case he decides to come back."

Sounded dangerous. And her uncle had just bought this convicted felon's *house.* As the pieces fell together, a sense of unease settled into Leslie's gut. No wonder the townsfolk kept staring at the property when they drove by—long, expectant stares as if they were looking for something hidden beyond the overgrown shrubbery and two stories of crooked shutters. "And you think this Dane person will come home?" she asked.

"Oh yeah. He didn't exactly leave peacefully, if you know what I mean. Says he was set up when they put him behind bars. Of course he got himself broke from all those legal fees, and his son couldn't afford to keep the place, so he was forced to sell it."

Which meant she was staying in what this Chappell guy probably still considered his house. Alone. Why hadn't anyone warned her before now?

Because she was an outsider who hadn't bothered to come out of hiding throughout her lengthy bout of failure-induced shame. Divorce proved to be more than she could handle, especially from a man who'd done all the cheating yet still managed to acquire half of everything they owned. Yes, Kyle bought her out of their downtown studio apartment and all its trappings, leaving her with enough money for a fresh start. But the emotional toll of being betrayed and abandoned by the man she'd adored at first sight bore no price.

Even now, just the thought of it threatened her composure, though it had been eight months since she and Kyle had settled. And Leslie was finally getting tired of it. Perhaps she needed a bigger distraction than Uncle C's junk heap of a home.

Since no one was in line behind her, she decided that there was no better time for a local history lesson than now. "You said his name was Dane Chappell?" When the cashier nodded, Leslie asked, "What did he go to prison for?"

"Attempted manslaughter." The clerk leaned in, giving Leslie a closeup of the scraggly hairs growing from her chin. "Long story short, he beat the mayor within an inch of his life. Lost everything, including his right to be here. If you see him, I suggest you call Sheriff Devine. She'll make sure he goes back to jail where he belongs."

"So coming back would be a parole violation or something?"

"Uh-huh. We expect it and so should you, *especially* you."

Leslie's bare shoulders broke out into a sudden rash of goosebumps. This wasn't what she needed to hear. Did Uncle Claven know what had happened to the previous owner of the home he'd just bought? No, she didn't think so. He was all about the peace and quiet. And the fallout shelter, which she had yet to locate. The thought of finding it both creeped her out and excited her at the same time—buried treasure that could contain anything from valuables to dangerous secrets.

Like a violent ex-felon hiding from the law.

Chapter 2

"Come on, Dad, rise and shine."

Dane pried an eye open and beheld his son, Oliver—or Otter to most folks—leaning over him with a mug of coffee in his grip. The full uniform he wore was an instant reminder that the knucklehead had once wanted to follow in his footsteps. A damn beat cop living on fumes and with a gym-rat roommate who idolized Dolph Lundgren. The stuff dreams were made of.

"Don't you have a parking ticket to write, Deputy?" he grumbled, pulling the sheet over his face and rolling over. The worn, leather couch beneath him creaked in protest. Dane's shins didn't like the arrangement, either, since they bore the constant weight of his feet, which dangled over the armrest. When he'd agreed to this living arrangement (not that he'd had much choice) he'd expected a bed of his own. A cot, maybe. Hell, even a blow-up mattress would be better than this patched-up piece of kindling.

How he longed for his own bed, in his own bedroom, in his own house. It was a goal that had kept him focused during the nineteen months of his incarceration, a goal that was achievable now that he was out.

The thought cleared the last dregs of sleep from his brain. As his son settled in the nearby armchair, Dane rolled over and sat up, blinking against the intense light breaking through the vertical blinds. "What time is it?"

"Late enough to question what time you went to bed," Oliver replied, his lanky frame folded over as he untied his shoes.

"You just get home?"

A nod meant it was after 8:00AM, but then the roommate walked out of the master bedroom in a haze of fresh aftershave. At six-foot five, Caleb Kennedy looked ready to leave for his shift complete with service revolver, groomed flattop, and skull-themed underwear, which Dane had caught a sleepy glimpse of when the man had come out for his first cup of coffee. Sharing a place sucked in so many ways…

"Morning, Kennedy," he said with a yawn. "Looking starched and steely-eyed this morning. Why the late start?"

Caleb gave a stiff nod as he plucked a pair of aviator sunglasses from the countertop and hooked them in the Vee of his uniform shirt. "I've been on the clock since seven, but someone already vomited on me. I had to come home and change." He lifted an arm and sniffed. Made a face. "I must have hung this dirty one in the closet by accident." He walked over to Oliver with his arm still raised. "Take a whiff, Otter. Too ripe?"

Dane's son winced and ducked out of the danger zone just in time. "Dude!"

"Seriously, man, I'm worried. This is the last clean one I have."

Dane watched the exchange with a small amount of guilt. He hadn't meant to wear the uniform long enough to stink it up, but it had been a damned long, hot night.

"I saw a can of air freshener in the bathroom," he grumbled, rising from the couch. "Use it on your pits and get going. I'll go to the dry cleaner's today."

Though Dane was fresh out of prison, the younger man still treated him with the respect due a police officer twenty years his senior. "Yes, sir," Caleb said as if he hadn't just been ordered out of his own home. He jetted toward the bathroom.

The two-bedroom duplex was cramped before Dane had graced its front doorstep with his meager belongings and broad, prison physique. Though the place was white-walled, simple, and fairly tidy, there just wasn't enough room for three grown men—four if one counted the life-size cutout of Dolph in all his armed regalia.

A typical bachelor pad, it was decorated with a variety of guitars, shaggy green rugs, and black retro furniture, all of which lacked design according to Dane. Give him the warmth of antique wood, or the comfort of plush cushions any day, just like his home in Rosemont.

Add a beautiful, reckless blonde to that and I'd be shitting in tall cotton.

Miss Downing's heart-shaped face popped out from the deepest depths of his mind where it had been lurking since the moment she'd opened the front door of his house. Even sleep-rumpled and bleary-eyed she'd hit him in the solar plexus with a terrible need to fuck. But she was dangerous. Would be tough to get around, especially if she ratted him out to the local police. It was still hard—even after time served in the dregs of hell—to imagine a life outside that particular black uniform. As a Summit County native and lifer, its county seat of Rosemont and the people's welfare had always come first for him, despite the ugly fact that no one wanted him as their sheriff anymore.

But that would change the moment Tosh fell. Even though Dane had spent every waking moment in his prison cell planning the mayor's demise, he still had no clue where to start. There were a million ways to kill someone's career and reputation, as Thurlow had done to Dane, but that was only if one were to venture beyond the boundaries of the law.

When the law was in a man's bones, however, his options were severely limited. Dane only had to broaden them, and his daring attempt to infiltrate his home earlier that morning had been a liberating experience. Something he could get used to. Something he would do again when—or if—he could, because he was a different man now and the anger inside him had festered far too long to control. The mission came first. His name, his reputation, his *future*, was worth the risk of added prison time in case he was caught violating the terms of his parole by leaving Kansas City, Missouri city limits. His *son's* home—or rather his new babysitter thanks to the cruel humor of irony.

"I'm turning in."

Dane blinked, refocusing on Oliver who was frowning at him with the shrewd, mesquite eyes of his mother. The two of them were alone, and it became apparent that Otter had been watching him while Dane blankly stewed in his underwear. He ran a hand through his messy finger-length waves. Mustered a smile. "Want something to eat first?"

The kid—though twenty-one years old and fully developed into the lithe, athletic shape Dane had once sported at that age—still held an edge of vulnerability that didn't fit the badge.

"I grabbed something on the way home," said Oliver. "But as long as it comes with the truth, I'll choke it down."

The guilt bubbled anew within Dane. Yep. Shrewd yet vulnerable. He'd have to keep that in mind before stepping out again in a stolen uniform. Not bothering with a lie that wouldn't be believed anyway, Dane simply stretched and headed for the bathroom.

"I believe in you, Dad."

Oliver's words stopped him in his tracks.

"But I won't risk my career over whatever you're cooking up."

Now who was lying? Dane spared a glance over his shoulder and locked eyes with his son. "Then never ask for the truth," he replied. "Not until after Tosh burns."

****

Leslie peered through the window-front of the laundromat where she instantly spotted three washers with her name on them. She'd been told the place was air conditioned by about four people so far, since the weather seemed to be the major news story of the day. If she heard one more heat-related idiom from someone who preferred to sit outside in it, she would scream.

Or was it the heat that was making her so grumpy? Perhaps she would fit in with the townsfolk better than she'd thought.

Bells clanked against glass as she backed through the laundromat's door with her fully loaded basket. Craning her neck to see over the mountain of clothes, she nearly tripped over the small person who was camped in the middle of the place playing with a pile of plastic dinosaurs. "Oops! Sorry."

"Son, get your toys off the floor," said a young mother with a protruding belly and pretty blush. "Sorry for that," she told Leslie while scooping up the scattered toys. "He doesn't get the concept of boundaries yet."

The pudgy boy peered up at Leslie through long, spiky bangs. She guessed him to be about four, his ornery smile a clear indication that he knew exactly what boundaries were and didn't give a fig. Returning his smile, Leslie muscled her load onto a nearby table.

"You live at the old Chappell place, don't you?" the young mother asked.

Wow, does everyone know that? Leslie had heard about small town grapevines, and according to Uncle Claven, this one was particularly organized. After dumping her load onto a table, she rested a moment and decided to try and care. To ask names. Blend, at least until she got home. This woman looked okay and appeared to be in dire need of adult conversation. "Leslie Downing," she said. "And you are?"

"Maxine Dillard. Call me Maxi." Mom nodded toward the boy. "And that there is trouble."

Leslie believed it—was glad the woman wasn't completely snowed by her child. She instantly liked the pair, and as she sorted colors, Trouble continued his game of dinosaur-battle, intent on keeping her his sole audience with frequent eye contact and coy smiles. He was cute, but it still didn't change her mind about not having kids of her own, no matter how much her family harped on her about it.

"No one usually comes here this time of day," Maxi said as she continued to fold her mountain of tiny clothes. "Still no washer and dryer out there?"

"Nope."

"There's a scratch and dent store in Topeka. They're having some kind of closeout sale through Friday, I think."

"I'll keep that in mind, thanks."

An awkward silence followed with exception to the juicy dinosaur battle unfolding on the floor.

"Not much of a talker, are you?" Maxi asked her.

That wasn't true. Leslie was a very social person, just not lately. "Sorry, I'm just tired. Didn't get much sleep last night because of that gas leak."

"What gas leak?"

"The one caused by the construction crew." Since Maxi looked curiously confused, Leslie elaborated. "The crew building the road behind my house ruptured a gas line. They tried to evacuate everyone within a two-mile radius."

"Last night?"

"Yes." But something told Leslie that the woman's obvious confusion was well founded. It was a feeling she'd had since Officer Kennedy left her house without further argument—after he had so easily found the hidden trap door camouflaged by decades of dust and cobwebs—after she'd realized the absence of a squad car, and that there was no activity to indicate other homeowners leaving the area. All had been eerily quiet afterward, as if the last forty-or-so minutes had never happened.

Because there had been no gas leak, she concluded with harsh finality. Such an event would be the talk of the town, and so far not a word about anything but the blistering heat. Chills raced down her spine, and they had nothing to do with the single A/C unit sputtering out cold puffs of air from the side window.

"Are you sure you weren't dreaming?" Maxi looked almost sorry for her. "I do that sometimes, have a dream so real I wake up confused or pissed off. Usually at my husband."

The last was said with a laugh, most likely an attempt to ease out of the subject since she obviously thought Leslie was wacko. But all Leslie could think of was the policeman who had come to her door. Was he even real? Was she going crazy? Could he have possibly *lied* to her?

There had definitely been a rumble of some sort, one big enough to rouse her from sleep, but Leslie now knew she'd been conned into leaving her home. It was just too strange the way Officer Kennedy had popped into her basement without a sound…as if he'd already been there. Lurking.

Thoughts of a certain parolee she'd just learned of entered her brain like a dark fog. Dane Chappell was his name.

If you see him, I suggest you call Sheriff Devine. She'll make sure he goes back to jail where he belongs.

But would he be so bold—so reckless—as to impersonate a police officer?

Instead of going home, Leslie stopped at the library where she obtained a card, signed a form, and in turn was given a password that would allow her access to one of the library's three computers. A quick Google search brought up four news articles about Dane Chappell—as well as all the damning photos of his familiar mug she could possibly hope for. There he was, Officer *Kennedy*, minus the week's-worth of beard and scruffy hair.

"Why you dirty rotten liar," she murmured to herself. No wonder he knew about the trap door. And if he was able to so easily break into the home's basement, he could have just as easily slipped into the home itself. And what? Stolen her stuff? Held her hostage? Raped and murdered her?

Yes, he could have done all those things, but he didn't. Instead, he'd very carefully devised a plan to get rid of her for a short period of time. When it had backfired, he'd left peacefully and without any indication that he'd been up to no good.

So, what was this guy's story? Her curiosity flared into a thirst for information, so Leslie hunkered down and started reading.

It didn't take long to learn that Dane Chappell was once the *sheriff* of Rosemont, which had her leaning back in her chair in a state of awe. Not that she couldn't see it. Having interacted with him, that one fact made more sense than anything else she'd read about him. What was so perplexing was the sheer amount of hatred directed toward the man. There were plenty of old, positive articles spotlighting a more respected peacekeeper of the community. From his start as a deputy, then to deputy sheriff, and finally his leap to the top spot. Yet he had not one supporter who'd spoken on his behalf during his trial. It was weird. Extreme. As if the people of Rosemont had all been brainwashed.

Brainwashed? Now *that* was extreme. Leslie guessed that as an outsider her opinion didn't amount to much, but she was also unbiased on the matter. All the negative articles started with the road, when Dane Chappell's land was first threatened by eminent domain, the government's way of claiming private property for the "good of the community." Interestingly, the town's new mayor had been sworn in only a few weeks beforehand. Was there a connection? "Apparently Chappell thought so," she murmured.

A few paragraphs down, the article mentioned plans for a chicken processing plant to go in on the town's western border. Twelve hundred new jobs were promised. The economic boost would benefit local businesses and cause land values to rise. No wonder the town was favorable of the idea, turning on their sheriff who was the only opposition to the plant's proposed road that would offer a direct trucking route from the highway, keeping the landmark county road and its flanking properties from succumbing to alterations and heavier traffic. Sheriff Chappell and a two-hundred-acre chunk of his spread were the necessary sacrifice.

And suddenly Leslie's problems seemed trivial. At least she wasn't *that* guy.

"Have you seen that man?"

Leslie jumped, looked over her shoulder to find another police officer standing over her, this one wearing a black uniform. She was tall, middle aged, her face filled out and sporting a tough, square jaw. She had raven, slicked-back hair that was pulled into a short ponytail at her nape. Her shiny badge read *Sheriff, Summit County*, confirming that the *blue* uniform "Officer Kennedy" had been wearing the previous night was indeed out of place.

"Uh…" She glanced back at the computer screen where Dane Chappell's clean-shaven face stared at her with a fair amount of gravity. "No," she heard herself say. "No, I…I just heard about him from the woman at

25

the grocery store. Thought I'd do my homework so I can keep an eye out."

The sheriff studied her with a discerning glare and pursed lips. "Good thinking. Dane Chappell is not someone you want to mess with."

Despite the news article's negative spin on the man, Leslie sensed there was more to the story than what she'd learn in any lopsided rag. "He assaulted a man?" she asked.

The officer—whom Leslie figured was the same Sheriff Devine the store clerk had mentioned—moved to the chair beside her and leaned on the back of it, squinting at the computer screen. "Nearly beat our mayor to death in his own home. They clashed from day one, and Dane always did have a violent side, getting into fights all the time as a kid, using unnecessary force on the job, that kind of thing." Her gaze grew heavy with concern. "I served this community under him for a handful of years, and I know the man. He'll come back for his pound of flesh. You happened to move in the same time he made parole, so you might want to get some kind of protection. Maybe even a dog. Just as an extra precaution."

Leslie wondered if it was bad that she found the town's comprehensive knowledge of her more disturbing than Dane Chappell's brief, early morning visit. She sensed he'd come to his old home in search of something, and *not* the aforementioned pound of flesh. Perhaps it was something he'd left behind...which would explain why she'd found him lurking in the home's basement. Even though she hadn't exactly made things easy for him, he'd handled her with the authoritative manner of a born lawman, not someone on the perpetual edge of violence.

No, he wasn't as dangerous as this woman was making him out to be, and Leslie had always been an excellent judge of character. "The town seems to be pretty scared of him," she said, her gaze sliding back to the computer screen. *Or they just wanted him out of the way.*

"Everyone in this town knew it was only a matter of time before he broke," the sheriff said. "We're keeping an eye out for him. You should, too." She retrieved a business card from her pocket and handed it to Leslie. "If you notice anything suspicious, no matter how strange, give us a call. We'll come out and have a look around."

Her smile was an attempted nicety that fell flat. When she left, Leslie glanced around and noticed several pairs of eyes on her. The resulting creeps reminded her of a Stephen King movie where she was the stranger in an old town full of secrets—secrets to be revealed just prior to the moonlit shimmer of a descending axe.

Shirking the urge to slink out of there, she instead turned back to the computer's screen and dug into the more recent articles.

All of which told the same tale of a violent lawman who'd finally gone too far.

****

"She didn't say a word," the voice told him over the phone.

Dane squinted against the late afternoon sun, his half-empty can of lemon-lime soda glinting with sweat as he carefully set it down on the patio table. "And you say Devine asked her straight up?"

"Yep. *Have you seen that man* were her exact words."

It was a question that couldn't have been interpreted any other way, yet according to his source Leslie Downing had flat out lied by telling the sheriff that she had *not* seen him. Always leery of hidden motives, Dane wondered why the lady would do that. It wasn't as if they'd particularly hit it off during their brief time together. In fact, she seemed quite *put off* by the whole thing, which was the reason for his phone call—to follow up before moving on to plan B.

What were the odds of him finally catching a break, of gaining an ally where least expected, which was under the very roof he still coveted as his own? The idea was plausible since Ms. Downing wasn't personally invested in the property, was only sprucing up the house until the legal owner arrived. Perhaps she was smarter than Dane had thought. Maybe she was able to read between the lines enough to get the gist of what was going on when no one else from the outside had ever bothered, let alone believed him or cared. He was a police officer, an unpopular figure during the height of a tumultuous, national war against police, making him as expendable as a week-old headline.

Not that he thought Ms. Downing cared about his problems, but she *had* lied…a curious gesture on her part. One that warranted a closer look.

"Listen…" He ran a hand over his beard, rehashing the wisdom of what he was about to do. "I need to borrow your car. Can you meet me at the state line?"

Chapter 3

The knock on her front door was confirmation that going into town had been a bad idea. Leslie put down her paintbrush, wiped her hands on her old *Omaha Zoo* T-shirt and began her loud clop across the house. Halfway through the living room she remembered the only other person who'd bothered to come over…an ex-felon with questionable intent. The mere possibility that he'd come back made her heart trip over itself. Why-oh-why had she covered for him? Where was the proof that Dane Chappell was a victim in anything?

Her steps cautious now, she reached the front door in silence and slowly leaned into the peephole. Breath held, she studied the figure that stood on the porch; trim, a slight bump around the middle, and finally the glimpse of a ponytail as it caught the breeze. Then another, smaller figure appeared within the circle of distorted glass, this one clearly on a mission to chase something that was headed toward the steps.

A familiar giggle brought it all into focus. Closing her eyes, Leslie took a deep breath and allowed the calm to still the tremble in her hands. Then she opened the door.

A grinning Maxi held out a paper plate loaded with cookies. "Hi. Thought I'd properly welcome you to the neighborhood."

Ignoring the cookies, Leslie focused on Maxi's

little boy, who was in the process of shoving a ground beetle into his mouth. "Um…Maxi…" She nodded in his direction.

The woman peered over her shoulder. Let out a gasp and bobbled the plate, which Leslie caught just before it was dropped.

"Trouble, how many times have I told you not to eat those things!" When Maxi swiped the insect away just in time, she hauled her son back to the door, a lame smile on her flushed face. "I swear he poops more bug parts than a rooster."

Swallowing hard, Leslie looked down at the cookies—oatmeal raisin by the looks of them—and quickly transferred the plate onto the small table just inside the entrance. "It almost sounds like you really did name him Trouble."

Her two guests followed her inside without a proper invite. Maxi shut the door behind her with a nervous laugh. "Well…it seemed fitting according to the inside of my uterus." She faced Leslie again with two hands flattened over her belly. "This baby'll be no different."

Leslie frowned at Trouble who was making a beeline for the stairs. "You mean that *is* his real name?"

"Actually, most folks call him TJ." Just when Leslie felt relief for the boy, Maxi added, "Stands for Trouble Junior. His grandma insisted that he'd be just like his daddy."

So the *dad* was named Trouble, too. Sweet America. "Um…" Leslie headed for the stairs also, catching the little tyrant around his middle as he lunged for the fifth step. "You know, I have an open can of wood stain in the kitchen. Perhaps this isn't the best time—"

"Look what you've done to this place." Maxi twirled around the living room, scoping out the fresh paint, polished light fixtures, and newly varnished wood trim. "No wonder you haven't showed yourself for weeks. You've been busy."

So Maxi was familiar with the house. Interesting. "Yeah…now that the painting's done I'm going to tear up the carpet." Leslie handed Trouble a cookie, figuring it was okay since Maxi didn't mind him tearing through a stranger's house unchecked. "You've been here before, then?"

"Of course. Otter Chappell and I practically grew up together, well…when he was visiting his daddy, that is. Ask me, he would have rather lived here than in the city. We were *almost* sweethearts, even gave each other our first kiss beside the pond out back."

As the influx of information whizzed past her, Leslie watched a cookie-wielding four-year-old circle into the dining room, then into the kitchen. She headed him off at the sawhorse island where sanded cabinet doors were in the process of being stained over a tarp-covered floor. "Let's go out into the back yard, shall we?" she suggested to Maxi who had followed them and was scoping out all the improvements made to that room as well.

The woman gave a dumb nod, but Leslie sensed her awe was born from nostalgia more than admiration. She picked up an unused paintbrush on the way out and shoved it in Trouble's empty fist. "Go paint some stuff, buddy. Show me what you can do."

She pushed open the screen door, its rusty hinges screeching in protest. With both fists occupied, his mouth full of wet cookie, Trouble produced a determined growl and hopped down the porch steps. What a handful, she thought, knowing now why Maxi had brought him—to be someone else's problem for a few precious moments. But why the hell did it have to be her, a busy woman who showed no interest in making friends let alone babysitting their offspring?

The paintbrush, Leslie decided, was a worthy sacrifice since Trouble seemed thoroughly occupied with his new job of "painting" everything in his path: stepping stones, tree trunks, clothesline, grass. Even the white, lacy yarrow flowers growing along the fence line.

Maxi laughed. "I think you found him a new career."

Worth every bit of the twelve bucks she'd spent on the brush, at least for now. "You can have it," Leslie said.

"Oh, I couldn't."

She gave Maxi a sideways glance. "You need it more than I do." A clear fact that halted further argument. Maxi was a young thing, nearly a kid herself. Her curiosity piqued, Leslie asked, "I'm guessing since you spent so much time here, you knew Dane Chappell as well."

Maxi's expression faltered a bit. "Of course. He was our sheriff."

"And hotheaded, I hear."

"I guess so."

Said with enough doubt to make things interesting. Leslie cocked her head. "Are *you* afraid of him coming back?"

Maxi shrugged, looked off in the distance. "I don't

know why he'd hurt *me*."

"But you know why he hurt the mayor?"

That earned her a brief glance. Maxi brushed off the question, instead finding a sudden interest in what her son was doing. "Trouble, stay away from the tall grass. There might be snakes in there."

"Everyone I ran into this morning warned me about him," Leslie said, unwilling to let the subject go. "Everyone except you, that is, and you were obviously close to him."

"I didn't say that. Sheriff Chappell was always working, so I rarely saw him out of uniform. Once or twice when I was over here, but me and Otter hung out by ourselves for the most part.

The names in this town… Leslie made a face. "Was his name really Otter?"

"It was actually Oliver. He liked to swim a lot."

Enough said. At least the poor kid had options. "And you two were the same age? What are you, eighteen? Nineteen?"

"Twenty. Otter is a year older than me."

Meaning Maxi had birthed Trouble at the tender age of sixteen. Leslie shivered at the thought, then realized that at forty-one, Dane had also been in his teens when he'd become a father. "Where was Otter's mother?" she asked.

"The sheriff was divorced. Otter lived with his mom and stepdad mostly, but he hated it. Said they were too strict, which is ironic since he's a police officer now. I know he idolized his dad and wanted to be just like him. Well…except for the attempted manslaughter part."

The sadness in Maxi's voice was hard to miss.

Leslie glanced at the thin wedding band on the young woman's finger, wondering if she really knew who Trouble's father was. At this day and age, first kisses had a way of turning into first times, especially for kids so young. "It sounds like you and Otter were pretty close."

Maxi pursed her lips. Nodded. "I wanted to be closer. He was an awkward kid, but you could tell he'd grow up to be good looking, just like his daddy."

Amusement laced Leslie's voice. "You think Sheriff Chappell was good looking?"

"Hell, yeah. If you'd seen him you would have been swooning just like the rest of the females in this town. Single guy, tall and confident, beautiful butt…"

Leslie checked herself before admitting that she *had* seen him. *And* his butt, which was quite nice. As evidenced in his photos, he was very handsome in a rugged, serious kind of way, but nineteen months in prison had hardened him, something noticeable even through his acquired facial hair. Had he grown the beard in order to hide? Was it camouflage for when he planned to come back to Rosemont and finish what he'd started with the mayor?

Possibly. Anyone who would risk going back to jail by violating parole harbored one hell of an agenda.

The two women talked some more, Leslie giving up very little about herself despite how Maxi pried. Her life was a sad bore, and she was much more interested in leaching information about the Chappell family and their nineteenth-century house. *Nineteenth century!* No wonder the place was a dump. A little neglect went a long way for a structure that old, but the more she learned, the more beauty she saw in it—was beginning to understand why Uncle Claven had wanted it, elusive fallout shelter aside. There was a new kind of peace in the view around her: sunlit hills blanketed with golden grasses, the shimmer of the pond's crystal surface despite the overgrowth surrounding it, the cool shade of the backyard cottonwoods…and the quiet was hard to beat.

"My uncle bought this place without even really looking at it," she said with wonder. "He was more interested in what was underneath it rather than the house itself, *or* this wonderful view."

Maxi rolled her eyes. "Yeah, if he lived here before, he knew about the bunker. Everyone did eventually, that's why Otter's grandpa had it taken out."

Leslie froze, and her eyes grew wide on the landscape. "He took it out?"

"Sometime in the eighties. I heard it was because a couple kids got trapped in there once, but that could just be a myth."

Rattled, Leslie looked back at the flaked, whitewashed siding of the two-story relic and wondered if her uncle had even asked about the underground shelter before buying it. "So it's not even there anymore?"

"That's what I said." Maxi laughed, the sound carrying over to Trouble, who straightened from his perch on a cinder block and sent her a toothy grin. "Too bad, though. I always thought something like that would be fascinating. Good for make-out sessions, at least."

Sure, Leslie thought, for horny teens with nothing but sex on the brain. And look where *that* had gotten Maxi. "Is that all there is for kids to do here?" she asked, wincing at the judgment she heard in her voice. "Sorry…it just seems like there's a lot of teenage pregnancy in these parts."

The woman's smile faltered. "I guess that's true." An uncomfortable silence ensued, then she glanced at Leslie. "You don't have kids, do you?"

A fact that had earned her a similar kind of judgment. Leslie shook her head. "Some people just aren't cut out for parenthood."

"You kept Trouble out of trouble for a whole five-minute stretch with that paintbrush."

Leslie looked over at her and grinned. "Sweettalk me all you want, but I'm not babysitting."

The two of them dissolved into a fit of giggles that effectively melted the tension. Maxi sighed, turning her face toward the sky. "It really is beautiful here. But I've taken up enough of your time. Trouble! Come on, sweetie, time to go."

"There isn't any need to rush off."

"I have a roast in the oven. Best get it on the table."

Leslie followed them around the house. In the driveway, she thanked Maxi for the cookies and told Trouble to stay out of trouble, a futile effort, she was sure. After the lengthy task of securing the child in his booster seat, Maxi waved goodbye before getting behind the wheel of her old Pontiac Sunbird. As the car backed out of the driveway, Trouble raised his new paintbrush and also waved at Leslie. Or was he painting her? It was hard to tell.

She felt herself smile regardless. So aptly named, the little pain in the ass got into stuff, but he didn't talk much, which was a delightful quality in any four-year-old. And through the unruly curtain of bangs, she thought she saw an old soul in the sparkle of his big brown eyes.

On her way back up the porch steps, Leslie concluded that her latest guests weren't so bad. Perhaps she'd even found a friend in Maxi, as well as a useful source of information. Getting some background on Dane Chappell helped humanize him a bit more, though she still wouldn't welcome him inside her home if he were to reappear on her doormat. The thought had yet to solidify when she closed the front door behind her, locked it, and slid the new chain into place. She was about to head back to the kitchen to resume her work when the half-eaten plate of cookies caught her eye. At first glance, the lumpy, bumpy texture of them brought ground beetles to mind. Then she realized…the plate was *half eaten.*

But by whom, if not she and her guests?

****

From his perch on the stairs, Dane watched the light come on in Leslie Downing's eyes. Was almost proud that she'd caught on so fast despite the new tremble in her shoulders. With her flaxen hair pulled back in a messy bun at the crown, she was a soft, sweet thing that reminded him of summer.

What he wouldn't do for a little warmth for a change. Everything he'd learned about her since finding out she'd covered for him solidified what he believed: Ms. Downing was a woman he wanted to get to know better, land struggle or no. And now that he was laying eyes on her again—in the flesh, her skin all flushed and warm—Dane knew he would someday end up in bed with her.

An image of her naked body beneath him as he

took possession of her passed through his thoughts like a brief flicker of film. Again, his dick began to shift as if it had suddenly forgotten how to behave. Yes, whether Ms. Downing knew it or not, her quiet time was over. Having been married once, she was already a graduate of the school of hard knocks. With him she would earn her masters. Something about that made him regret how he was about to use her.

And something about it made him want to smile.

From the stack of cookies in his hand, Dane brought another one to his mouth and crunched into it. Chewing, he scoped out the delectable treat as he felt Leslie's gaze fly toward him. He sensed that initial moment of fright when one discovered an intruder in their home, but the new breed of asshole in him saw the beauty of his quiet re-entrance into her life.

"Wha—what are you doing here?" she stuttered, backing against the door with a *thump*.

He swallowed his mouthful. "Taking in the flavors of home," he replied before shoving the rest of the cookie in. His next words were muffled by an orgasmic combination of sugar, butter, and oats. "Maxi always did make a fine batch of oatmeal raisin."

"I know who you are." Her voice shook, but she swallowed and put some strength into it. "If you don't leave, I'll call the police."

A corner of his mouth curved upward. He wiped his fingertips against his jeans and got to his feet. Took the three steps down to the ground floor and leaned against the banister. "I'll go in a minute. But first I'd like to finish these cookies." He held the three up that were in his hand.

Still plastered against the door, Leslie snatched the

paper plate of remaining cookies and hugged it to her chest as if it were her most prized possession.

Amused, Dane added, "While I do, I'd like to ask you some questions."

"Questions?"

"You were awfully curious about me today." His gaze darted toward the open windows at the rear of the house where he'd heard every word exchanged between Leslie and Maxi in the back yard. "Now I'm curious about you."

When she followed his gaze, a pretty blush formed on her cheeks. "I'd just learned that the so-called cop who'd ordered me out of my house last night was an ex-con committing a serious parole violation."

"Then why didn't you turn me in when you had the chance?"

"Believe me, if I had cell service out here—"

"From my understanding, there was a perfectly good sheriff standing right beside you at the time."

After a thoughtful moment, her mouth dropped open. "You're talking about the library."

He took another bite. Crunched slowly.

"You didn't seem like a threat," she said through her teeth. "Unlike *now*."

"Then why aren't you running out that perfectly good door behind you?"

Just like anyone fielding tough questions, Leslie took her time processing them until her cool, sexy eyes lit with an answer. She lifted her chin. "Because you're right. I *am* curious, at least until you finish those cookies in your hand. And then, by God, I better never see your face around here again."

"Fair enough."

Keeping her gaze on him, she took a few cautious steps toward the dining room where she deposited her crushed plate of cookies onto the table. Then she took up a Phillips screwdriver, which she held at her side in a white-knuckled grip. Though Dane could easily relieve her of it, the act of doing so would work against him and his primary goal. Trust. It had to start somewhere.

"You have two and a half cookies," she pointed out. "Better make them count."

He raised the half eaten one to his mouth. Said, "You don't seem surprised that I know about your encounter with Sheriff Devine." And then took a much smaller bite than the previous ones.

"From what I read, *you* were the sheriff here once," she said. "I'd be surprised if you didn't have an ally or two in the wings. In fact, it makes sense."

"How's that?"

"From my experience with the media, it can pick and choose what it wants people to know. I've learned to spot the bias, and they pulled no stops when it came to you."

The lady was beautiful *and* smart. Way too good for the likes of him, but Dane was getting used to the idea of taking what he wanted, consequences be damned. "Don't blame the papers," he replied, hiding his smile. "Smear campaigns are always bought and paid for by a higher authority."

"And who would that be? Rydell Foods?"

He dismissed the notion as another bite went in. "Rydell can build their chicken plant anywhere. In fact, they had plenty of other offers."

She cocked her head. "From towns that want the

economic boost? Like Rosemont?"

"The people of Rosemont don't know what they're getting into. Hell, they didn't even know the city council voted on the project until months after the deal was struck."

"How can they not know?"

He leaned a shoulder against the dividing wall between the living and dining rooms, getting comfortable with the view if not the idea of conversing with this woman. "It was all done under the table. When I got wind of it, I brought it out into the open."

She chewed her bottom lip, as if she were seriously considering it all as a legit possibility. "And you're saying this 'higher authority' turned on you for it? That you were framed and did time as an innocent man?"

"You make it sound so cliché." Dane always owned his mistakes, an honest quality that may earn him that ticket out of Hell when the time came. "But the only thing I'm guilty of is *pretending* to beat a man within an inch of his no-good life."

Leslie's expression lost its spark of curiosity, but the fear had yet to return. "The mayor," she said.

He grunted an assent, wondering if he should just shove in the rest of his cookies and leave. The subject of Tosh never failed to bring on the darkness, like a disease that ate at him from the inside out. Dane fought it back, knowing he'd frighten this woman if he succumbed to it now. "I lost a lot because of that crooked son-of-a-bitch. Yeah, I wanted to knock his teeth out and then some. But someone else beat me to it."

"Who?"

"Got no idea. What matters is that Tosh pointed the

finger at me and, thanks to my beat-down with an honest to goodness punching bag, I had the bloody knuckles to show for it."

"And you're here risking a trip back to prison because you feel like you have nothing to lose?" she asked him, her loose strands of hair dancing around her face as they caught the breeze from the open window beside her.

Dane watched them, feeling an instant calm that had never been achievable before. "That depends."

Her soft, beautiful eyes narrowed. "On what?"

"On you."

Chapter 4

The caged-animal look that had developed in Dane Chappell's eyes softened to the polished steel Leslie remembered from before. She swallowed hard. Backed up a step, afraid of that intensity he was capable of implanting within her like a mating of minds. She always liked strong men, leaders that charged ahead of the front lines without fear of what may come at them. Her ex, Kyle, was like that, and had made quite a name for himself in the world of media. But he would never jump in front of a bullet meant for someone else. The image of Dane doing so, however, was an easy one to conjure. So why was she so damned afraid of him? "The sheriff said you've always had a temper," she added, tightening her grip on the screwdriver in her hand.

His gaze followed the slight movement as if he were in tune with every thought going through her mind. "Devine would say that."

"The people are afraid of you."

"The people have been fed a lot of lies."

The anger was gone, his mention of "the people" shrouded by a fondness one would exude for family or children. Leslie had the feeling she'd gotten her first glimpse of Sheriff Chappell in his true element. Her grip on the screwdriver loosened a bit. "So why are you here? What do you want from me?"

Dane studied the last cookie in his hand. He was a strong presence with his muscles, his tight expression, and throbbing testosterone. But that one cookie and the way he stared at it—as if eating it would symbolize the end of all hope—made him seem tragically vulnerable.

"I wanted to ask for your help," he said, his tone thoughtful. "You're an outsider who has no vested interest in this town or its future." He looked up at her then, their gazes locking. Unbreakable. "But you *are* interested in the truth."

"Why would I be? I'm literally just passing through."

His eyes sparkled. "I've done some research of my own. You're an editor with the drive of a journalist. Isn't that what Kyle Downing said about you in one of his interviews?"

So much for privacy. Riled, Leslie folded her arms across her chest. "Ah. The small-town lawman is suddenly a big city detective."

A simple shrug accompanied his answer. "Doesn't get much more 'big city' than prison."

She could imagine. His world must have grown exponentially in the confines of a tiny cell. "If you want to butter me up, mentioning my ex-husband isn't the way to do it."

"How about if I mention what a narcissistic fool I think he is?"

Some of the starch drained from her shoulders. "That'll do."

A deep chuckle rumbled from his throat, the genuine nature of it surprising her into a smile. Though he'd barely smiled himself, the tension around his eyes and mouth had softened, making him appear almost…beautiful. She could see where Maxi was going with the whole handsome thing. Could imagine the ladies fawning over their big, strapping sheriff. She had seen for herself what a uniform did for that powerful physique of his. As she lost herself in the recollection of it, the parts of her that had been dormant for months stirred back to life, waking a warm need that almost made her fidget.

Suddenly she wanted him out of there before she really did start to fidget. Steeling herself against the urge to run out the back door, she said, "I think you should go now."

A myriad of emotions raced across his face, ending with stony regret. As the pulse at his jaw began to thrum, he raised the last cookie to his mouth. It was an act of acceptance on his part, one she believed would end any interaction between them.

"Don't."

He paused just before the point of no return.

"Hang on to it for a bit," she continued, almost rankled by her weakness. Despite her plans to remain detached throughout her brief stay in Rosemont, Dane Chappell had nailed her in one, astute breath. His story, his losses, his personal quest to right some wrongs were simply too profound for her to ignore. "I just need to think on it, that's all."

With the hope restored to his gaze, he palmed the cookie. Gave her a nod of gratitude. "At the risk of sounding like a dick, you'd better think fast. That road going in behind us is about to cut through our last chance at stopping this chicken plant from happening."

She frowned. "What do you mean?"

"Without it, Rydell Foods will pull out of the deal.

45

Build somewhere else."

To think a multi-million-dollar project of that caliber would hinge on a simple road... "Are you sure?"

"Yes. It was non-negotiable on their part."

Leslie crossed her arms. "And tell me again why it would be such a bad thing to have a prosperous factory in Rosemont?"

His gaze went down to the screwdriver in her hand, which she realized had gone lax in her grip. "That's something you should learn for yourself," he replied. "You can start by going to Rose Park on the west side of town and sitting on one of the benches by the pond. Watch the old folks feed the ducks. The kids play some ball. The sun lower over the ridge. And when you soak it all in, keep in mind it'll all go away when that plant is built."

The wholesome image he'd painted popped out of her head like a busted balloon. "The plant is going where the park is?" she asked, already bothered by the prospect.

"Close enough to make an impact."

"How so?"

His gaze turned shrewd as it read hers. "Go to the library and look up pollution and environmental complaints about Rydell Foods over the last decade." The pulse in his jaw was back. "Then do a search of Clearwater, Iowa."

She stared at that pulse, fascinated with how the man conveyed his emotions without even moving or saying a word. "You can't just *tell* me about Clearwater, Iowa?" she asked him.

He gave her a tight smile. "Not without

accidentally eating my last cookie."

When she smiled back, it was a genuine one, and the angst he'd built up while telling his story about the park slowly dissipated as he watched her. And watched her.

"But if it's okay with you," he added, his voice a bit rougher than before, "I'd like to take one last look in the basement while I'm here."

"You never found what you were looking for," she guessed. "What is it exactly?"

"A way to stop the road."

She thought about that, and finally decided not to pry any further for fear of falling too deeply into a cause not her own. "Go for it."

But when he moved to the back porch, she couldn't help but follow, her curiosity getting the better of her. At the bottom of the steps, he turned and arched a brow at her. She crossed her arms again. Stuck her chin up. "You didn't think you'd go without supervision, did you?"

Dane looked only mildly annoyed by that. "Think I'm gonna steal from you, Ms. Downing?"

When she took the last step and reached the grass, he hadn't bothered to move or back up. They stood only a few inches apart now, so close she caught his scent. Fabric softener, a little copper, and whatever animal magnetism smelled like.

And hell if his gaze hadn't grown hot. "You know what I think?" he murmured.

"What?" she breathed.

"I think you're getting sucked in, Ms. Downing."

Those eyes looked like they wanted to devour her now, so much that it took what little breath she had left right out of her lungs. "N-no." She inhaled a hearty dose of air. "There is absolutely no…no sucking."

How long had he been in prison again? Surely the first thing he did upon his release was find a willing one-night-stand to purge all the sexual tension he was aiming at her that very moment.

His mouth moved with a slow smile. "Too bad."

Reeling from the sheer strength of those vibes, she totally missed him walking away until she found herself alone and blinking at the carnage of the back porch. She caught up to him at the top of the steps leading down to the basement door. "If you're implying—"

"By the way," he interrupted, "I like what you've done with the place."

Right. She took a deep breath, telling herself not to put too much thought into it. Dane Chappell was a hard man to read. Hard head. Hard ass. Hard stare. Hard shoulder muscles that moved like powerful sin beneath the shirt he wore.

Quit staring at his muscles.

The last thing she needed was a quick fling with a guy who was probably on his way back to jail. Once they were in the basement, she perched on the second to the bottom step and watched him search. He seemed intent, knew exactly where to look for whatever he was looking for, and Leslie was loath to interrupt. But as he removed bottles of liquor from an overhead cabinet, she couldn't help but do so. "My uncle bought this place because of the fallout shelter," she told him. "He'll be upset when he finds out it isn't here anymore."

"Upset enough to sell it back to me?" Dane asked over his shoulder.

"You'd like that, wouldn't you?"

"Very much so."

Her gaze narrowed suspiciously on his backside. "I would hate to think your son lied to him about it when he sold him the house."

His backside stiffened a bit. "Otter wouldn't do that. The subject must not have come up."

Probably. It certainly wouldn't be Uncle Claven's first impulsive move. Leslie continued to watch Dane and his careful scrutiny of each bottle. "What exactly are you looking for?"

He took a small flashlight out of his pocket and shined it in the back of the now empty cabinet. "A bottle of single malt whiskey," he said finally.

Whiskey? That was what made the man risk his freedom by showing up here? "Mr. Chappell—"

"Call me Dane." Blowing out a breath, he made a visual sweep of the entire basement, his lips pursed in thought.

"Dane," she said sweetly. "It appears to me that you don't need any more whiskey, you need an AA meeting."

His eyes narrowed on something in a dark corner and he headed that way. "The whiskey is worth eighty dollars alone, but the papers it came with are priceless. I just found out from a friend that he'd sent both here via courier, but I was arrested before they arrived. My son remembered seeing the box of whiskey and told me it should still be here."

"I'm sure there was a lot of foot traffic in this place when it was up for sale," she said, hating to burst his bubble. "What's to say someone didn't pilfer your liquor stash while they were here?"

"Nothing. But I have to try, don't I?"

He sounded miffed, as if he'd heard the same thing a dozen times already. Something told her he was still fighting a battle he'd lost a long time ago, one everyone else in his life wished he would concede to already. "Sssssoo," she drawled, "what exactly was in this envelope that makes it important enough to violate your parole?"

Dane came out of the shadows with a black box in his hands. There was a gold bow on top, and a tag that he was in the process of reading. As he held it under the light, the look on his face spelled pure excitement, and was powerful enough to get Leslie off her butt. She approached him, peering around his shoulder as he set the box down and opened it. Out came a sophisticated looking bottle of dark brown liquor that sported a black label with a red wax seal above it. Then he pulled an envelope out of the box, but when he opened it his face slowly fell. It was empty.

No papers, though whoever had taken them left plenty of evidence that they'd been there at one time.

She took the envelope just before it slipped through his fingers. The printed seal on the return address line read *Kansas Department of Wildlife*. "What were the papers, Dane?" she asked again, sharing his sorrow down to her bones.

He turned dead, listless eyes toward her. "It doesn't matter anymore."

Leslie watched him gently set the bottle of whiskey down on the emptied cabinet's shelf. She moved aside for him as he approached the stairs empty-handed. Only when she glimpsed his profile again did she realize that he wasn't sad.

He was angry. Very, very angry.

"Is there anything I can do?" she asked in a small voice.

He stopped mid-stride, knuckles turning white as he gripped the edge of the doorway. "Meet me again tomorrow evening, after you've done what I asked."

She swallowed, unsure of whether to duck, hide, or just take a face full of gray matter when the man's head exploded. "Okay. But no more break-ins. I'll come to you."

He twisted around then, giving her some semblance of a smile. "I'd like that. Just make sure you aren't followed."

"Why? You're safe as long as you aren't caught outside state lines."

The smile disappeared. "I'm more worried about you."

"Oh." Definitely a natural born protector. Once his reply sank in, though… "Wait a minute," she said. "You think someone could be spying on me?"

"Just keep an eye out. Devine is very resourceful. Meet me at a place called Moonlight's, in Westport. Lower level. Eight o'clock."

If the man aimed to make her as paranoid as he, mission accomplished. Feeling crummier than ever for his run of bad luck, Leslie watched him jump the fence. On the other side of it, he was almost immediately swallowed up by thick scrub brush and vine, and the lowering light of dusk. He stopped. Patted the cookie in his pocket as a reminder that they had a deal. "No pressure, Ms. Downing," he said in a low voice. "But without those papers, you're the only hope I have left."

Uh-oh. The man was in deeper trouble than he knew. "I'm very sorry you didn't find what you were looking for," she replied softly, meaning every word. "And if I come across the papers, I'll bring them to you."

"You won't. Someone already found them, and I think I know who."

"Mayor Tosh?"

His lips thinned into a grim line. "I'm going to get seven kinds of fucked up tonight, just so I don't come back and finish that bastard off."

She answered him with a wobbly smile. "In that case, I know of an eighty-dollar bottle of whiskey with your name on it."

A bitter laugh. "Staring at it will only make me madder."

Understandable. Not another word was exchanged as he disappeared into the woods, taking his barely controlled anger with him…and leaving Leslie with an unsettled feeling that eclipsed all others. What was she doing getting mixed up in all this? Now that Dane was gone, it was as if a curtain had been lifted, and she found herself standing in the quagmire of someone else's problems.

But at least that quagmire was no longer her own.

****

"Mayor Tosh, the sheriff is here to see you."

Without taking his eyes off his laptop, Thurlow Tosh reached over and pressed the speaker button on his desk phone. "Send her in." Then he addressed the man who was at his open door, finishing up with the new sign marking it his. "Carl, take a break, will you?"

The new City Hall still smelled of fresh paint and crisp carpeting, but it also surrounded him with an incomparable elegance that the doublewide trailer of old failed to offer. As soon as he was sworn in as mayor, he'd vowed to upgrade despite the city council's grumblings of low funds. Thanks to his wooing of Rydell Foods, they'd enjoyed an influx of cash from the sixty-acre sale of land on which to build the plant—at an inflated price, of course, in exchange for tax-free benefits.

Now he was sitting in luxury and enjoying the remote-control lights and window shades his new building had to offer. Its brick-and-mortar façade, white columns, and circle drive exhibited the look of a mansion. Perhaps he and Peggy should move in, he thought with a chuckle. Or with his next kickback he'd just build them a bigger family home.

There was no trace of Carl by the time Devine entered his office. As she shut the door behind her, Thurlow sat back in his chair and regarded her with an expectant air, which she ignored as she thumbed out a text on her phone. "Well," he prodded. "Any sign of him?"

Devine must have hit send because she pocketed the phone and gave him her full attention. "I just put out a bolo on Chappell. John Watson, who lives down the road from Chappell's old place, said he saw a strange car pull over in front of his house last night and pick up a stranger. No plate number to go off of and no evidence at the scene, but if he's paying visits to Ms. Downing, we'll be waiting next time."

Thurlow regarded his reflection in the now darkened screen of his laptop. His full cheek bore a permanent scar that nearly ran into his hairline. Three of his teeth were now fake, but looked fantastic, nonetheless. His near-white brows and hair—blond at the time of his beating—had once been mired in blood. He ran a hand through the full mass, remembering the photos he'd been shown of his pulverized face. It was pure luck that he'd survived with his eyesight intact. The traumatizing event was almost a blur, only coming in brief flashes of memory—of brutish knuckles pounding at him over and over again, of him begging his attacker to stop. He gritted his teeth, cursing his weaknesses while he fisted his trembling hand before him.

"Don't worry," came Devine's voice from across the desk. She was still standing, her olive-green eyes regarding him with something akin to sympathy. "I won't let him get near you."

Anger flourished anew. He stood up with enough force to send his chair flying backward. "I don't need you to act as my bodyguard," he sneered, hands on hips as he rounded the desk and approached her. "Makes me look like a fucking pussy."

A pulse began to jump in her thick jaw. She was a tough looking bitch when she narrowed her eyes like that, but in a sexy, predatory way that worked with her full-figured physique. "I may be a woman," she said, squaring off with him. "But I'm also the sheriff. Your manhood isn't in question."

He closed the remaining distance between them, getting in her face so that he had to refocus for clarity. "Damn right it's not."

With the push of a button on his special remote, his office door locked with a faint click. Then he grabbed Sheriff Devine's hand and placed it over his hardening crotch. "And it really wants to fuck something right now."

Her thin, un-glossed lips stretched into a slow, burning smile.

****

Rose Park was a modest little break in the woods that backed the western side of town. There wasn't much in the way of playground equipment, Leslie noticed, but the large pond, bike trails, and groomed flora made for a beautiful place to sit on the grass and enjoy the sunshine or a good book. The town square was still outfitted in the cobblestones and shade trees of old. Most of the buildings surrounding it were the original brick and mortar storefronts. Except for the county courthouse, which had burned down four decades prior and sat in the center square with a more modern architecture.

The police station and jail were situated in the northwest corner of the square, harmoniously sharing space with the Sheriff's Department.

There wasn't much activity at high noon on a hot Tuesday, but Leslie could imagine people walking their dogs at dusk. Eating their lunches on a park bench in springtime. And just like Dane said, an elderly couple holding hands as they got their steps in amid the sunrise.

A fountain in the middle of the pond displayed a sparkling, fan-like formation while fat ducks teetered across the grass in the foreground, searching for a handout or a juicy grub.

Yeah. She could totally see the appeal. It was peaceful here and, as the many colorful flowers would attest, loved by enough people to remain well tended. It would be a complete shame to have the prettiest section of Rosemont sullied by the presence of a three hundred twenty-million-dollar poultry complex, its factory-emitting productivity poorly hidden behind a razor-wired, chain-link fence.

Sure, the people saw what they wanted to see: prosperity, booming businesses, rising property values. It's what had been promised them by not only their mayor, but Rydell's own hired guns. And after reading all about Clearwater, Iowa, Leslie now understood that Dane only wanted the people of Rosemont to make an *informed* decision, for them and the whole of Summit County.

If it wasn't already too late.

Would they have so quickly accepted the shady tactics of the city council's secret vote if they'd known about Clearwater? How Rydell Foods had deposited thousands of pounds of toxic pollutants into its waterways, causing the biggest environmental disaster in the state's history? How the population boom had caused the overcrowding of schools and soaring crime rates? And that over seventy percent of the promised jobs went to foreigners who worked for lower wages?

Probably not. Then again, that's what made paid-off politicians so damned rich and slimy. And now *Leslie* wanted to beat the snot out of Mayor Thurlow Tosh.

Well played, Dane Chappell. Well played.

"Saturday is movie night in the park," came a familiar voice behind her.

Leslie sat up and turned with a smile for Maxi. "Hey, you." Her gaze lowered to the four-year-old staring at her from around Mom's backside. "Mister Trouble. What are you doing out in this heat?"

Maxi produced a near-empty bag of sandwich

bread. "Trouble's favorite activity. Feeding the ducks."

"Duckth!" Trouble yelled, coming out of hiding and jumping up and down with hands grabbing.

Leslie reared back, surprised to hear such an explosion of sound from the usually quiet child. "How exciting," she exclaimed, feeling the exhilaration herself. She'd never fed ducks before. "Can I join you?"

"Of course you can," Maxi gushed, her thin maternity sundress blowing sunshine right between her legs as she led Trouble closer to the pond.

Leslie got up from her park bench and followed, but almost changed her mind when an army of waddlers came barreling down on the mother and son duo. They and their bread were definitely known to these particular locals. "Are you sure they won't bite?" she asked warily.

Maxi laughed as she tore a slice into little pieces. "Not if you throw it. Show her how, Trouble."

The little boy grabbed a handful in a squished fist. He gently took one piece out and gave it a wild toss. Ducks descended on the bread in a furious mosh-posh of quacks and waggling tails. Trouble let out a roar of delight that didn't faze the wildlife one bit. He tossed another and got the same result, his audience growing and oh-so loyal.

Maxi handed Leslie a few pieces. "Go on, throw some over there."

Feeling much like a kid herself, she mimicked Trouble's technique; however, an untimely gust of wind kicked up and blew the whole fistful out of her hand. Bread scattered around her feet. As the feathered beasts dove for it, Leslie yelped. Danced. Jumped up and down. Wild laughter rose above the sound of furious quacking, and Leslie sent her companions a quelling look that only made them laugh harder.

"I don't think I like ducks very much," she complained, scoping out her pinky toe, which had taken a small nip by a particularly overzealous waddler. "Tell me they don't carry rabies."

Still laughing, Maxi bent low and inspected the toe, which was dangerously exposed in a pair of aqua bejeweled flip-flops. "You're fine. Didn't even break the skin." Holding her belly, she slowly straightened again. "I haven't laughed that hard in a long time."

"So glad I could entertain," Leslie griped, though a smile broke through as she gingerly made her way back to the park bench. "I think I'll just watch you from here."

"Speaking of entertainment, you should come to the movie Saturday night. I think this week they're playing that romantic comedy with Chris Evans and," she snapped her fingers, "that girl who played the daughter in that movie. What is her name... crap that's gonna bug me." Then her eyes got big. "Oh my gosh, Leslie, it's so much fun. People come with their lawn chairs or picnic blankets, and a cooler of whatever, and then they blow up this big movie screen and people just hang out and—"

As Maxi rambled on, Trouble chased her dangling bag of bread in an attempt to grab another piece. Imagining Maxi and her family partaking in movie night in the park put such a wholesome picture in Leslie's head that she suddenly wanted more than anything to be a part of it.

On her way back to her car, she passed a storefront

with a changeable message board in the window that read: "Movie night in the park. This week's feature: *Rain In Your Hair,* starring Chris Evans and Maggie Grace."

She backed up a few steps, peered around the side of the building and yelled at Maxi. "Maggie Grace!"

Maxi turned and bopped her forehead with a palm. "Yes! Thank you!"

Chapter 5

That evening, Dane waited in the underground bar of Moonlight's. It was a dark place with just enough noise to hear without being heard, which made it a great public establishment to talk business. Bathed in blue neon, he stood at the bar with a club soda in hand. Scanned the crowd. Knew that once Leslie showed up, she may turn around and walk right back out again.

The swinging door behind the bar opened. Out came a short, thick-chested black man wearing a sophisticated white coat and hat. The hat came off revealing a close haircut with a side part etched into it. The man's dark eyes met Dane's and crinkled when he smiled. He approached with a hand out and Dane met it with his own. They clasped, pulled in for a one-armed bro hug that ended with some fond reflection.

"How ya doin', Sugar Free?" Dane asked. "Keeping things honest?"

The ex-gangbanger shook his head, his smile remaining as he retrieved a glass. "As the day is long, Five-O. To what do I owe this pleasure?"

"Just checking on my favorite roommate."

Terrell Washington—or *Sugar Free* to those who knew him on the streets—squirted something from the fountain over ice. He came around the bar and pulled out the stool next to Dane's. "Or you want something."

Dane chuckled and held up his glass. "Well, you do

owe me."

They clinked in a toast that faded their smiles. Prison had been a special kind of hell for them both, for different reasons. Surrounded by rival gang members and cop haters, Dane and Terrell were biding their time until some scumbag figured them out and decided to end their lives. It would have happened for Terrell if Dane hadn't watched his back. And Terrell was the only fellow prisoner who'd known Dane was a cop.

"I saved your life just by keeping my mouth shut," the man preened. "That's the only reason you didn't get parole through the *back* door."

"True dat, brother."

Terrell's jovial laughter carried across the bar. "Don't even start with the ghetto talk, Five-O, you know you suck at it."

An "exercise" they'd laughed through before when time was their worst enemy. Their first few weeks as cellmates had been wrought with tension. Both had slept with one eye open, waiting the other out. But it had been the third cellmate, a screwball named Fido who'd made an actual attempt on the illustrious Sugar Free when his back was turned, and Dane had put the man down quickly and without thought. Not because there had been any love between he and Terrell at the time, but no one deserved to die while taking a piss.

It was enough to shake the hardened gangbanger up a bit. Terrell had actually trusted Fido, a turn of events that taught him a most valuable lesson—trust came in many colors, even blue.

Now Terrell Washington was an honest-to-goodness member of the working-class. He was a good man, one Dane had grown to respect more than most—

for turning it all around if nothing else. "Your brother still directing films?" he asked.

Terrell's smile faded. "Ah. Now we're talking."

"I just need that buried footage I told you about brought back to life. Preferably in high definition."

"Resurrection is one thing. Birthing's another."

"Depends on the religion."

Terrell's gaze shifted to an object behind Dane. His brow smoothed out and his eyes warmed. "You expecting company?"

Dane turned and felt an immediate surge of lust as Leslie Downing came into view. Her gaze was intense, unbreaking as she skirted around a few male gawkers and headed straight for him. Her hair was down, like spun gold as it framed her soft face and creamy, bare shoulders. The woman knew how to dress, how to look, how to float like an angel. He guessed she couldn't help it when her radiant skin outshone the colorful, sleeveless dress she wore. So caught up in her, he failed to hear his friend until a low whistle broke through the fog.

"No way, convict. That chick has vanilla written all over her fine ass."

"Watch it," Dane said through the side of his mouth as he stood to meet Leslie. "Let's grab a booth," he suggested to her in lieu of the usual greeting. At that point, any effort at one would come off as a schoolboy attempt to flirt.

She nodded her reply, her gaze flickering over the African-American man behind him. Dane put his hand against her lower back, keenly aware of how good the minor touch felt as he ushered her toward the farthest of glittery black booths along the wall. He had her get in first, then slid in beside her, always on the outside. Always with the wall at his six.

When Terrell slid into the seat facing them, her look turned wary. The guy still appeared every bit the hoodlum despite the chef's attire, and Dane guessed it was because the life was sewn into his deepest fibers. Would always be there in his language, his walk, his habit of zeroing in on someone with crosshair-eyes. And if he took the coat off, Leslie would be treated to a whole host of other reasons to be wary. Sugar Free still wore his colors in the ink on his arms and torso, tattoos—real-deal scary shit—that he'd decided to keep as-is as a reminder of where not to go when temptation called.

As Dane introduced them, he felt a reluctant pride in her ability to pretend that she wasn't crapping herself right now. Any other woman who was thoroughly trapped in a booth with two horribly questionable characters would. She'd had no reason to come. No reason to trust him. No reason to think she would make it out of there unscathed.

But he would change all of that tonight. "Leslie is a journalist," he told Terrell.

While the man scrutinized, she cleared her throat. "Um…not a journalist," she added, and slid the drink menu in for a closer look.

"Oh, right. She's an *editor*," Dane amended, "who should be a journalist." Because she would become one for the cause if he played his cards right. "I take it you did some research today, Ms. Downing."

Before she could answer, a slip of a waitress came up to their booth, her glossy curls lightened to the same shade as her cocoa skin. The girl flirted with Terrell for an adorable moment, which brought a sweet smile out of him. When she asked what everyone was having, Leslie shoved the drink menu with its fruity cocktails aside and ordered a vodka neat. "And bring a water," she added. "And a straw, please." Her hands went back in her lap in tight fists.

"And you, sir?"

Dane held up his near-empty rocks glass. "Club soda."

Leslie's gaze darted upward, her petite little brows scrunching in that confused way of hers. "Nursing a hangover?" she guessed when the waitress left.

Terrell's chest rumbled with laughter. "I see you already made an impression with the lady."

"Look who's talking," Dane mumbled in return. But Terrell was right. Even with his groomed hair and sport coat, he felt the prison on him—a stink that would never go away thanks to Thurlow Tosh and his thirst for power. Worse yet, Dane would never be able to legally own or carry a firearm again, a fundamental need that left him fidgety enough to fuel his desire for revenge. "I guess it's no secret by now that I wanted you two to meet."

Terrell leaned forward and laced his fingers on the white and black speckled tabletop. "I think you better get specific before she climbs over you and runs outta here."

"Terrell has connections," Dane explained to Leslie. "Ones that could be useful when it comes to public service announcements."

Her lips parted with a speculative, "Oh."

"And don't let the bling fool you." He indicated the diamond "S" in each of the ex-gangster's earlobes, as well as the metal on his teeth. "Terrell's a regular pussycat."

The man grinned. "I won't bite. Promise."

"You know…" Leslie's eyes narrowed on the silver display. "You aren't exactly instilling me with confidence."

The waitress came back with her loaded tray. "Club soda for you, sir, and a shot of liquid courage for the lady."

Terrell laughed again as she set the vodka shot and glass of iced water down in front of Leslie. "Better keep 'em coming," he told her.

Nine songs and three shots later, Leslie sat in rapt attention while Terrell told prison stories, half of them untrue, the other half watered down to suit a more tender palate such as hers. Dane watched her with amused fascination as she annihilated a plate of nachos in the process.

"You mean he actually killed a man over a bag of corn chips?" she asked between bites. Her wide-eyed gaze slid over to Dane for confirmation.

He shrugged, thoroughly enjoying drunk-Leslie. "It was the last bag."

"No way!"

"Seriously," Terrell said. "That's why they called him Fido Lay."

"And Dane saved you from this sicko?"

"We had each other's backs," Dane offered with a fair amount of reverence. "We may not have survived otherwise."

The two ex-cons shared a prolonged look of understanding. Amidst the shifting atmosphere, Terrell nodded. "I hear you, Five-O. But we're out now. Free.

You should be starting over like me, not nursing old grudges."

"I'm not free," Dane said with a level stare. "I won't be until I get back every last right Tosh took from me."

After a moment, Terrell nodded. "Okay, then. But after this we're even." He tapped the table to emphasize his point. "No more favors. I don't want the smell of your shit blowing in my direction."

"Are you expecting Terrell to break the law for you?" Leslie asked, her voice incredulous beside him.

Without bothering to acknowledge the frown he could feel aimed in his direction, Dane sat back. Held Terrell's gaze. "I'm asking him to help me right a wrong."

Terrell shook his head. Observed a few patrons who'd passed by on their way to the restrooms. "How soon?"

"Three days," Dane answered.

"How buried is this footage?"

"Deep enough."

"We talking Nat Geo or Jerry Springer?"

"A little of both."

Terrell produced a cellphone, thumbed in a quick text. "This'll ruin lives, brah."

Dane watched him, knowing he was about to get a small portion of the justice he'd been dreaming about every second of every day of the nineteen months he'd rotted in prison. "At least it'll be the right lives this time," he said without a single shred of remorse.

Leslie shoved her plate of nachos aside. "Why did you want me and Terrell to meet, Dane?"

He sent her a stiff smile. "Got plans for Saturday

night?"

"Actually, yes. I—" A hiccup broke through "—thought I'd take my uncle to movie night in the park."

The woman was full of surprises. She'd already solved half his problems and he hadn't so much as broken a sweat.

Almost an hour later, no matter how many coffees Dane had forced down her, Leslie still exited Moonlight's on unsteady legs. It had been a mistake letting her get all liquored up, but he'd needed her agreeable. And he got what he wanted that night, in more ways than he could hope for: help from Terrell to gather the necessary dirt on Tosh and help from Leslie to expose it. His life was turning around already. He could feel the positive vibes with every smile Leslie aimed at him, drunken or no.

But as he'd watched her give Terrell a big, warm hug before parting ways, Dane couldn't help but wonder if his restoration of life was worth the cost of her virtue. She was a good girl despite her own hardships…though he thought she could use a wake-up call of her own. A naïve, single woman living alone needed better protection than a Phillips screwdriver. Didn't Midwest city-girls know these things?

Terrell had appreciated her hug a little too much if the man's clandestine, twinkly smile was any indication. Dane knew of six ways she could have put him down, ending with a robust *"Back away, asshole!"* He'd make it a point to show her every one of them in preparation for Saturday night.

"See you in a few days, Sunshine," Terrell had said to her. "And stay away from this convict, here. He'll do nothing but get you in trouble."

Leslie had sent Dane her best attempt at a scowl. "I should say the same to you, Sugar Free." Terrell's street name had rolled off her tongue as if she were talking to Santa Clause. "Hey—how did you get that name, anyway?"

Terrell steadied her teetering form with a light grip on the shoulders. "I'm diabetic."

"Really? I've never heard of a diabetic gangster before."

Dane hid his amusement behind a sudden need to scratch his beard as Terrell continued to feed her bullshit. He'd earned the name for his brutal tendencies on the streets. Being the smallest kid on the playground, he'd had to prove that he was the biggest, and he'd shown no love, no "sugar" to anyone who'd fucked up. Sugar Free gave no second chances, a rep that caught up with him in prison. Something had happened to him there, something he wouldn't talk about. But it had made Terrell Washington a different man, vowing to never earn a return trip to that particular playground.

As Leslie walked to her car, Dane followed, keeping a sharp eye out for anyone suspicious. He hadn't meant to venture out into the open with her, but drunk-Leslie needed a ride. "Give me the keys," he said as they approached her silver Camry.

"I'm fine."

"Good girls don't drive drunk."

She stopped. Swayed a bit as she blinked up at him. "I'm not."

He couldn't keep his amused smile from breaking through. "You're drunk enough to be dangerous."

"No, I mean I'm not a good girl. Kyle always said that, and it drove me crazy."

That nugget of info put a damper on his mood. "What's wrong with good girls?"

She dug through her purse in a vicious search for her keys. "Apparently they make bad lovers."

When she produced the keys, he removed them from her hand without receiving any further argument. As they stood by her car, her words resonated through his mind. He doubted she would have blurted out such a thing without the help of three vodkas, but she did. And it was telling.

"It's pretty obvious to me you weren't married to the right man," he said, his voice a little too rough for his liking.

"And?" she returned with attitude.

"Is it obvious to *you?*"

Her scowl faded with a sigh of resignation. "I don't care anymore."

He wanted to pull her in and hug the hell out of her. She was an adorable, wounded soul with so much to offer, but until she was sober, there would be no offering of anything. Hugging would lead to kissing. Kissing would lead to heavy petting. Heavy petting would lead to—

Aw hell. He pulled her in anyway, unable to resist her clear effort to stay cool. She didn't try to pull away, just burrowed in as if she were bone tired. The feel of her against him, all soft and compliant, tugged at the parts of him down below, but it also tugged at his heart. Yes, the two of them would fall into bed one day and test that theory about bad lovers. His inner alpha-male couldn't turn down such a challenge, but it would be when her eyes weren't so glassy.

"Come on, Leslie Downing." He pulled away but

kept his arm around her shoulders as he led her to the passenger side of the car. "We're going to my place."

She sagged against him, her fragrant hair just below his chin. "So you can take advantage of me, Mr. Chappell?"

"So you can sleep some of that off before you drive yourself home." He opened the door for her.

Before getting in, she squared off with him. Looked at his mouth. "Whose bed am I sleeping in?"

"Mine."

"I thought so," she smirked.

"It's called the couch."

"Oh."

She actually looked disappointed. Dane hid a groan as she finally got in and shut her door. He circled around the car, giving his stirred-up cock a stern talking-to along the way.

"Nice night for a rendezvous," came a voice beside him.

Dane aborted his attempt to open the driver's side door and slowly turned around, taking in the familiar figure standing in shadows by a white Caddy five cars down. The fact that Leslie had been followed after all wasn't the big surprise to Dane.

It was that Mayor Thurlow Tosh had waited this long to show himself.

"You aren't too bright, are you, Tosh?" Dane asked the man, hands in pockets as a reminder not to use them. At that moment it was a good thing he wasn't armed. "Always poking the bear."

Thurlow unwrapped a piece of gum and stuck it in his mouth. He chewed lazily in the night, his light hair standing out against the dark sky. "Are you going to beat me up again, Dane?"

Dane stared at the gum wrapper as it went into Thurlow's pocket. It was white with the brand name printed in red, just like the one he'd seen beside the box of whiskey in his basement. "Wish it was me the first time," Dane replied with faux calm. "The least I could get for losing my freedom is the satisfaction of feeling your bones break under my knuckles."

"So barbaric. And now you're using Ms. Downing to continue this crusade of yours." Thurlow was unmoving from his relaxed position by his car. "I'd advise you against it. You have no sympathizers, and you don't want to risk the community turning on her, too."

"That a threat?"

"Just a reminder. No one deserves to be victimized by you."

There was some truth to what he said, enough to put the taste of guilt in Dane's mouth. "At least I'm not destroying a whole town."

"I'm saving Rosemont. Despite being the county seat, it was on its way to becoming a ghost town and you know it."

"If you really believed that, you wouldn't have kept the city council vote a secret. The truth is you're an outsider. You have no real home, no family roots to speak of, and not a shred of compassion for the people of Rosemont." Dane pointed a finger. "But that town still comes first for me, and I'll stop you no matter *who* I have to use to do it."

"At least you admit you're using Ms. Downing." Tosh removed the gum and smiled as he wadded it back up in its wrapper. "This was nice, but I have to get home to my wife. We're going over plans for a new house."

The man was good at rubbing shit in, especially at a distance. "Say hi to Peggy for me," Dane threw in as an exaggerated pleasantry. "Oh…by the way, does she know you're fucking your sheriff?"

"Don't gossip, Chappell," Tosh threw back without so much as a flinch. "It doesn't suit you."

As the white Caddy drove away, Dane yanked open the Camry's door and slid behind the wheel. He sat there for a moment, using the time it took to adjust the seat in order to count down from twenty.

Leslie was staring straight ahead, her blonde hair glowing under the dome light. Dane glanced over at her. "You heard that, didn't you?"

"Kind of hard not to."

"Look, I didn't mean it to sound like I was using—"

"I get it, Dane." Her words were sharp, in stark difference to the last time she'd spoken. "You've been dealt a bad hand. But like Terrell said, after this thing on Saturday is done, I'd prefer that you don't contact me again." When her eyes met his, the dome light faded to dark. "Do we understand each other?"

Chapter 6

The ride back to Dane's place was wrought with tension, Leslie staring out the window the whole way and watching the city pass by in silence. When they arrived in front of a quiet, side-by-side duplex, she was stone cold sober and in no mood to come inside.

"Don't make me call the cops on you," he teased in an apparent attempt to lighten the mood. "Unless you want to get out and do the sobriety test for me in this very driveway."

She rolled her eyes. "Fine. I'll do the test if it will get you off my back."

The fact she wanted to leave so badly resonated between them, and Dane blew out a frustrated breath as they both got out of the car. On the vacant side of the driveway, she kicked off her heels and waited for him to start issuing commands.

His first came with the authoritative ring of a cop. "I want you to close your eyes and touch the tip of your right index finger to the end of your nose." She did. "Now your left."

That one landed with only a minor misalignment. In her opinion it wasn't enough to slap the cuffs on her.

"Now, following the edge of the driveway, I want you to walk toward me heel-to-toe in a perfectly straight line until I tell you to stop."

Starting at the sidewalk, she did as she was told,

looking down at her feet, her arms out and keeping her balanced. "If you're going to ask me to say the alphabet backward," she said, "I can't even do that sober."

"Look up at me, please."

She brought her head up, watching him and his intent focus on her steps. The shift caused her to wobble to the side, so she stopped and corrected her balance with one foot still in the air.

"I didn't tell you to stop."

"Oh, for the love of…" Leslie took a deep breath, centered her chi, and continued walking. And walking. His gaze came up, locked with hers. The heat she saw there slammed into her with hurricane force. Her step faltered again, and this time she just shut down.

"Ms. Downing," he said low. "I didn't tell you to stop."

But she couldn't move. So he came to her, closing the meager distance with a humble air about him. "Don't go," he whispered, their bodies barely touching. "Sleep, at least for a little while. I promise I'll be a good boy."

Was this him caring about her? Or caring that she survived the drive home in order to carry out her part in his crusade? It was hard to tell anything other than that his intense, masculine heat was making her break into a sweat. "Does this mean I didn't pass your test?"

"Failed miserably."

"You tripped me up. That's hardly fair."

"Tell that to him." He jerked his chin, making her turn and look behind her.

There, at the end of the driveway, was a white police car idling in the road. Her heart lodged in her diaphragm, and she fired a look back at Dane that killed. "Asshole. You really did call the cops."

"Relax, it's only my son." His lips twitched and he took her elbow, ushering her toward the squad car as its window rolled down. He leaned over and rested a forearm on the windowsill. "You have some weird timing, deputy."

Beyond the stationary laptop and scary looking rifle, dash lights illuminated the handsome young officer behind the wheel. With his father's dark hair, strong forehead, and compelling stare, Leslie could see why Maxi was so attracted to Otter Chappell.

She could also see the resemblance between him and a little boy named Trouble.

He nodded at her, though his gaze moved between her and Dane. "It almost looked like you were giving the lady here a sobriety test."

"I was," Dane answered. "She failed."

Annoyed, Leslie stuck a hand through the window, which the young deputy took. A handshake ensued as she introduced herself. "You must be Otter—uh—Oliver. You sold your dad's property to my uncle and I'm staying out there for a while."

Oliver's expression remained pleasant, indicating he wasn't a bit surprised to find her loitering at his place of residence. "Pleasure to meet you, Leslie."

"And I didn't fail that test. Your father cheated."

Sensing some sign language going on behind her, she looked back at Dane who stood cool as a cucumber.

Otter didn't miss a beat. "Well, I do detect a hint of alcohol on your breath. At this point I'd advise that you stay off the road."

****

Leslie woke the next morning with a minor

headache and lots of confusion. The air was cool on her exposed arm, a different kind of cool than the early morning breeze flowing through an open window. The smell of already-brewed coffee hit her olfactory system just as her phone began to buzz beneath her left thigh.

All systems go. Rolling her eyeballs forward, she got them ready for the grand opening, knowing they would be God-awful-red and rimmed with crusty mascara. As her lids finally parted, she remembered exactly where she was.

In Dane's bed.

Leather creaked as she sat up and rubbed the sleep from her eyes. The couch was pretty comfortable all things considered, and there was only room for one person. Not that Dane had made advances other than supplying her with a pillow and blanket.

Phone! By the time she remembered to dig it out from under her butt, it was warm to the touch and had already stopped buzzing. With a yawn, she checked the screen, loving that she actually had bars for a change.

Unknown number. Whoever tried to call would leave a voicemail if it were that important.

Coffee appeared, held in the grasp of a very big, very masculine hand. She looked up into Dane's stoic countenance, dropped the phone on the coffee table, and took the mug in both hands.

"Thank you." She buried her face in its rising column of steam, trying to ignore how primal and sexy he looked in his maxed-out T-shirt, jeans, and wet hair. Yes, the ex-sheriff of Summit County was climbing the ranks as one of the most incredibly handsome men she'd ever met in her adult life. Even more handsome than Kyle, a feat she didn't think was possible.

In fact, her ex-husband was becoming less important as the days progressed. When did that start happening?

Dane shoved his hands in the front pockets of his jeans. "Need an ibuprofen?"

"Maybe?" she replied, not sure of anything at the moment. When he disappeared again, she got up with coffee in hand and headed to the bathroom, a part of the duplex she'd become very familiar with since her agreement to sleep for a few hours. That few hours had turned into six if the time on her phone was correct.

On her way, she stopped at a life-sized cutout of what looked to be Dolph Lundgren. She studied the Swedish actor's bold display of machismo and decided that the fierce smolder had nothing on Dane Chappell.

Ten minutes later, she emerged with her hair up and face washed, feeling much better and more than ready for that drive home. But when she spied the bottle of ibuprofen beside her phone, she knew the drive would have to wait. First—an apology.

In her bare feet and wrinkled dress, she went in search of Dane. Found him on the back patio where he stood by a table and chairs, facing the sunrise. He drank from his own coffee mug, his broad shoulders making one hell of a silhouette.

She stepped outside and closed the sliding glass door behind her. "I'm sorry for giving you so much grief last night."

He looked down at her, amusement crinkling the corners of his eyes. "No need to apologize."

"I wasn't right to drive. You of all people would know that, so thank you for stopping me."

"You were…emotional."

For some reason, the outdoors gave her more room to consider why she'd been emotional. She took another sip of coffee. "I'm not anymore. In fact, I want to help you now more than ever. You were right about that mayor character. He must have had me followed. And just showing up like that, and what he said…" She shook her head at the brazen nature of the man. "It was an obvious attempt to goad you."

Dane nodded, his ever-watchful gaze perusing the neighborhood. "He wants me to get another nineteen months so he doesn't have to worry about what I'll do next."

Leslie hugged her coffee mug to her chest despite the fact it was warmer outside than indoors. "With all that talk about you using me, he did the same thing. I won't let him do it again, especially now that he knows we're working together."

"We aren't working together." When their eyes met, his were solemn. "You're going to the park to watch a movie, that's all. As far as last night goes, we were just two people enjoying a drink." His lips curved up. "Or three."

His words confirmed what she'd wondered last night. He *was* worried about her. And she was worried about him. "What if I need to contact you?" she asked, her chest suddenly heavier than before.

"Terrell is your contact. It's best if you and I keep things limited."

She felt his sincerity now, knew that he wasn't necessarily *using* her to further his cause. He was just asking for help—but not at the cost of her safety. "I want you to promise me something," she said, their gazes still locked. "Don't eat that last cookie."

She could tell by the way he looked at her mouth that he wanted to kiss her. For the first time since her split with Kyle, she entertained the idea of being with another man. A *real* one who exuded the perfect combination of strength, determination, and concern for others. Whose eyes said the same thing his words did.

He reached out and tucked a loose strand of hair back into her up-do. "I'll get the damned thing bronzed if it means we'll bump into each other again some day."

Her pulse tap-danced its way right into her groin, making her ache with need. The temptation to grab his face and drill him with a passionate kiss was getting harder and harder to fight, especially now that her juices were flowing. So, she put on a bright smile, said, "It's a deal," and turned back toward the sliding glass doors.

Once the air conditioning hit her skin, she realized just how warm she had become. When she retrieved her phone, it showed that she had one voicemail. She grabbed her purse and keys from the end table, deposited the coffee mug in its place, and got out of there as fast as she could without looking back at a man she knew was watching her hasty departure with equal want.

Only when she was on the road did she listen to that voicemail. And only when she heard the sound of Sheriff Devine's voice did she realize how big of a mistake she'd made in agreeing to help Dane Chappell.

****

It was eight o'clock in the morning before Leslie arrived at Rosemont's police station, pulling into one of the many empty diagonal parking spaces along the front. The native stone and iron-accented windows advertised that there was a jail inside and stood out against the brick fronts of the buildings around it. Since the area was largely empty, her silver Camry may as well have been a billboard stating she was in trouble. That she had been summoned by the law for reasons that would be heavily broadcast among the gossips before the coffee ran out that morning.

She took a deep, fortifying breath before peeling her hands from the steering wheel, removing her sunglasses, and shutting the car down.

As she walked through the front doors, a multitude of odors hit her at once, food-type ones that didn't help to improve the bad vibes one bit. Though visually interesting in an 1800s time-warp kind of way, she found no comfort in the dark wooden floors, paneled walls, and iron light fixtures.

No one waited to greet her behind the Plexiglas partition. There was no noise to speak of. No signs that she would leave with her dignity intact. Finally, a skinny fellow in a black uniform showed up with a half-eaten granola bar in one hand and a steaming paper cup in the other. Upon seeing her, he jerked his chin in greeting but failed to put down his breakfast. "What can I do for you?"

Like he didn't know. "Leslie Downing. I'm here to pick up my uncle, Claven Gallagher."

"Ah." He nodded. "The butt man. You're lucky Ms. Hathaway didn't press assault charges, or you'd be forking out bail."

"Excuse me, the *butt man?*"

"Uh-huh." The deputy clamped his granola bar between his teeth and pushed a button while she showed him her ID.

The door buzzed and unlatched. When Leslie walked through it, he met her in the adjacent hall, crunching noisily as he led the way. "Mr. Gallagher claims he was only joking when he rammed one of those dashboard hula girls into Ms. Hathaway's backside." His eyes popped with incredulity. "Guess those two have an interesting history."

Leslie knew he put one of those dolls on the dashboard of every car he'd owned. As a child, she'd been fascinated by the beauty of the hula girl, as well as the seamless movement of her little grass skirt. But of all the crazy things Uncle Claven had done in his life, she couldn't see him ramming her into someone's rear. "Did he admit to doing this?"

The deputy sent her a droll look. "There were witnesses. Who, by the way, say he tried to poke her a second time."

"Where did this happen? I didn't even know he was in town. I was supposed to pick him up at the bus stop this afternoon."

"It *happened* at the bus stop. Rolled in about 5:00AM."

Which would explain the witnesses. *Damn you, Uncle C.* He was already starting trouble, if in fact the story was true. She still couldn't rule out the possibility that Sheriff Devine was harassing her for meeting with Dane.

If this town wasn't already in trouble because of the mayor's plans with Rydell Foods, it had no chance with Uncle Claven. The seventy-year-old train wreck would level it for sure. "I must have gotten the time of day wrong," she grumbled. "If I'd been there to pick him up, none of this would have happened."

"Don't blame yourself. My mother grew up with the man. Said it sounds like he hasn't changed all that much."

It was never a wonder as to why Uncle Claven hadn't married. The family saw him as a black sheep. Kyle always said no sane woman would have him, and that it was better to keep the kind who *would* have him away from the Thanksgiving table. Leslie was always inclined to agree. Now she thought Kyle just sounded like an asshole.

A protective surge took over, giving Leslie's chin a slight lift as she was led into an office with Sheriff Devine's name on it. It reminded her of Dane's crusade, of how she was involved and really pumped about it, and how she should make her uncle's welfare a crusade of her own. Someone had to care, didn't they?

The deputy told Leslie to have a seat in one of the boxy, black leather chairs, which she did. The office was packed with shelves of books and wood furniture that emanated an old-fashioned smell. It was kind of nice, especially since the space seemed immune to the food odors from outside it. She could see Dane sitting behind the desk, and sensed that not much had changed since his departure.

"Ms. Downing."

The sheriff walked in behind her and closed the door. To keep from feeling so cornered, Leslie pondered Dane's remark about Devine and the mayor. Wondered if the two really were involved in an illicit affair. The thought grossed her out, especially as she watched Devine adjust her utility belt before taking a seat behind the desk. Her dark hair was slicked back in its usual, low ponytail, and her tough scowl was in place.

"I'm sorry we had to meet again under such awkward circumstances." Devine dug through some papers. Found a pen. "I need you to sign this. It just states we're releasing your uncle into your custody."

Leslie took the offered form and read it clear through, showing that she wasn't going to simply take her word for it.

"It has also come to my attention that you've been in contact with Dane Chappell."

Leslie peered up from the paper in her hand. "And it's come to my attention…" *that you've been sleeping with the mayor.* "…that neither of us did anything illegal."

As much as she wanted to voice her first thought, no good could come from poking *that* bear. So she backed her lie with a smile. "Relax, sheriff. He tried to convince me to help him, but I refused."

The woman angled her head, her look narrowing. "Help him in what way?"

"To prove that he was falsely accused of assaulting Mayor Tosh."

"Why did you refuse?"

"Because it isn't my fight. I'm only here for a few more weeks and I want them to be just as uneventful as the last few have been."

"Was last night uneventful?"

The implication hovered between them like a stale draft. Leslie broke eye contact to lean forward and sign her name on the bottom line. "I guess since you can't come right out and ask if I slept with him, I'll give you an equally evasive answer." She put the pen down. Beamed across the desk. "Yes."

The sheriff's look turned to stone. "Yes it was uneventful, or yes you slept with him?"

"Exactly."

The deputy chose that moment to come in with the alleged criminal in tow. Fuming, Leslie got up from her chair at the same time Sheriff Devine rose from hers. Uncle Claven looked so tired and stank so badly it nearly broke her heart. His normally groomed white hair and mustache were all over the place, and his paunch of a belly gave off a loud, hungry growl. Sensing it wouldn't be wise to hug him at that moment, Leslie ran a hand down his arm instead. "How are you doing, Uncle C?" she asked, her voice harsher than what she had intended. "I hear you've been catching up with the locals."

The old man kept her gaze with a set of puppy-dog eyes, the blue of his irises a startling contrast against the bloodshot white. "All I did was say hello to an old friend, String Bean," he stated. "I swear."

She could already feel her cheeks redden at the use of her nickname. It had been years since she'd heard it, and Leslie couldn't help but wonder what Uncle Claven's game was. "I think in this case you should have used your words."

"I did." Sinking against the chair, he was the picture of a crestfallen man. "I said hello. When she ignored me, I showed her the doll and the next thing I know she's threatening to ram it up my ass."

Leslie turned to the sheriff who simply shrugged and said, "Witnesses claim you were the one who actually attempted it. *After* Ms. Hathaway tried to walk away."

His look became indignant. "I thought it was an

invitation."

As his words resonated among the blinking law officers, Leslie closed her eyes. Searched out his hand and gave it a squeeze. "May we go now?" she asked, really wishing she'd taken some of that ibuprofen Dane had offered earlier.

"Fine with me," the sheriff answered. "Just make sure he stays out of trouble from now on."

The woman may as well have asked her to stuff a live squirrel in a breadbox. Impossible, at least without getting bit. "Not a problem," she said through her teeth. "Come on, Uncle C. Let's go home."

Chapter 7

The small diner was packed with morning traffic, half of them police. After his shift and still in uniform, Oliver passed by and clapped Dane on the shoulder. "You look tired, Pop. Get laid last night?"

Across from Dane, Caleb snickered in his coffee. The younger man was on duty, but decided to take an early break in order to have breakfast with him and Otter, as they occasionally did. Dane ignored his son's remark and continued to plow through his scrambled eggs.

"Forgive me for saying this," Oliver pulled out a chair and sat beside him, snatching up a menu on the way down, "but that Leslie is way too young and pretty to be dating an old man like you."

Dane glared. "We aren't dating. Last night was business."

"If that cute blonde I saw sleeping on the couch was business," Caleb said between bites, "I'd like to see how you do pleasure."

"It's best you two leave me the hell alone about it."

"Oh, come on, Dad, we're just playing around." Oliver half-mouthed, half-signed his order to the busy waitress behind the counter, who nodded an affirmative in return. "I just hope you don't get her into trouble with whatever you're cooking up."

"Leslie Downing can handle herself."

From what Dane had seen so far, she could handle anything, including a badass gangster like Terrell. But he feared Oliver was right. If Tosh was dirty enough to frame an innocent man for aggravated assault, there was nothing to stop him from framing an innocent woman. Dane's concern for Leslie had grown beyond what was expected, not only robbing him of sweet indifference, but also his plans to use her for other things. He cared. And it sucked.

His phone buzzed inside his breast pocket. He dug it out and checked the screen. "It's Reko," he said to Oliver. He put his fork down and pushed his half-eaten food away, suddenly wishing he'd waited to eat until after this particular phone call. "Give me some good news, buddy," was his greeting.

"Sorry, man, no can do."

The bacon and eggs in Dane's stomach became official weapons. "Shit," he grumbled. "I was really hoping it was you."

"If it were me," Reko replied, "I'd have taken the booze, the envelope, the whole damned box and given it to you with a side of fries. But that would have been breaking and entering."

"I know." And it was wishful thinking to hope that Reko, the conservation hero, would stoop to subterfuge. "You just confirmed it was Tosh," Dane thought out loud. "Or one of his lackeys. Those papers are as good as gone."

"I checked with Betty and she said my copy machine saves only so many files before they get erased from its memory banks. Wish I'd checked it when the originals went missing, but I thought you'd gotten the copies I delivered with the booze."

His heart officially sunk, Dane rubbed at his eyes. "It's probably too late anyway with the road already started."

"Maybe. But it'll take them another week or two to reach your hill. If we can find those copies before then and prove you filed them before imminent domain, you have a good shot at stopping Rydell."

"Any chance in getting the activists involved?"

A deep, pensive sigh. "Sure, I guess. They'll get their signs out for anything not human. But will the state listen? Kansas owns your property now. Yes, your whippoorwills are endangered, but there are other refuges around, and the conservation board has bigger fish to fry—no pun intended. Your best shot was at finding those papers and proving your dates. That and the notary's testimony together may do it. Otherwise, Rydell wins." When a heated silence ensued, Reko's voice became sympathetic. "Look, it's obvious Mayor Tosh is in their pocket. He's a special kind of prick, and he likes his morning coffee spiked with leverage. Only way you're going to beat him is if you have a little leverage of your own. Those papers would have been it. Sorry, man."

Dane hung up. Gripped the phone tight. Everything around him went dim as images of Thurlow Tosh touching a flame to the corner of his conservation papers flickered in front of him. "That rotten motherfucker," he murmured calmly, when in truth he felt like tearing the diner apart.

"Who, Reko?" Oliver asked.

"Tosh. Someone must have tipped him off about those copies, just like they did when I filed the initial paperwork on our hill."

Caleb took up a napkin and wiped his mouth. "Sorry to hear that, Mr. Chappell. I know how important your family's land is to you." He scooted back his chair and threw down a ten-dollar bill. "I better get out there and look important. See you fellas later."

As Dane and Oliver were left to sit and brood alone, the coffee pot was brought around. Dane held his hand up to the waitress, indicating he was done. At the moment, nothing but a bottle of pink bismuth would sit right.

Now that Caleb was gone, Oliver moved into the vacated seat and faced Dane with an air of sadness. "I really wish I could've hung on to that farm, Dad. I'm really sorry."

The Chappells were one of Rosemont's founding families, had been a part of its history since the civil war. Eight generations had called it home and had farmed there for nearly one hundred fifty years. Dane was never much of a farmer, and since his parents died, all two hundred and forty acres of the land had been enrolled in the Crop Rotation Program. His neighbor, Howard Diedricksen, harvested and sold the hay from it, and Dane had never taken a percentage of the profits since Howard and his family needed the money more.

But everything that meant anything to Dane had taken place within the boundaries of Summit County, and thirty-nine years of memories flowed through him like brief flashes of a strobe light. Not just memories of his family, but his coming of age, league baseball tournaments, his first car, returning home from college with a job already waiting for him at the local police station. That first job preceded seventeen years of law enforcement—a career that had come under heavy fire since Thurlow Tosh came to town five years prior.

When one carried authority and a firearm, they were bound to use them on occasion. Dane hadn't had to use the firearm but once or twice, and his authority had never been questioned until Tosh—an attorney at the time—started lighting fires, pulling "victims of harassment" out of the woodwork from past to present. The man was a snake charmer, was elected mayor on his first try. But he was mayor of only one city. Dane had influence over the whole county, and was by far the biggest threat to Rosemont's industrialized future. When the smear campaigns weren't enough to unseat him, and when Dane refused to sell his land, it was Tosh who resorted to criminal tactics in order to end him for good.

The mayor had sold his soul to Rydell.

"Losing the farm is not your fault, kid." Dane stared at the remains of his meal, his stomach roiling now. "It's mine. I'm the one who let Tosh run me out of money by fighting those assault charges. If I'd have just done the time, I'd still have a home to go to when my parole is up."

Otter shook his head with an incredulous laugh. "You were innocent. Hell, you were the goddamned *sheriff*. You had no choice but to fight."

That's what Dane had thought at the time. But there was something to be said for hindsight.

"Maybe now that you have six figures waiting for you in the bank," Otter continued, "Leslie can convince her uncle to sell what's left of the farm back."

"Baby steps," Dane replied, sitting back and resting his arm on the adjacent chair. "Rosemont isn't big enough for both Tosh and me. The locals are about to become enlightened, and then they'll have to choose. My hope is that they'll kick that son-of-a-bitch and his chicken plant to the curb. If not…" Though the thought made his heart hurt, he had to accept the possibility. "I may as well forget about ever going back."

"Let's hope they see the light before your new homeowner gets too comfortable."

In a perfect world, maybe. But even though his plan with Tosh was progressing smoother than expected, thanks to Leslie, Dane knew better than to think her uncle would be so accommodating, especially if he found that fallout shelter.

But nobody knew it was still there, let alone where the new hatch was located. If what Leslie said was true, and if there was a chance her uncle would voluntarily move, then Dane would just have to go back and make sure that hatch was hidden good enough.

Reko's comment about leverage swam around Dane's brain like a hungry piranha. If there was a god, he may not need any leverage once Rosemont got wind of the truth. And if that god saw fit to bless him with a little mercy, Otter would have sold his property to a man who may not want it after all. "I have seventeen months until my parole is up," Dane murmured, lost in his reverie of new possibilities. "Sure would be nice to have a home to go back to."

✳✳✳✳

Thurlow loved the roar of track hoes, black smoke shooting into the air with each push of the throttle, trees going down, land being cleared for the next set of explosives. Facing a sunrise of incredible pinks and blues, he stood and watched what looked like progress with hands on his hips and a smile on his face. The plan was being explained to him by the job foreman who yelled above the noise. There were two more rises to level before hitting Chappell's property. *My property*, he corrected in his mind. Actually, it was the state's property, but none of this would have been possible if it weren't for him. Prosperity was what he was all about, and a hero in the eyes of many. Business owners were already backing him for his upcoming race for governor. There were already discussions for a dollar store to go in on the east side of town, and the fast-food joints were starting to make noise.

Which reminded him of the full schedule he had that week. Back to work. Sometime later, he reentered his office with a bagel in his mouth, his phone in one hand, and his travel mug in the other. As he cleared out his usual plethora of new emails, a shadow appeared in his peripheral vision, causing him to drop the bagel. "God dammit, Peggy," he grumbled when he saw who loitered by his windows. "I told you not to come here without telling me first."

His wife—a mild, sandy-haired beauty he'd wooed fresh out of college—regarded him now in her stylish blazer and jeans. She wore an odd expression he'd never seen before. "Why is that, Thurlow?" she asked, her voice tight. "So I won't catch you in an untoward situation with another woman?"

His suit rasped against his shoulders as he bent to pick the bagel up and throw it in the trash. "What's that supposed to mean?"

"I received a message on my cellphone this morning from an unknown sender." She put her phone gently down on his desktop, the screen lit with motion.

Thurlow picked the thing up and propped a hip on

his desk while he watched what looked like a porn video. At first he was repulsed by the obvious prank sent to a public figure by an obvious sicko. His look of disgust faded, however, when he recognized the size and shape of his own penis. The trousers bunched at his knees. The wedding ring on his own finger as he wrapped his hand around Cicely Devine's dark head.

And it was his own voice that streamed through the speaker.

"Oh, yeah. That's it, baby, suck my cock. Suck it hard."

His shock didn't come from the existence of the video. It was his own, after all, taken so that he could watch it repeatedly until he decided to delete it. No, his shock came from the knowledge that someone had stolen it off the Cloud and purposely sent it to his wife. Only a talented hacker with a focused agenda would even bother, because he *had* deleted it after his interaction with Chappell the other night. That comment the man had thrown out about his affair with Devine had rattled him. How did the asshole know?

"Peggy—"

"Don't, Thurlow." She went to the window, hugged her arms, and gave a disgusted laugh. "I've suspected for quite some time that you were cheating on me. We haven't exactly been a romantic couple since my family influenced you to bring me back here."

"It was just this one time," Thurlow vowed. One time of many that his butch sheriff had blown him, but the only time he'd taken video of it. Now he regretted doing so, knowing it had been a mistake to get so comfortable with a woman he'd bought and paid for with a little romance and a lot of lies.

When he reached out to touch Peggy's arm, she flinched and backed away. Her eyes were dry, her rose colored lips pursed in a fierce line. "That video proves I was right all along. You have a sickness, Thurlow, and I want a divorce."

Thurlow dipped his head, cursing the fates that kept him in this repeated loop from hell. "Do we really need to do this again, Peggy?"

"Yes!" she snapped, piercing him with her dagger-like gaze. "And this time I mean it!"

"We can't get a divorce. You signed a contract that says you will love, honor, and cherish me until death do us part."

"You haven't exactly honored your vows," she fired back.

"And then you signed a real one that says as the wife of a politician, you will not defame my character."

"Your character was defamed before I even met you! You will never be more than a sleazy lawyer, and I will always be the fool who fell for your act."

His smile was wrought with patience. "Be that as it may, you are stuck with me until the end, Mrs. Thurlow Tosh."

In a visual effort to compose herself, Peggy swallowed. Lifted her chin. "I refuse to accept those terms. You can expect to hear from my attorney."

"Are you forgetting that between us you were the first to cover up a lie? A lie I *protected* you from?"

Thurlow knew he had her before the words even left his mouth. She was near the door now, her perfectly coiffed hair resting atop stiff shoulders. "I won't let you continue to hold that over my head," she said, though it was apparent her confidence was slipping.

"You killed a man, Peggy. Left him in a sinking car to drown while you saved yourself and kept it a secret. People go to prison for that. This may be your hometown, but I guarantee the people of Rosemont won't protect you if they learn you were the one who killed their beloved Reverend McCabe."

The ensuing silence was deafening. "It was twenty-two years ago," she whispered finally. "I was just a child."

"And now you're a respected member of the community." Her family name alone helped in that regard, but his title as mayor had shot her to the top. "We both are. Together we can make this town the prosperous place you always wanted it to be."

She turned around to reveal an unusually pale complexion. "I don't love you anymore, Thurlow."

Considering the fact she'd had a hard crush on Dane Chappell when they'd met, Thurlow felt nothing for her heartfelt declaration. "That's okay, Peggy," he said calmly. "I never loved you."

The tears began to flow then, in earnest as she regarded him with hatred in her countenance. "You're a monster. I wish I'd never laid eyes on you."

With his lewd video continuing to play in his mind, he could only grant her a sympathetic smile. "I'll see you when I get home."

****

Leslie once again studied the text bubble that had just appeared on her phone. It was early Friday morning and Terrell had finally contacted her. Was ready to meet. She looked back at her laptop's screen and realized she hadn't typed a darned thing since the text had come, messing up the groove she'd found upon sitting down that morning. Dane's words had settled in her head, planted roots and grown into a desire to actually write her own article. Not that it was her first one by any means, but this one seemed special. Different than the fluff pieces she'd attempted before and discarded as junk.

She took a deep breath, shut down her laptop and rose from her place on the window seat where she'd been enjoying the morning sunrise with her coffee. Then she went in search of her uncle, who she found in the upstairs bathroom scoping out the new fixtures the plumber had just installed. He seemed pleased.

"Morning, String Bean." He removed his readers and stuffed them in the pocket of his bathrobe. "Have I told you yet what a nice job you've done with this place?"

Only a thousand times. "Yes, Uncle C," she replied with a warm smile. "But I'll never get tired of hearing it."

She backed out of the doorway as he turned out the light and moved into the hall. "I'm adding you to the deed." He took her face in his hands. Gave it a light jiggle. "You're the only one who cares about me, you know."

"That isn't true. And you don't have to put me on the deed. The last few weeks have been great therapy for me."

"After your husband left you in the lurch?" He barked out a humorless laugh as he left her in the hall and went into the master bedroom. "Yeah, I can see that. You know he was never good for you, right?"

The theory, popular among her entire family, was becoming more credible every day. Her hope that Kyle would realize his mistake and come crawling back to her was no longer what got her out of bed every morning. With Dane constantly taking up her thoughts lately, she rarely thought of her ex anymore. "Those brownie points were really racking up until you mentioned Kyle, Uncle C," she said dryly.

"Sorry."

No, he wasn't. She couldn't help but smile at his profile as he rifled through the top drawer of his dresser. She aimed for her own bedroom door, which was right beside her. "I'm going to the city this morning and will be gone for about three hours. Will you be alright? Can I get you anything?"

"I was about to head out myself." He pulled out a pair of socks. "Be back in time for lunch?"

"Yep."

Since it was barely after seven, she assumed he was going into town for breakfast, a meal she rarely partook in. And since he'd just purchased an old GMC pickup truck from a family down the road, he was probably anxious to test his newfound freedom.

In her room, she donned a summery T-shirt and tattered jean shorts. She put her hair up in a ponytail and slipped on a pair of sandals. It would be a hot day, especially since the dew had already burned off the grass. Though she had no reason to be nervous, Leslie couldn't help but check her appearance in the mirror. Perhaps a pair of really big sunglasses were in order, to hide behind in case anyone followed her. Before the thought had a chance to solidify, she wrote her paranoia off as ridiculous and chose the skinny ones instead. After all, Terrell was only giving her something. The hard part was yet to come.

By the time she made it downstairs, her nerves were completely in check. She poured some coffee into a travel mug, turned the pot off and grabbed her keys and purse. As she passed by the front dining room window, though, the view outside made her stop dead in her tracks.

There was Uncle Claven, dressed in nothing but a pair of 80s-style jogging shorts, running shoes, and a terrycloth headband. The massive amounts of exposed, saggy skin stood out like a bad meme just waiting for a caption.

She rushed outside, hoping to deter him from going to breakfast that way. Cars whizzed by on the highway, one honking as he stood in his yard beneath his waving American flag. It was a superhero pose that beat all. Uncle Claven was feeling way too good about whatever he was planning, causing her nerves to frazzle anew.

But before she could yell out to him, he took off in a lazy jog, looked both ways before crossing the highway, and disappeared down the dirt road on the opposite side of it.

"Good lord," she breathed, hand to chest as she let the blood flow again. How about that? Honest to goodness exercise. Maybe moving to Rosemont was what the crazy old coot needed after all.

Her plan had been to stay a while to see that he was properly settled. The sight that had just been burned into her retinas, however, made her think she'd better get while the getting was good. Go back to Omaha before he gave her a heart attack.

In her haste to prevent a disaster, Leslie had developed a sudden, nervous bladder. With the hour-long drive before her, she decided it was better to be safe than sorry, and went back into the house. When she came out of it again, she began to lock up before realizing her uncle may not have a way to get back in without his truck keys. As she stood there on the welcome mat trying to figure out what to do, heavy breathing sounded behind her. She turned, her eyes widening once again as Uncle Claven stumbled back into the yard. His face was ashen, his breathing labored, and he held a fist to his chest.

"Oh, my God." She dropped everything and ran to him.

As she approached, he fell to his knees. There were leaves and brambles stuck to his terrycloth headband, and dirt mottled his entire front. "Call the police," he wheezed.

"What happened?" In a panic, Leslie hovered over him, wondering what one would do for a heart-attack victim when they were still upright. "Do you need an ambulance? No, it would be faster if I just took you to the hospital."

"I don't need a damned ambulance," he wheezed. "Some lunatic in a short bus just tried to run me over!"

"*What?* A what-bus?"

"You know, a school bus for little handicapped kids. That thing had to be going eighty miles per hour."

She looked down the dirt road and past the trees, failing to see even a hint of a dust cloud that a vehicle would have left behind. "Where was this? I didn't see a school bus."

He pointed. "The road comes to a T down that way. Whoever the driver was aimed right for me so that I had to dive into the ditch. She tried to kill me!"

"You're sure it was a she?" Leslie asked, her

doubts growing.

Claven scowled and grumbled as he swayed to his feet. "Quit asking dumb questions and help me get inside. I'll call the police myself."

Aside from a few minor scrapes and a bad temper, Leslie deemed him free of serious injury. She called the police, shortly after which a Deputy Forester arrived and took her uncle's dramatic statement. They were informed that there were only two handicapped busses in the district. Two drivers, whose names he would not mention, would be questioned. Gauging the young officer's resigned attitude toward the whole thing, however, Leslie figured the story would be dismissed as one of great exaggeration.

After the deputy left, she was keenly aware that it was too late to meet with Terrell. She sent him a quick text, asking if they still could.

Terrell—*Have to be somewhere at 11. Will leave package with LaShonda at Moonlight's*—

Leslie—*LaShonda?*—

Terrell—*Waitress from the other night*—

Aside from the very real worry that someone had, indeed, tried to run her uncle over, Leslie supposed it was for the best. At least her nerves seemed to prefer the arrangement. If anyone were spying on her, a rendezvous with LaShonda wouldn't raise so many red flags. After settling a freshly-showered Claven on the couch with the remote control and a bowl of oatmeal, she once again grabbed up her purse and keys.

"You're leaving me?" said the old man, his puppy dog eyes on full sympathy mode.

So much for the superhero. "You're going to be fine, Uncle C," she replied, "and I have to meet someone. I'll be back before you even miss me."

"Hey, bring a pizza, will you?" he yelled before she closed the front door. "And a pint of cherry ice-cream!"

Chapter 8

Leslie entered the darkened foyer of Moonlight's, her pupils slowly adjusting as she removed her sunglasses. The stairwell was even darker, but the lunch crowd was considerably lighter than the dinner crowd at least. Once she reached the basement level, LaShonda instantly recognized her, held up one finger, and disappeared into the kitchen. Moments later she came out with a lunch-size brown paper sack and handed it to her over the bar.

"There's a little something extra in there," she explained, indicating the weight of the bag, which was considerably heavier than a movie disk should be. "Courtesy of your friendly neighborhood ex-con." She ended that with a wink.

Leslie's smile appeared. "Which one?"

"Open it and find out." The woman leaned closer and added in a whisper, "I'd do it in the bathroom, though."

Intrigued, Leslie headed toward the back where the bathrooms were located. She closed herself in a stall, locked the door, and opened the bag. Inside was the expected Blue-ray disk of *Rain In Your Hair,* the movie they would be playing for Rosemont's Saturday night event.

With the disk was a cellphone. When she removed it from the bag, she saw that it was one of those cheap, disposable phones with the prepaid minutes. She woke the screen and immediately saw a text bubble from someone named Dick.

—*Keep hidden and use with caution. -D.*—

As a giddy feeling entered her stomach, Leslie grinned at the phone and began to explore it as if it were her favorite birthday present. There were only three numbers programed into the address book, which belonged to Oliver, Terrell, and "Dick." "Appropriate alias," she mumbled to herself, glad to learn that Dane had a sense of humor beneath all that anger. She texted him back: —*Got it. Thank you, Dick.*—

He must have been waiting for it because he immediately replied: —*Thought you'd like that. Delete this convo before you leave.*—

Leslie—*Boss bag.*—

Dick—*You have no idea.*—

She laughed, loving that she now had access to Dane whenever she needed him. The only thing better would be if the phone came with a cell tower she could plant in the back yard of the house. But the important thing, she guessed, was that it would work at the park when they really needed it most. Movie night was tomorrow. He'd want to know how it went.

With the items safely tucked in her purse, Leslie threw away the bag and left. She beamed at LaShonda on her way out, and the young waitress grinned right back. "Bye, Sunshine," she yelled after her, and Leslie remembered that it was what Terrell had called her the other night. Much preferable to String Bean, she decided, though Claven was the only one who used that horrid nickname.

Her mission accomplished, she hit the parking lot

with confidence in her steps. Then came someone else's footsteps, matching hers from behind. Leslie took a tentative peek over her shoulder and made out an unfamiliar shape in dark clothing. It was a man, too close for comfort and walking fast.

It doesn't mean he's following you.

But her blood began to race through her veins anyway. Leslie tightened her grip on her purse and walked faster. Hers was one of a half-dozen cars in the parking lot and didn't take long to reach, but as she hit the unlock button on her keys, a hand closed over her shoulder.

"Give me the purse, lady."

Leslie whirled around just as her purse was grabbed and tugged at, but her arm was already clamped down on it, and her key was already out. With an instinctive roar, she jabbed at her attacker, aiming for the forearm and scoring a hit. The hooded man yowled in pain, let go of the purse, and looked as if he may try for it again. Leslie then flipped her keys and showed him the nozzle of her pepper spray. Her finger on the button was enough to change his mind. As the man took off holding his bloody forearm, a panting and furious Leslie committed his description to memory.

White male, early twenties, six feet plus, navy blue hoodie and jeans.

Vague, but she would remember his face. It was a healthy face, one that wouldn't normally be found on a typical, drug-addicted mugger. He also wore a ring on his right hand—a class ring if she ever recognized one.

Thoroughly rattled, she got into her car and immediately locked the doors. Once she was back on the road, she drove to a department store a few blocks away and parked again. With her eyes on her surroundings, she took Dane's phone out of her purse and dialed.

"Leslie?"

His voice offered a type of comfort she'd never felt before. Her heartbeat slowed a bit though she kept her eyes peeled for anyone who may be following her. "Someone just tried to steal my purse," she said, her own voice surprisingly calm. "It could have been a random thing, but he didn't look at all like your typical mugger."

"There's no such thing as a typical mugger," he replied heatedly. "Are you alright?"

"Yes. He didn't make out so great, though."

There was a lengthy pause. Then, "What does your gut tell you? Did the attack feel random?"

"My gut tells me it was too much of a coincidence that the one time I have something irreplaceable in my purse, someone tries to steal it."

"I agree. Where are you? I'll meet you."

As she waited for him, Leslie brushed aside the nagging feeling that this was a bad idea and welcomed the anticipatory pleasure of seeing him again. Ten minutes later, her burner phone buzzed with a text.

Dick—*Black truck right behind you.*—

She looked in her rearview mirror and saw a tall, shiny black truck parked behind another car. The windows were tinted and it was hard to see the driver, but she knew it was Dane. She shut down her car and its running air conditioning, and grabbed her purse. As soon as she stepped outside, heat blasted her from all angles. The smell of hot asphalt assaulted her nose. She walked at a leisurely pace, careful not to draw unwanted attention. This sneaky stuff—thrilling as it was—was starting to work on her resolve.

When she got close enough, the truck's doors unlocked. She pulled the handle, opened the passenger door, and stepped up to get in. Only when she was safely closed inside did she allow herself to breathe. Without looking at Dane, she said, "We have to quit meeting like this."

And she meant it. She wanted to meet him in the open without all the caution and the danger, just two people finally getting the chance to know each other. They were allowed.

Yet they weren't. When she finally looked over at him, she could tell he was thinking the same thing. His mouth was grim beneath the light beard. His hair curled loosely around the edges of a black ball cap, and beneath the brim his eyes bore into hers with thinly veiled meaning, making her heart skip a beat.

"When I gave you that phone," he said, "I didn't expect you to have to use it so soon."

"I'm sorry."

He let out a wry laugh. Draped his wrist over the steering wheel and looked around. "No, I'm sorry. I dragged you into my affairs and now you're scared."

"I don't know that I'd call it scared. Pissed, maybe, but not scared."

He nodded as if he truly believed her. "Do you know how to protect yourself?"

"I just thwarted an attacker, didn't I?" She held up the pepper spray on her key ring. "Breakfast of champions."

She thought she saw a flash of amusement in his eyes before he said, "Your best defense is to know your surroundings. Be wary of everything and everyone around you at all times. Treat all strangers as a potential threat, no matter what they look like."

"Stranger-danger. Got it."

"Have you noticed anything else? Anyone lurking around the house or following you around town?"

"Not really. Just that…" She paused, wondering if she should even mention the incident that made her miss her rendezvous with Terrell.

"What, Leslie?" he prodded gently, sounding very much like a lawman.

She let out a pent-up breath. "My uncle claims that someone tried to run him over this morning."

His gaze grew sharp. "You don't believe him?"

"I honestly don't know what to think. He went for a jog on the dirt road across from your—er, *his* house and came back filthy. I didn't see anything, but he said someone driving a handicapped school bus was going too fast and aimed right for him."

Dane shook his head. "Della Hathaway has that route. She's as harmless as they come." His features softened a touch. "That's right, this is the middle of August. Today would be the first day of school."

Leslie wondered if he knew how openly he wore his heart on his sleeve at that moment. She held back the urge to touch him then, to tell him it would all work out and that he would be going back home soon— because the odds were that he wouldn't. She cleared the emotion from her throat and focused on the familiar name he'd just blurted out. "Hathaway…Uncle C knows her, I think. They had a slight confrontation when he arrived in town."

"What kind of confrontation?" Dane asked.

The kind that had landed him in jail, which wasn't exactly a rare occurrence for Claven Gallagher. "Believe me, you don't want to know," she mumbled. "But do you think it's possible that she could have wanted to get back at him?"

He appeared doubtful. "Della can be a grumpy old thing, but she isn't *capable* of speeding, let alone harming someone."

If the woman had such a stellar reputation, surely she wouldn't be overcome with a desire to sully it over the likes of her uncle. "I guess you would know," Leslie conceded, not feeling much better than before. She glanced over at him. "I can tell how much you miss the town, but do you miss being sheriff?"

"Yeah." The word was drawn out on a breath of frustration. "I miss being there for the people. The way things used to be."

A deep sadness descended over her, for Dane's misfortune as well as his plight. He seemed genuinely upset for the people of Rosemont, perhaps more so than for himself.

After a moment of reflective silence, he looked over at her, his mouth set in a strange smile. "You up for a drive?"

****

Feeling unusually good about himself, Dane pulled into a spot at his son's gym and shut the truck's engine down.

Leslie squinted up at the sign with a look of pure distaste on her visage. "These things are meat markets, you know."

She was right, and when they walked through the front doors, she would be the prime cut. "Otter gave me a visitor's pass," he said before they got out. "There's a sparring room in the back."

She met him around the rear of the truck. "So…why do we need a sparring room?"

He noted her wary gaze through the sunglasses and suppressed a smile. "I want you to show me what you got."

Her lips formed an "O" right before her expression melted with foreboding. "I wish I'd worn better shoes."

Something told him he was lucky she hadn't. She already held an advantage in those sexy little shorts of hers. Those things offered a distraction as well as movability. Wearing jeans as he was, his movements would be hindered. And his focus even more so.

When they entered the establishment, it was pretty sparse, its many rows of equipment occupied by a handful of folks on treadmills, a couple of big guys on weights, and the few athletic trainers on staff. It was a good thing. Dane checked the two of them in, and as they walked through the gym, he knew exactly who watched them—or more like who watched Leslie and her progress toward the back. The sense of ownership within him was strong, as useless as it was, and he resisted the childish urge to put his arm around her shoulders.

Safely enclosed in their private little room, she put her purse down in a corner. He removed his cap and emptied his pockets in the same place, both of them prepping for what he was already deeming a bad idea. Which only allowed time for the sexual tension to rise.

Could she feel it, too? When he looked over at her, it was pretty evident by the flush on her cheeks that her mind was in the exact same place.

Good.

No, bad. She ought not to look at him like that if she expected him to be a good boy. Then again, he was an adult male and fully capable of keeping himself in check, which he would do if it killed him.

Leslie shook out her limbs and cracked her neck as if she were prepping for a marathon. "The place doesn't smell as bad as I expected."

He watched her with amusement. "Don't tell me you've never been to a gym before."

"I prefer the outdoors. Well…when I care about exercise, anyway."

Yes, he could see her jogging in a park with lots of creeps waiting behind bushes. "Have you ever been mugged before?" he asked.

She shook her head. "My friend was and we took a self-defense class together."

He wanted to ask about the friend, but too much small talk would give his libido time to peak. "Show me your fist," he said instead. When she made a solid one with no protruding digits, he nodded his approval. "Know how to use that?"

"Of course."

"Show me."

And it began. For the next few minutes, she lightly demonstrated what she'd learned. As test dummy, he lightly coached, showing her better ways to land her punches and on what parts of the body. His attempt to keep it positive, though, was constantly thwarted by a competitive side she had absolutely no control over. And he liked that side of her. A lot.

The room's energy began to buzz with the rising thrill of battle, and they went with it. Leslie's half-hearted attempts to nail him turned into serious ones. As a card-carrying tough guy, Dane took the abuse with an air of utmost patience...until she followed his advice a little too well and aimed for the softest part of his body. He blocked her kick with both hands, giving her a look that warned.

She answered it with a lame smile that belied the fire in her eyes. "Sorry."

He couldn't help but smile back, then he laughed at her obvious show of spirit. "I can see that. How 'bout in my case we practice on the *other* soft parts we talked about?"

"Other soft parts. Got it." She was all seriousness again, unapologetic and vibrant with energy. "I forgot there were so many of them. Nose. Eyes. Throat."

He grabbed her wrist and she levered out of the hold with more speed than before. He followed up with a feigned punch to the face. She deflected his arm and jabbed the heel of her hand against his nose. She was decent at defending herself, and he was pleased if not a tad surprised. "Very good," he said. "Now walk away from me and we'll practice that bear hug technique one more time."

It was his favorite move. Dane suspected she knew it, too, since this whole session had been laced with sexual tension, despite his efforts to keep it clean.

Sure enough, her brow went up. "Why don't you walk away from me this time?"

"Because I'm bigger than you."

"So?"

She was feeling empowered. Cocky. In prison, those types ended up either dead or in the infirmary. Dane accepted her challenge with a shrug, turning

111

around so that she could do her worst. As soon as her arms circled his middle and squeezed, he dropped his weight. And as he anticipated, she went right down with him. They both ended up on the floor, her shrieking as he twisted to avoid crushing her. He recovered first, and with lightning speed was on top of her, pinning her wrists to the mat.

Her blonde ponytail was fanned out on the floor. Her chest was heaving, and her eyes were alight with fire—and defeat. "Point taken," she breathed.

She could have gone for the jewels again if his legs weren't between hers. Dane had the advantage of bulk and weight, but Leslie Downing had the power to incapacitate him with one small wiggle of her hips. The mere thought made his interest rise before he had a chance to squelch it. "What are you going to do now, Ms. Downing?" he rasped, his words rough with longing. "I have the high ground."

Her gaze went to his mouth. "I guess I'm at your mercy."

He could see the desire there, knew that if he kissed her, she would probably kiss him back. He also knew she could feel him hardening against the apex of her thighs. When he'd brought her here, the plan had been to prepare her in case she was attacked again.

Not to attack her himself.

But suddenly he was the one being kissed. Her head was off the floor, and as her honeyed lips moved against his, his insides imploded, giving up all control. His body hardened with the need to devour, as if bracing for a good pounce. Unable to help himself, he advanced and plundered, sampling her sweet mouth for the first time. She opened for him, allowing full access as a soft moan left her throat. Yes, she was every bit as affected as he was, tasting him with equal curiosity and hunger.

And then she did it. She moved those hips against him, inciting a full-on riot down below. He was a grown man, losing control like a dumb kid climbing the ropes in gym class. "Jesus, Leslie," he groaned against her mouth. "You aren't making this easy."

As soon as the words were out, she somehow managed to flip them over until he was on his back. Now he was the one with pinned wrists, facing the ceiling—as well as a grinning blonde woman with triumph in her eyes. Her smile was big, her lips all pink and fired up. "Now I have the high ground," she said with spark. "What do you say to that, Mr. Chappell?"

His aching groin would say she was a tease, but his head said she was a survivor. The fact his hormones were still hung up on that kiss spelled nothing but trouble for him—trouble his conscience couldn't afford if his quest for truth and vengeance were to put Leslie in danger.

No, he couldn't have her. Not yet. But right now, he would bask in the vibrant look of her, remember this light in her eyes and the heat of that kiss still lingering on his lips. "I'd say you had me beat since the first night I came knocking," he answered in all honesty.

She must have liked that answer because she grinned, stood up and offered him a hand. "I'll remember that next time you ask me for a favor."

Chapter 9

Dane's parting words to her had been to listen to her gut, to be watchful since she and Uncle Claven could be targets. Her close call with a mugger was evidence of that.

He then assured her that the phone he'd given her used a better carrier for the Rosemont area and would work from the farmhouse. For a while, Leslie was more thankful for it than a kid at Christmas.

But then the memory of their kiss rose to the top of gifts she'd received that day…and she hoped they'd get a chance to do it again. The feeling of empowerment as she'd taken control, followed her desires, and came out on top was like no other. When she'd kissed Dane, something inside her changed. She was no longer a divorced woman struggling to find the surface. Her self-confidence had come out of hiding. Her sex drive had been slammed out of neutral. She felt alive again, ready to conquer anything, and it was all because of Dane Chappell.

"Have you grown a hollow leg since I moved in, String Bean?"

Leslie glanced up from her plate as she shoved the last bite of breakfast into her mouth. Uncle Claven was watching her above the rim of his white coffee mug, a gleam of satisfaction in his eyes. What was it about old folks and their fascination with younger people's appetites?

So she was in a diner, enjoying a fatty, caloric meal of the traditional American variety with her crazy uncle. Alert the media. Leslie shoved her plate away, picked up her own coffee, and beamed back at him. "I guess I forgot how good pancakes and bacon are."

His smile appeared. "Keep eating like that and I'll have to call you Pork Chop."

While he laughed, she glared with humor. "Leave it up to you to come up with a worse name than String Bean. "

Watching him across the table, in a public place and on his best behavior, Leslie realized how much she cherished these rare moments of normalcy with her uncle. Perhaps that was why she'd stuck with him through the years, because she knew there was a good man beneath the loony façade. She'd drawn him out enough times to keep trying for more, unlike her mother and siblings. It occurred to her then that perhaps Uncle Claven just didn't like the rest of his family. Maybe his crazy was a deterrent.

If so, it worked.

She put her cup down and regarded him with a curious smile. "You know…I don't like the thought of you living here alone. I mean, why Rosemont? You always talked about it like you weren't happy here." He especially wouldn't like it when Rydell Foods moved in. The sound of trucks in the background, invading his peaceful countryside experience.

His hair was the whitest of white against the morning sunlight as he pondered her question, making him appear even older than his years. "I'm still not quite sure why. I feel as though I have unfinished business here, and that if I don't figure out what it is I won't accomplish what I'm supposed to. I don't want to die that way. Hell, I don't want to die at all, which is why I scooped up that old Chappell house when it became available." He glanced around. Lowered his voice. "When the nukes fall, I aim to be one of the smart ones."

The bomb shelter again. She'd almost forgotten that was her uncle's reason for choosing Dane's house. She folded her arms across the table and cleared her throat. Her next question came out a near whisper, though she knew no one was within hearing range. "What if—what if there is no bomb shelter on the Chappell property? Would you stay?"

"Hell no. I'd sell it and put my money on that missile silo in Salina." He winked. Leaned back again with a secret in his smile. "The future is *below* ground, String Bean. Mark my words."

Her stomach began to roil again. "Have you even looked for the shelter?"

"Don't have to. I know where it is."

Or, rather, he knew where it *used* to be… "Maybe we should put that on our to-do list for this morning." She sent him a lame smile. "I'll help you."

When the waitress came around with the coffee pot, Claven held out his mug for another refill without taking his gaze off Leslie. He waited until they were alone again before he said, "You almost sound as if you don't think it's there."

The hint of accusation in his words caused her cheeks to heat up. "Well…"

"Leslie Grace Downing, do you think I'm crazy?"

Of course she did, sometimes of the bat-shit

variety. But her guilt came from knowing the bunker was no longer there and not saying anything to him about it. She never thought he'd believe her, anyway, not until he saw proof. And the sooner that happened, the sooner they'd find out if Uncle Claven was willing to sell his place back to Dane.

"Well, I'll be a son-of-a-gun."

Claven's gaze had shifted, was now trained out the window and was cold as ice. Leslie followed it. Her attention was instantly drawn to a short, yellow school bus exiting a car wash down the road. It was slowly approaching the diner on the twenty-mile-per-hour, two-lane road that cut through Rosemont's business district.

There was a thump. Dishes rattled. Leslie turned back around to find Claven up and headed for the diner's glass doors. Panic assailed her as he blasted through them, leaving her to either wait him out, or pay the check and hope to catch up before anything bad happened. Leslie opted to pay the check.

On her feet now, she dug through her purse, pulled out some cash and threw it on the table. Then she was out the door, but only in time to hear the screech of brakes and see the bus come to a jarring halt just inches away from a fuming Claven Gallagher. He stood in the middle of the lane, hands at his sides, his distended belly rising and falling with heavy breaths. Other cars were coming, soon to be caught up in the standoff that could only end with another trip to the police department.

Leslie should have known her rare moment of normality would end this way. "Hey!" She crossed the street and took her uncle by the arm. "You can't just stop traffic like this, Uncle C."

Just then, the double doors of the bus came open, and the old man's arm tensed beneath the palm of her hand. Leslie saw the outline of a person through the windshield. Whoever the driver was had risen from their seat and was now descending the steps.

A woman appeared, small and frail with the very distinct look of the grandma in Little Red Riding Hood. Her gray hair was in a neat bun at her nape. Her eyeglasses were perched at the end of her nose. She wore a mint green sweater with a navy-blue skirt, crew socks, and a pair of slip-on loafers—and there was a glare of hatred in her wrinkle-lined eyes of pale blue.

"You." Claven waggled a finger in her direction. "I knew it."

"What are you doing standing in the middle of the road like that?" the woman groused.

Leslie had wanted to ask the same thing, but all *she* could do was stand there and watch, a helpless slave to her curiosity. So, this was Della Hathaway—the woman her uncle had assaulted with a dashboard hula girl. What had the man been thinking?

His cheeks now jiggled with rage. "You tried to run me over."

Her petite head reared back with affront. "I did no such thing."

"Don't deny it. Ever since I came back, you've been aiming to kill me."

"And why would I waste my energy?"

"Because you're a vindictive old tart!"

As horns began to honk, Leslie doubled her efforts to bring Claven back to sanity. "That's enough. I'm not bailing you out of jail again. Let's go." She threw an apologetic smile at the incredibly harmless looking Ms. Hathaway. "I am so sorry for all of this. He won't bother you again, I promise."

"You have no business driving that bus, Della Hathaway," Claven shouted as he allowed Leslie to push him back toward the diner. "Shame on you! Shame. On. You!"

"Would you be quiet," Leslie hissed, daring a look over her shoulder, though it was a relief to see that the woman was in the process of re-boarding her bus. The doors closed. The brakes were released. And as the bus began to roll again, a red-faced Della shook her fist through the closed side-window. Luckily there were no kids on board, much to Leslie's relief.

When she managed to get him in the passenger seat of his truck, she slid behind the wheel, closed the door, and stared at him in amazement. "Exactly what kind of history do you have with her?" she asked. "I've never seen you act like this toward a woman."

"According to her," he grumbled, "we never met before. But I know she remembers. She just doesn't want anyone knowing the truth."

"The truth about what?"

He looked at her then, his eyes bloodshot with temper. The seconds ticked by, heavy with indecision. Then he clamped his mouth shut and trained his gaze out the windshield. "Did you tip her good?"

Leslie's brain was officially scrambled. "Tip? Who, Ms. Hathaway?"

"No, the waitress. Do I need to go inside and throw a few more dollars on the table?"

At her wits end, she inserted the key and started the truck. "I tipped her plenty. And I think you've shown your face enough around here for one day."

Back at the house, there was a large brown box waiting on the porch. Leslie put the truck in park, got out and eyeballed her uncle as he did the same. "Don't touch it," he warned as they approached the steps. "Could be from her."

By now, Leslie knew exactly whom the man referred to. "I seriously doubt Ms. Hathaway would put something harmful on your doorstep."

"Ha!" He grabbed the broom that was leaning against the corner railing. "Don't let those innocent eyes fool you. She's mean as a snake." With the broom's handle, he poked at the box a few times. "That's probably what's in there. She's hoping I'll get bitten and die."

"Okay, you have got to tell me what happened between you two." Leslie bent over, jabbed the top seam with a key and slit it down the middle. While he loudly protested, she wrenched the rest of it open and peered inside. "It's a bunch of brown packets."

Claven stepped closer. Took a peek. "Oooh, my MREs." The broom hit the deck. He picked up the box and motioned for Leslie to hurry and unlock the door.

"What are MREs?" she asked as the door came open.

"Meal packets for my bunker." He walked inside and headed for the kitchen with his box. "I should have three more of these coming, so keep an eye out."

As if he hadn't just accused an innocent woman of attempted murder. Closing and locking the door behind her, Leslie began to question the wisdom of bringing Uncle Claven to movie night in the park. He was obviously disturbed no matter how many spells of lucidity she'd glimpsed in him. Besides all the crazy conspiracy theories, the precipitous purchases, and the harassment of a poor elderly woman, he was hoarding supplies for a shelter he hadn't even seen with his own eyes yet.

Perhaps the digging should wait until after Saturday night's big event, when he may be *relieved* to learn of just one more good reason to sell.

****

A cool evening breeze teased the miniature white lights strung from the trees in Rosemont Park. A snack stand on wheels was perched near its grassy entrance, and it appeared as if the city's entire population had made their way to the grounds with coolers and blankets in tow. True to Maxi's word, a big blow-up movie screen sat front and center, ready to project the evening's feature film.

Or what was *supposed* to be the feature film. As Leslie walked away from the projector stand, the bundle of nerves in her stomach had her looking over her shoulder to see if anyone had caught her clandestine act of switching the DVDs. Now the real copy of *Rain In Your Hair* was in her purse, and Terrell's copy was waiting to be loaded into the player. How to return the original was a problem she would deal with later. Right now it was all about the future. These people had a wake-up call coming. Uncle Claven had yet to arrive. Life was good.

She took a deep breath of fresh air, knowing that this town would now have a good chance of keeping that fresh air. As long as the people fought, and as long as the road was unfinished, it wasn't too late. If the majority wished it, The Rydell Foods invasion could be stopped. Her article was the added boost Dane had hoped she'd write, and it was loaded with blatant, fact-based truths. He would be pleased.

And that alone made her smile.

"Oh, good, you made it!"

Maxi appeared with little Trouble in tow, and with who had to be her husband. Big Trouble. The man was tall, sported a heavy red beard and ball cap with an archery logo on it. A loose, camouflage tank top hung from his shoulders, showcasing a set of muscular arms and furry armpits. When the introductions were made, he gave Leslie a sweet nod. "Ma'am."

She immediately liked him, but quickly deduced there were no similarities between him and the little four-year-old with whom he shared a name. Little Trouble's paternity was none of her business, but she couldn't let go of the possibility that Otter was a dad. Who else, she wondered, shared her suspicions? Or perhaps knew it to be true?

While Leslie packed her things, Maxi invited her to sit with them. "I'd like that," Leslie replied, "but I'll have my uncle with me. He should be arriving any time."

In fact, she wondered what was taking the old coot so long. He'd wanted to finish an episode of his favorite game show, which should have been over a half hour ago. It wouldn't take him more than six minutes to drive into town from the house.

"Isn't he the one who stopped traffic in front of the diner yesterday?" Maxi asked as they all walked through the park's entrance together.

Leslie hid a cringe behind her curtain of hair. "That would be him."

Big Trouble let loose with a loud guffaw. "I heard he accused Ms. Hathaway of reckless driving. If that don't beat all."

Feeling somewhat obligated to defend her uncle, Leslie shrugged. "Someone *did* almost run him over." Or so he'd said.

Maxi joined in the laughter. "Not Ms. Hathaway. She's *the* town blue-hair, always driving below the speed limit, always with a line of cars behind her."

"That's why she's transported the special needs kids all these years," Big Trouble added. He picked up his son and threw him on top of his shoulders. "Word is, Claven Gallagher is a little off-kilter himself. No offense."

Truth be told, Leslie wasn't sure of anything when it came to Uncle Claven. Just that she cared about him and hoped like hell it wasn't a mistake. With a sigh, she hoisted her loaded beach bag further up her shoulder. "None taken."

She decided to sit with them until Uncle Claven made his appearance. While among friends, she was less paranoid, less conscious of the strange looks she was getting from the main populace. Trouble Junior engaged in a game of keep-away with a Golden Retriever that bore the vest of a service dog. Leslie believed such distractions were a no-no in the world of service dogs, not that Maxi and her husband appeared mindful of it. Perhaps it was a regular thing with this crowd.

A man was camped at the projection system, talking to some of the town folk and completely unaware that he was about to become part of a historic coup. When he began to fiddle with the equipment,

Leslie's blood started to pump. She watched him. Knew exactly when the movie went in. Waited for the screen to light up. Wished Dane were there so he could witness this moment—a moment he'd spent a lot of time planning.

When the screen did light up, Leslie's concerns about her uncle's absence dissipated like smoke in the wind. Instead, she took great interest in watching the people. Having already previewed the movie in the comfort of her home, she knew what was next, and was addicted to the real-life drama about to unfold around her. At first the reactions were limited as the documentary appeared more like a pre-film advertisement. Then the mumbling started. A man stood up and pointed at the screen. "That's about Rydell," he said to the family next to his.

Then the park came alive with movement as more folks became aware. Another man by the gazebo started cutting through the maze of blankets, heading right for the projector. It was Mayor Tosh with his white hair and business-casual attire. His mildly handsome face was wrought with a mixture of anger and panic. Then Leslie spotted Sheriff Devine following suit.

Well, hell. She hadn't thought of what would happen if they were in attendance and wanted to stop the damned thing. Had Dane? Probably, but it didn't appear as if anyone was going to get in their way.

Without wasting more precious time, she shot to her feet and pointed, too. "Hey, I know where that is," she shouted. "That's Clearwater, Iowa. Rydell Foods polluted so much of its waterways the place is now a ghost town." Then she turned to Big Trouble, who stared up at her with a look of unadulterated confusion.

"Help me," she hissed. "We need to keep it playing."

But it was Maxi who got up next. The woman moved surprisingly well despite the large baby in her womb. "What is this, Leslie?" she asked.

"Something the town needs to see." Leslie jerked her head in TJ's direction. "For his sake if not your own."

Then all hell broke loose as the Golden Retriever went tearing across the grass. Trouble screamed and went after it. Maxi went after him, followed by Big Trouble who finally found the wherewithal to take action. The four of them formed a zig-zaggie sort of line until the dog faked left just before plowing straight into a determined Mayor Tosh. The man was tripped up enough to fall to the ground. When Sheriff Devine bent to help him, he screamed at her to stop the player. But then she was avoiding a four-year-old kid on the rampage, and then was faced with a pregnant mother who'd stopped and was now bending over with apparent abdominal pains. Only Leslie was privy to all of that since all other eyes were glued to the movie screen. As soon as Tosh got back to his feet, the service dog once again tackled him to the ground, licking his face with gusto. Trouble held his tummy and giggled so hard a wet spot appeared on the front of his shorts. Then he tackled the mayor, too.

Leslie's concern for Maxi took front and center, but when the woman looked up at her and winked, she gave in to the joy. With her bottom lip tucked between her teeth, Leslie watched as Big Trouble hijacked the sheriff in order to gain her assistance with Maxi. Meanwhile, the video documentary played on, even capturing the operator's full attention. She doubted anyone would *let* Tosh stop it at this point. But it was better to be safe than sorry.

When she moved toward the projector with every intention of guarding it with her life, her pocket buzzed. She reached inside it, checked the burner phone that Dane had given her. The screen was lit up with a text.

—*Flower Shop.*—

With a frown, she looked up at the row of brick-front buildings next to the park. From that angle, she could see the backs of the shops. A lone person stood next to an open door. Whoever it was, he was oddly clothed in a jacket-hat combo that shaded his features from the lamplight overhead. As soon as she spotted him, he slipped through that open door.

Dane.

Her nostrils flared with excitement. With a clandestine look over her shoulder, she headed that way, but went to the front of the buildings instead of the back in case anyone watched her. As she followed the sidewalk, she was somewhat shocked to see her uncle's truck parked in one of the diagonal spaces ahead. One peek through the windows showed no sign of him. He must have failed to text her when he arrived, or found some old acquaintances to sit with, yet she was unwilling to worry about it right now. This was *her* time, and by God, she needed it.

Sure enough, the third store down was a flower shop, the only building in the square that was painted a gaudy light purple. As she climbed the few steps up to the landing, the doubts began to form. Would Dane even try to come here? Every time he did, he risked getting caught. Didn't he trust her enough to carry out his plan without chickening out?

It could be a trap. But she brushed away the thought as soon as it formed. It didn't keep her heart from racing beneath her breastbone, though, when she tested the shop's door…and found it unlocked.

The noise from the park faded as the door closed behind her. Now that she was inside, she moved into the darkness, beyond the window's sparse light. It was quiet save the muffled boom of sound from the projection screen's dual speakers outside. The place offered a smorgasbord of fragrances, all of them heady and wonderful. The aged wood floors beneath her creaked out her presence, but she kept going, using her phone's screen to light the way. "Hello?" she whispered. "Dane?"

A hand covered her mouth from behind, causing her stomach to turn over. Before she could produce one iota of sound, she was whirled around and suddenly engulfed in a hard, emotional kiss.

And Leslie would know that pair of lips anywhere.

Happiness and good vibes filled her entire being. The kiss broke long enough for them to smile at each other before Dane moved in again, hungrier this time to the point that Leslie's knees went weak. She kissed him back with equal vigor, every bit as ravenous as he. It felt so good just being with him, this strong, enigmatic man who had come into her life under the guise of a lie.

They stopped for air. Dane put his forehead to hers. "Let's get out of here," he whispered.

She nodded, too breathless to attempt words.

He had shed the coat and hat, and instead of heading toward an outer exit, he pulled her to a side door that led into the next business. They crossed through that one and into a third business, which was a garage of some kind with a variety of cars packed inside. Dane pulled her to an 80's model Oldsmobile that was in the front of the pack, its nose nearly touching the clouded glass garage door. He reached for the front passenger door handle, but stopped when a sound broke through the silence. A moan? No, a giggle. He looked back at her with a questioning frown. It was then Leslie noticed that the Oldsmobile's tinted windows were fogged up. She pointed it out to Dane, a movement that must have been caught by whoever was inside because a bump was heard, followed by some scuffling and a loud curse.

That curse sounded awfully familiar.

As the car wiggled back and forth, Leslie removed her hand from Dane's and simply stared, horrified by the possibilities. "Uncle C?" Though she spoke low, her voice sounded like a gong within the cavernous walls of the garage.

After a prolonged moment of silence, another voice came, this one from inside the car.

"String Bean?"

Chapter 10

Leslie closed her eyes, her high completely gone as the Oldsmobile's rear door opened. Out came a sweaty Uncle Claven, his rumpled shirt missing the top three buttons. There was color in his cheeks unlike any she'd ever seen.

He was eyeballing Dane just as shrewdly. "Who are you?" he asked gruffly.

Another person popped out, this one a bit smaller but even more of a surprise than the first. "Why that's…that's Sheriff Chappell!" the woman exclaimed.

While Leslie gawked, Dane inclined his head, as if it were every day he encountered two elderly folks getting it on in the back seat of a parked car. "Ms. Hathaway."

The prim little woman who'd shaken her fist at Claven the previous day was buttoning her sweater like a teenager in love. Her gray hair was loose and long, streaming down her back in a wild mass. She looked much younger than before, aided by the flush of energy on her visage. "What are you doing inside county lines?" she asked Dane.

He hid his smile and retook possession of Leslie's hand. "I guess trying to accomplish the same thing you are, only you beat me to my getaway car."

Said without apology or humility, even in the face of her uncle. When the old man shot her a scowl, Leslie felt like dying. Before he could question the logic of getting romantic with such a controversial figure like Dane Chappell, she pointed out, "I thought you and Miss Hathaway hated each other."

Both elders took a sudden interest in straightening their clothes. Claven cleared his throat. "We've come to an understanding."

"Yes, even though he is certainly no gentleman," Della said primly. "And he fibs a lot."

"I do not fib. You remember wrong."

Leslie could feel the tension rise all over again. Before the two could get fired up into another argument, Dane thankfully stepped in. "Look, we're in a bit of a hurry, so if you two could pick another car..."

As Claven began to look around for something else to defile, Della lifted her chin. "I don't know whatever for. As far as I'm concerned, neither one of us saw or heard anything here tonight."

"Same thing she said fifty-two years ago," Claven muttered under his breath.

Ignoring that, as well as the old man's gaping zipper, Leslie kept her imploring gaze on Della. "You won't tell anyone you saw Dane here?"

"Of course not," she replied with a look of distaste, and turned slightly to address her partner. "I can't say the same for him, though."

Claven glared at her. "Never been a snitch, and I don't plan to start now."

As soon as the words were out, a cacophony of noises came from their left: the opening of a door, a shuffle of footsteps, multiple voices... "I know it was him, ma'am, there ain't no one else 'round here built like Dane Chappell."

"I believe you, Willie." That was Sheriff Devin's voice. "Just keep guiding the way."

Dane, Leslie, Claven, and Della all hit the floor. The beam of a flashlight appeared, zigzagging through the packed, dimly lit garage. It took one moment of wide-eyed, ragged breathing to realize that there was no way they *wouldn't* be caught.

Because now that they were boxed in, the closed garage door was their only way out.

****

Dane met Leslie's terror-filled gaze. Their little run-in with her uncle and Della had cost them precious time—and quite possibly his freedom. The sheriff's footsteps were scuffling ever closer, then they were accompanied by another set of footsteps.

"Is he in here?"

Dane's blood instantly ran cold. Thurlow Tosh had joined the small group, and Dane felt the sudden need to welcome him with an open-armed tackle. Leslie's hand on his was the only thing staying him—his only link to sanity.

"Still looking, sir," Devine answered.

"Don't fuck up, Cecily. I want him brought in."

Since his focus was centered on Tosh, it took Dane a precious moment to realize that the elders were escaping…back inside the Oldsmobile. When Claven waved him and Leslie in from the back seat, Dane thought he was crazy. Why would they want to trap themselves inside a car?

His question was answered when the garage door in front of the Oldsmobile began to lift.

The beam of Devine's flashlight shot toward the front, illuminating the garage's shifting façade. The

Oldsmobile's engine turned over and roared to life. Leslie's foot had just disappeared inside the car's rear door when a hand shot out. Dane took it and launched himself inside the back seat just before the car jetted forward.

"Hey! Stop!"

Dane's door slammed closed, narrowly missing his feet. They barely cleared the lifting garage door before springing onto the street and cutting a hard left. The interior was packed with bodies, most of them unsettled and bouncing around like loose change. They banked right. Then another hard left. Tires squealed, and the rear fender scraped pavement as they tore into another parking lot. Amid the chaos, Dane could barely put a clear thought together beyond the fact that the enclosed air was hot, humid, and reeked of sex. They zoomed beneath a streetlamp which illuminated Leslie's face long enough to show that her pallor was a little off. He followed her gaze and saw something white hanging from the window's crank-style handle.

A pair of panties.

Claven was in the process of rolling over the seats until he finally made it to the front. When he settled behind the dash, only then did Dane realize who was driving. His gaze widened in amazement on the petite head of Della Hathaway, then it zoomed to the speedometer.

Holy shit.

Claven Gallagher let out a whoop of triumph. "You see?" He pointed to the woman beside him. "I told you she drives like Andretti!"

One look through the rear window showed flashing lights in the distance. As they shot through the grocery store's loading zone, Dane knew that their pursuers were coming fast and knew why Della felt the need for speed. "We should switch places," he told her. "Stop here."

"No, let her drive." Claven grabbed the dashboard. "Trust me, she knows what she's doing."

It had come out a half grumble, but Dane was following along just fine. He remembered Leslie's story about the school bus incident, but it would take time for it to make complete sense. The question now was—who the hell had opened that garage door and helped them escape?

The Oldsmobile careened back onto the street. A police car was zooming toward them head-on, so Della cut a hard left and headed east through the back of a neighborhood. Then a right, and another left. The flashing lights behind them had yet to reappear. The houses thinned out until a dead-end sign loomed ahead. "You may want to buckle up here," Della instructed calmly.

When she cut the headlights and drifted right past the sign in complete darkness, they all dove for their seatbelts. Lost in a continuous state of bafflement, Dane watched the road's barricade drift by. The hum of pavement turned to gravel, then to dirt. Everyone was shouting, throwing around orders like be careful. Turn the damned lights on. Don't get them killed.

All except Della Hathaway who finally removed her foot from the gas. The car coasted over an embankment and pitched forward. Beside him, Leslie groaned and put a hand over her mouth as Della rode the parking brake all the way down a steep hillside, the moonlight overhead illuminating trees and other foliage just enough for her to avoid them. It was a bumpy ride that Dane wasn't sure Leslie could survive, so he rubbed the back of her neck and silently prayed that she not make the situation any messier than it already was.

They somehow ended up down on another road in a completely different part of town, the street following the natural curves of a wooded hollow. It took a moment for Dane to zero in on the area, but as soon as he did, his anxiety began to rise again. "What the hell, Della?"

Della's eyes lifted and met his in the rearview mirror. "I heard this is where all the hooligans hang out, sheriff."

****

Every instinct Thurlow possessed told him Chappell was close. Not only could he *feel* his presence, he knew that the bastard wouldn't want to miss his chance to witness the chaos his little Rydell production had incited. Unfortunately, when the movie had begun, Thurlow was too wrapped up in conversation with friends to notice what was going on. Until it was too late. Peggy had gotten out of her lounge chair and descended the gazebo's steps as if in a trance. When he'd followed her gaze and noticed what was playing on the movie screen, his vision wavered. His surroundings became a blank until all he could see was that screen. All he could hear was a narrator's stilted voice detailing the misfortunes of a small town that had been decimated by Rydell Foods and their careless handling of the environment.

After his crazed flight toward the projection equipment, and after his unfortunate tussle with a dog and small child that left him smelling like urine, he decided whatever damage the movie had caused was nothing he couldn't fix. People would have questions and he would dispel their fears with talk of new EPA standards. Maybe throw in some bullshit statistics. He would figure it out later. Right now he wanted Chappell.

But it seemed as if the white Oldsmobile they'd been chasing had disappeared into thin air. "Where the fuck did it go?" he barked.

Devine slowed at an intersection, but still saw no sign of taillights in the distance. She shined her spotlight on a few driveways, then sped on to the next intersection. She'd been in constant contact with the other deputies on the hunt, but it was almost as if the damned car had disappeared.

Until the radio chirped. "Suspect spotted at Fifth and Schlitz Creek. All units respond."

Thurlow grabbed the skyhook and held on while Devine mashed the gas. So far her brand new fleet of squad cars had been unable to outmaneuver the rusty old boat that Chappell had escaped in, and Thurlow's blood pressure had skyrocketed during the chase. Now, with the promise of victory close at hand, he kept it in check with visions of Dane Chappell in handcuffs.

"Schlitz Creek is miles from the county line," the sheriff said, zooming down a steep, curvy hillside. "It's treacherous and there's only one way out, so he's as good as caught."

Thurlow's smile was mean, the taste of power and dominance sweet on his tongue. Up ahead, red and blue lights appeared, throwing the surrounding woods in constant motion. He squinted until he could make out the white, spotlighted rear-end of a car stopped on the road's narrow shoulder.

And there, by the right taillight, was the Oldsmobile symbol. "Yeah!" Thurlow shouted with a clap of victory. "I got you now, you stupid bastard!"

Devine pulled up behind the deputy's car and skidded to a stop. "Stay inside until I give the all clear," she ordered before getting out with her gun drawn.

Thurlow watched as she disappeared from view, only the top of her head visible above the other squad car. She was talking to the deputy who was slightly taller, his expression much too calm for having just caught up with a dangerous suspect.

A sick feeling entered Thurlow's gut. Ignoring Devine's warning, he unbuckled, got out of the squad car, and approached the two police officers. Devine moved to stop him, but he pushed past her and approached the white car without further caution. The windows were rolled down, making it easy to see the headrests sticking up above the seats.

And that the seats were completely empty.

****

Leslie laughed, her hair blowing in the wind and adding to the celebratory chaos of the moment while Dane sped past the county line and outside Sheriff Devine's jurisdiction. They were safe, back in the borrowed black truck with the windows down and the speedometer resting at a cool sixty-five miles per hour. Dane had assured her that this was friendly territory since the neighboring sheriff's department loathed Tosh, Devine, and their dirty politics.

The dash lights illuminated his profile, and she caught a rare glimpse of him in happy mode. He smiled at her, then back at the road as a chuckle shook his chest. He eased off the gas pedal, giving their hearts a chance to slow and their thoughts to organize.

"That was an interesting escape," she said, grinning at him with staggering relief. "I'd be happy to never experience it again."

"Della Hathaway." He removed the ball cap long enough to scratch his head. "Who'd have thought?"

Her smile melted into a look of chagrin. "My uncle. He was right about her. I'll never hear the end of it." The two elders had been safely deposited at Della's doorstep, which was conveniently located on the edge of town. Leslie looked over at Dane. "You were pretty freaked out when you realized Della was taking you right to your truck."

He ran a hand over his whiskers. "You have to admit, it's a scary coincidence."

"So she wasn't part of your escape plan?"

Though his lips were scrunched in thought, he shook his head. "Not that I know of, at least. Neither was whoever opened that garage door, unless Della was somehow able to do it remotely."

"Do you think that man who led Devine to the shop will be able to identify you?"

"Nah. All a lawyer would have to say is that he spotted someone with a similar shape to mine. Nothing that would hold up in court. I'm more worried about your uncle."

So was Leslie, at least until she could sit down and have a talk with him. "When we left them, Della seemed pretty sure he'd stay quiet."

"Probably because he'd just gotten laid," Dane replied. "Men are easy to mold when you heat them up."

A shudder ran down her spine as she relived her dire need to roll down a window. Groaning, she sank further into her seat. "I touched Della's underwear."

He laughed, a sexy rumble that changed his entire persona. For the first time, Leslie could see him as a man with a sense of humor, and what he must have been like before Tosh ruined his life. Was it possible Sheriff Chappell really did have a soft side at one time, as Maxi had suggested? While she pondered the idea, thoughts of her uncle's sex life slowly gave way to thoughts of her own. That kiss she'd shared with Dane in the flower shop had awoken her wonton side, and it was still kicking despite all that had happened since.

When they approached the next town, Dane slowed to the thirty-five mile-per-hour speed limit. Music reached them, distant and upbeat with a buoyant country twang. He pulled into the parking lot of what looked like a honky-tonk, its outdoor deck crowded with patrons. Dane cut the engine and palmed his keys. "I need a drink." He glanced at her, his eyes crinkled with suggestive humor. "You up for it?"

Moments later they were armed with cold beers, which they took to an empty table among the hubbub of saloon goers. Though she'd never cared much for country music, it was loud and surprisingly appropriate for her mood.

"I learned a few things tonight," Dane said as he pulled out her chair. "Maybe even solved an old mystery."

When she sat down, she took a long drink from her bottle, thoroughly enjoying this chance to relax with Dane. "Does it have anything to do with Della Hathaway?"

"I'm thinking so." He took his own seat, his posture as casual as his T-shirt and jeans, his broad shoulders lacking the tension that seemed to be a part of him. "Back in the sixties, our area had a rash of interstate shipment thefts," he explained. "Trucks carrying everything from TVs to fashion dolls were getting hit. They'd get stranded with engine problems, and when the drivers went for help, their cargo would be gone by the time they got back." He took a pull from his beer, observing the crowd with the watchful interest of a cop. "The FBI came to Rosemont's sheriff's department with suspicions that one of our residents was involved. They set up some surveillance, got enough evidence to organize a sting. One night after a robbery, they managed to catch up to a box truck they believed was loaded with stolen rotisserie ovens, but only because it had broken down on a dirt road just east of Rosemont. Then the suspect's car—or rather one matching the description—came out of nowhere and whisked the driver away before the dust could settle. The team surveying the suspect's home was given the green light to search it, but instead of coming in to an empty house…they found the suspect." Dane's eyes twinkled. "He was finishing up dinner with his wife and an episode of Perry Mason."

Leslie listened in rapt attention. "Then who was driving the getaway car?"

"They never did figure that out, or if it was even the same car. Turned out the suspect's car had been in Pete's Garage for two weeks, waiting on a new transmission. When they realized they'd been watching the wrong man, the FBI left with their tails between their legs. Local law had their laugh and moved on." He leaned toward her with a mischievous light in his eyes. "A month later, every housewife in Rosemont had a rotisserie oven."

"No! Who was the suspect?"

He paused, a slight smile on his mouth. "Charlie Hathaway."

Her expression went flat. "Don't tell me…"

Dane nodded. "And if I remember the story right, his fourteen-year-old daughter, Della, was at a friend's house that night."

"Fourteen!"

"But she was always a straight arrow, not even a parking ticket. I'm probably wrong…"

In light of all that had just happened, Leslie didn't think so. "Sometimes it takes an outsider to spot things that the insiders are blind to," she said. "My uncle's been back in town for less than a week and he managed to expose a side of her you never knew existed." Her brow went up and she paused before taking another pull from her beer. "You aren't wrong, Sheriff Chappell."

He looked at her for a good long time, his shrewd gaze burning a path from her thoughts to her loins. Then he put his near-empty bottle down, removed hers from her grip, and stood up. "Dance with me," he said, pulling her up with him.

She followed without hesitation, wondering what had taken him so long to ask. The song was a fast-tempoe'd number that inspired her to be-bop behind him on their way to the dance floor. No way would she attempt the twists and twirls of the western-bedecked ladies that were already there with their partners. Surely Dane wouldn't expect her to.

And then the world started spinning. Leslie yelped

in surprise, but his full spin was so effortless that it was over before she knew it. Now she was pressed against him with one of his strong arms clamped firmly around her waist. His free hand captured hers while she hung on to his shoulder for dear life. Unable to keep up, she stumbled.

But he had such a firm hold on her, she doubted anyone noticed.

"Put your feet on mine," he instructed above the music. When she did, he said, "Now just relax and enjoy the ride."

Mission accomplished. As she moved with him, she concentrated on his steps, learning the dance that everyone else seemed to be doing. She observed the others. Bit her lip and focused as if her life depended on learning this thing called the two-step. After a bit more coaching from her partner, she stepped off his feet and continued on, only once bumping toes with his.

Dane beamed down at her with pure pride in his smile. "You're a natural."

Before she knew it, he was swinging them both in circles, which went okay as long as she remembered to switch her feet. Then he tried a little push-and-pull maneuver that was by far her favorite, because the feel of their bodies coming back together was pure heaven in her book. The music upped its beat and her heart skipped right along with it. Dane's enthusiasm made her laugh. Her feet moved as if they had wings, and by the time the song ended, she felt like she'd been just a little bit possessed by Ginger Rogers.

There was clapping. Laughter. The lights overhead bathed them in colors, but she and Dane were stopped in the middle of the dance floor, glued to each other in an embrace that made their surroundings seem far away. Another song started with a warble of fiddles, but she couldn't move as he held her captive with the longing in his gaze. He lowered his head. She met him halfway. Their lips came together in a kiss that seared her insides from her heart down to her toes. Her soul was soaring, and she felt so carefree at that moment she didn't care who watched them, because all she wanted to do was swallow him whole.

Her body arched into his, and she could feel how much he wanted her. His tongue took complete possession of her mouth. Their breathing was labored, hot and ragged while they stood among many and simply devoured each other. Then he broke the kiss, but her eyes remained closed until he ran his hands through her hair.

"Leslie."

Her lids slowly opened to reveal a hot, viral man with a one-track mind. Sex. It was coming, or at least she damned well hoped so.

His mouth moved into an ornery half-smile that stoked her nether regions. "Let's get out of here."

Chapter 11

He'd rendered her so dumb with that kiss, all she could do was nod. The two beers were forgotten as, hand-in-hand, they cut their way through the moving stream of bodies until they were off the dance floor and heading toward the door. Once outside, the music became a muffled mosh-posh of beat and twang. The truck's alarm blipped, greeting them as they approached. Dane's eyes were watchful, as he was always wary no matter his mood. Leslie thought that was sexy as hell.

They walked to the driver's side door. He opened it and had her get in first. It was an old move that suggested she stay close and cuddly until they got to wherever they were going. When they were both inside, he grinned at her before inserting the key. "I want to show you something," he said.

She grinned back. "I'll just bet you do."

Moments later they zoomed past the Clearwater County sign once again. The man seemed to have no boundaries, nor care that he wasn't allowed to cross this one. The excitement from their earlier run-in with the law was a distant memory at that point, even for Leslie. They would probably never expect him to come back, at least not so soon.

When he turned onto a dark, dirt road in the middle of nowhere, Leslie was completely lost. Had no clue where they were or even where they'd been. For most of her stay in Rosemont, Kansas, her world had been tucked inside an old, ramshackle farmhouse that had started out just as desolate as she'd felt inside.

Now she was experiencing life from here to the moon, all within a sixty-mile radius.

Dane slowed, then drove the truck off-road where they went bouncing over uneven pasture for a bit before finding another, more patchy stretch of gravel. Leslie put her head back on his shoulder, content to stay there for a while. "Where are we going?" she asked.

"You'll see."

At one point he cut the lights, pulling Della's trick and using only the moonlight to see by. He definitely knew the area, even though the overgrowth had surely changed some since he'd been gone. As they headed up a small hill, he followed the edges of the road. The truck crested it and then went down. The next hill was bigger, steeper than the last, and before they reached the top of that one, he stopped right there in the middle of the road and put it in park. When all was quiet again, Leslie looked up at him with furrowed brow. "We're just stopping? Right here?"

"We walk from here."

He opened his door, got out, and gave her a hand. They left the truck and continued upward on foot. Her light canvas shoes were too thin on the bottom for gravel, but she couldn't care less. The air maintained a balmy heat that was gradually cooling as the night progressed. Sweat began to bead on her upper lip. The gravel ended and was replaced by a path of large, flat stones that were soon swallowed by grass. Dane led her around the side of the hill until they came upon a slightly wooded area that hissed against a sudden breeze. The air against her skin felt like a dream. She opened her arms to it. Closed her eyes as her hair billowed around her shoulders.

It took a moment for her to realize that Dane had stopped. She stopped too and glanced back at him. He was standing there in a clearing of soft grass, watching her. "Now that I'm here," he murmured, "I don't know what's more beautiful. You or the scenery."

Scenery? She looked forward again, only to lose her breath. The lights of Rosemont shimmered in the distance, set deep against a silhouetted backdrop of the bluffs behind it. They were far, far away, and much closer were a few random lights from tiny houses that dotted the countryside. Farmhouses. She squinted at the closest one…and spotted a familiar red truck parked beneath the light of the utility pole. "Is that my uncle's truck?"

Dane walked up behind her, put his hands on her shoulders and pulled her back against him. His whiskers grazed the top of her ear. "My family called this Whippoorwill Hill. We used to sleep here under the stars, generations of us dating back to the mid-nineteenth century. I remember doing it as a kid, and I'd always hike back home at about three in the morning."

Though he kept his voice light, Leslie felt the sadness creep in. "Why?"

"Because the damned whippoorwills wouldn't shut up."

Her answering laugh came out a hiccup as her eyes began to fill. "It's breathtaking."

"Yeah, well…it isn't ours anymore."

She turned in his arms, looked up at him through a distortion of tears. "I think if I can convince my uncle that there is no bomb shelter, he might sell the land back to you. That was the only reason he bought the place."

His wry smile appeared. "I won't lie to you. I want my land back, but your uncle doesn't own this part. The state does."

"Oh." She stared at his chest for a moment. Then horror struck and her gaze flew back upward. "Is this where the road is going through?"

He nodded, his lips thinning into a grim line. "There are some old graves over there that they'll have to move. Wasn't good enough to avoid eminent domain, so I filed papers with the conservation agency to donate this land as a wildlife refuge. I figured if the state was going to own it, it would at least be under my rules. And it would stay untouched." His voice got even quieter. "But something happened to those papers. My guess is because Tosh knew I had a chance of winning."

"Those were the papers you were looking for in the basement?"

He nodded. "Copies Reko sent me before I was arrested. I didn't know they existed, or I would have had Otter use them to finish the job."

Leslie wrapped her arms around her middle. Turned back toward the sparkling view ahead. "My uncle always said it ain't over till the napalm runs out." She wiped at a stray tear that had finally escaped. "As of tonight, there are a lot of confused people down there, wondering what they've gotten themselves into."

"I hope it's enough." He turned her back around

and cupped her face with his hands. The moon was behind him, capturing his hair in a silver glow and his features in darkness. His thumb came up. Wiped the wet trail off her cheek. "Thank you, Leslie, for helping me. You didn't have to, and I know what it could have cost you. What it might still cost you."

Her smile came from deep down. "I haven't thought of my own problems since I found you eating cookies on my staircase. To me the reward far outweighs the challenges."

He was still for a moment. She could feel his gaze on her as she waited with parted lips. Then he bent again and kissed her, finally giving her what she'd been hoping for since the last one. She wrapped her arms around his middle and kissed him back with something that felt an awful lot like love. Whatever it was, she simply went with it. The moon, the land, the wanderlust wind that caressed her bare arms, all added to the magic of Dane's touch. Perfection in its purest form.

His big body shivered against hers. He lifted his head, and when he spoke, his words were husky with longing. "Leslie…"

"What?" she breathed, her lips tingly and hungry for more.

His smile was lewd. "I want to show you something."

She smiled back, her body screaming that he fill her already. The setting for this moment was perfect, an enchanting place of magic and memory—a place Leslie hoped would exist forever. She toed her shoes off. He drew his shirt up and over his head and laid it on the grass. For a moment Leslie was struck dumb at the array of muscle covering his upper body. Yes, she'd fantasized plenty about what he'd look like without clothes on. But nothing could have prepared her for this.

When she realized she'd been gawking, she cleared her throat under the heat of his inquiring gaze. "You're so…fit," she explained.

His shoulders flexed, then relaxed, and he removed his hands from his fly. "I won't hurt you, Leslie."

A part of her cried inside, the part that wanted him to take her without caution. "I'm not afraid of you, Dane," she whispered. "And I'm certainly not breakable."

She lifted her fingertips to his collarbone. Traced the many ridges and plains of his chest, then his abs, then downward along the thin trail of hair that disappeared under his still-buttoned jeans. His muscles danced beneath her touch. His intake of breath showed her just how much she affected him. When she worked the button loose, his fly popped open under the pressure of his rock-hard shaft. She dipped her hand inside. Touched him. Knew he was barely hanging on to his control. Leslie liked him that way, so wound tight that one nudge in the right direction could undo him. And she held all the power.

When she moved her hands around to the back, she cupped his bare buttocks for a moment, then pushed his jeans and boxers downward. His shaft came out, finally bared to her in all its glory. Damn he had assets, and she was about to sample them all.

Dane must have sensed where her thoughts were going because he stopped her before she could kneel at his feet.

"I wouldn't last two seconds, honey," he rasped.

"It's been a while for me."

So, he *hadn't* found pleasure in a woman since getting out of prison. She could see him focusing all his energy and frustrations on his quest for vengeance. He was a warrior, self-disciplined and battle-ready. The image made her blood run even hotter, if such a thing were possible. He upped the heat by undoing her blouse, slow and sensual, one button at a time. When the blouse came open, he dipped his hands inside and moved it off her shoulders. He got to his knees, cupped his palms around her breasts, and gazed at them through the fabric of her bra. The attention made her nipples tighten and pucker. His thumbs grazed over them, wringing a ragged moan from her throat.

He loosened the clasp at her back. The bra came off, baring her breasts to his gaze and to the cooling air. Never before had she felt so wanton, so willing to do anything. *Anything*. "You're driving me insane," she hissed, her hands digging into his shoulders.

"I just want to look at you for a bit," he explained, touching her as if memorizing every contour with his fingers and palms. "Give myself a moment."

Her heart went out to him then, knowing this was his first time in so long. He wanted it to be perfect, and to give as much pleasure as he would take from her. But when his lips grazed her nipple, soon followed by his tongue…Leslie found herself in a whole new, undiscovered world of sensuality. She threw her head back, vying for the same control while the heat of his mouth closed over the sensitive peak. He sucked it, swirled his tongue over it, then released it to the night breeze. The sudden cool made her gasp. Her body wept for him, in constant motion and tight with longing. She laced her fingers through his hair, willing him to do that again. And he didn't disappoint. Took his time worshiping her breasts as if they were the most beautiful things he'd ever seen and tasted. While her everything was occupied by what he was doing up top, she missed that he'd pulled her shorts and panties down until his fingers grazed her sensitive opening.

When he groaned, Leslie let go, losing the battle with her own control. With a few expert strokes, he brought her to climax. She exploded, crying out as the pleasure flowered throughout her body. Before she had a chance to recover, she was on the ground, her back resting against the soft cotton of his T-shirt. Dane was on top of her, his warmth covering her as he took possession of her mouth. His jeans were gone, and she moved her bare legs up and down the length of his much larger ones. Dane positioned himself, pushed inside her slow and deep. She felt the protection he wore and was glad he'd had the scruples to don it since hers were apparently missing in action. There was no need to prepare as she was wet enough for them both, but never before had she been so filled by a man, with such need that she felt as if they were one body.

Dane stopped. Buried his face against her neck. They were joined, naked beneath the stars in a moment that needed to be savored. Then he began to move his hips in deep, slow thrusts. The feel of his length gliding in and out of her was the sweetest, most torturous kind of heaven she'd ever experienced. Not even her husband had felt this good, as if she and Dane were connected in more ways than just the physical. Perhaps it was the magic of this place; the small victory that had instigated such a celebratory mood, her feelings for this man and his plight soared far beyond what she thought possible.

Leslie hugged him to her hoping to take him in even deeper, though she knew it was physically impossible. Dane answered her needs, wrapping an arm around her middle and lifting her so that they fit even more perfectly together. For a moment they *were* one, inseparable in the face of their pleasure. His breath was a rasp of ecstasy against her ear as he spilled forth endless months of celibacy, of heartache and anger, of lost faith and resurrection. Leslie felt it all, reveling in the connection they shared in every fiber of their being.

Moments later, her sated body taking his full weight, Leslie lay there in a state of exhaustive wonder. "Wow," she breathed. "You certainly haven't forgotten how to do it."

A chuckle shook his chest. He rolled them over, taking her with him so that she was nestled in the crook of his arm. The grass was soft enough and somehow more appropriate for the occasion than his T-shirt, as if nature were aiding them in their short time together. He played with her hair, both of them gazing up at the billions of stars above. Clear as ever, just like her wants and desires. "Dane?"

"Hmm?"

"This was as perfect as it gets for me."

How dumb that sounded, but she couldn't help it. Her heart was so full she needed him to understand how important he'd become to her.

"It isn't over yet, Ms. Downing," he replied. "I want to do a lot more things to your body before this night is through."

More? Could she handle more? She looked up at

him, at the thick whiskers covering his jaw, and she wondered how long he would feel that need to hide. "You almost sound as if you're on borrowed time," she said softly.

His gaze searched the stars for a moment before he answered, "I've felt that way since my parole hearing. Hard habit to break, I guess."

"You won't go back to prison. Too many of us are on your side. Me, Maxi, Della...whoever your inside contact is." She thought about that for a moment. "It's Maxi, isn't it?"

"What about Maxi?"

"She's your contact. She told you about my first run-in with Sheriff Devine, and then you just happened to show up in my house when she was distracting me in the back yard."

Amusement crinkled his eyes. "Maxi is a good kid, but I would never put an expectant mother in that position."

Oh yeah. She'd forgotten about that. "Della, then?"

He laughed. "If I'd known Della was so crafty, she would have been my first choice."

Yeah, he was obviously surprised about Della. "Okay, what about that Reko guy you mentioned?"

Dane shifted a bit and looked down at her. "Why do you want to know so bad?"

She shrugged a shoulder. "Because I care, and I want to know who to turn to if you need help."

His rugged features turned soft and sexy. "You care, huh?"

Feeling his mood, she smiled up at him. "Yeah. Don't you know that already?"

"I just thought you wanted my body."

She dissolved into a fit of amusement. He pulled her on top of him and they gazed into each other's eyes for a moment, completely at ease. Unafraid of who may come looking. No one was around, it was just them and the Milky Way above.

A curious call came from the west, carrying around the curvature of the hill. Leslie looked up, her smile fading. *And the whippoorwills.*

Yes, they were there, too. Dane pulled hair away from her eyes as he watched her with wry humor. "They like to hide in the Osage trees by the graves."

The graves. A shiver wracked her spine. "Okay, so this was perfect until you said that."

He rolled his eyes. "Trust me, the dead people are too old to care." He lifted his head and kissed her, igniting another spark within her belly. "And if they aren't, they're about to be thoroughly educated."

But just when he was about to carry out his promise of more pleasure, a faint jingle came from the direction of his jeans. Dane groaned against her lips. Sat them both up so that she was straddling his lap as he reached for his pants. He dug out his phone and checked the screen. "Damn."

"What?" He gave her such a look of chagrin that Leslie knew exactly what was coming. "You have to go?"

"My parole officer just showed up at the duplex."

Her heart dropped down to her diaphragm. Damned Mayor Tosh… "What are you going to do?"

"Hightail it over to Sugar Free's place." Dane gently lifted her off him and got to his feet. "He'll cover for me."

His mention of Terrell made Leslie instantly feel

better since she trusted the ex-gangster and his loyalty toward Dane. Suddenly cold, she too searched for her clothes and rushed to put them on. "When will I see you again?"

"When it's safe for you," he replied. "If Devine harasses you for any reason, use that burner phone and call Otter. He'll know what to do."

****

The next day, Leslie drove to town with her laptop and grocery list. Uncle Claven had been curiously absent, but a text from him assured her that he was okay and in the company of one very needy woman. If the thought of doing it near dead people had freaked her out last night, the thought of *those* two doing it was much, much worse. Uncle Claven must not think Della was trying to kill him anymore. *Or* the man wanted to go out with a bang instead of a whimper.

Leslie had also gotten word from Otter that Dane was in the clear. She'd been unable to sleep, worried about him and wondering if he was back in handcuffs. She should have known, though. He was a survivor and way too smart for Thurlow Tosh.

At eleven o'clock in the morning, the temperatures were already high enough to create a ripple of arid heat above the blacktop. One mile into her drive, a flash of white caught her eye. It was a large wooden sign propped up in someone's yard. As she got closer, she made out the red hand-painted words on the sign.

NO RYDELL IN ROSEMONT!

Passing the sign, Leslie craned her neck, wondering if she'd just read right. As the vision solidified in her brain, a smile appeared. "Well, I'll be damned."

****

Thurlow sat at his bright, sunny breakfast table, scouring the local newspaper for any fires that may need putting out. There was a big front-page article about last night's movie in the park, but he'd paid the editor enough to keep it vague. The public would expect a story, and for it to disappear altogether would only create more buzz.

But still he was restless. There was a familiar stirring in his gut that he didn't like. It always meant there was more coming, and to get ahead of it he needed to act fast before someone else acted first. To go big or go home. That's how he'd ended up in Rosemont in the first place, and he'd be damned if he were going to let anyone topple him from *this* kingdom. Not when it was about to thrive.

Peggy entered the kitchen, her hair coiffed and complimented with a complete set of jewelry. She pulled out a drawer, sifted through some receipts while her purse dangled from one forearm. Thurlow frowned at her polished and pressed appearance. "Where are you going?"

"To church," she replied without looking up.

Was it Sunday? He looked out the dining area's wall of windows, past the vast front lawn, and noticed the traffic headed toward town. His mind had been on one single track since Dane Chappell had slipped through his fingers the night before.

Oh well, there would be other chances. The man was too arrogant to stay away, and next time Thurlow would be ready for him. He downed his orange juice and stood up. "Give me ten minutes."

She closed the drawer and stuffed a receipt in her

purse. "I'm leaving now or I'll be late. You can meet me there."

With one foot on the stairs, he threw over his shoulder, "You'll wait for me, Peggy."

"No, I won't." Her high heels tapped out her progress toward the garage.

His bathrobe flared open as he ran to catch up with her. He grabbed her wrist and forced her to stop. "We will go to church together like we always do, or we won't go at all."

"Get your hand off me."

"Peggy." He took a deep, cleansing breath, his head filling with the powdery scent of her perfume. In a valiant attempt to meet her halfway, he lifted his hand in a show of utmost patience and understanding. "It's important that we present a united front, especially in lieu of what happened last night." When her chin stayed at a stubborn angle, he moved in closer. "We need each other. Remember?"

Her rouged cheeks flared red against the light cream of her blouse. She cleared her throat. Put her purse down on the end table beside the living room couch. "Please hurry."

Chapter 12

Dane looked down at his cellphone and couldn't keep the smile from his face. Every time it dinged, he knew it was another photo from Leslie showing yet another sign she'd run into throughout her day spent in town. They were popping up now like mushrooms after a good rain. It was only Sunday and already the people were rising toward an angry majority that would demand an emergency town hall meeting by mid-week.

"You gonna stare at your phone all day or hand me some damned shingles?"

Terrell's voice came down at him with the chill of iced-water, and Dane realized he'd been slacking on the job. Grumbling, he stuffed the phone in his back pocket. With his load of shingles tucked under an arm, he began to climb the ladder.

"Careful, now, Five-O. I wouldn't want you to break something now that you gettin' some."

"I never said—" Dane huffed his way up to the last rung and swung his immense load onto the roof "—that I was getting some." He stopped for a moment, catching his breath in the intense heat of late morning. "And what grade are you in anyway, talking like that."

Laughter filled the air. They were both shirtless, sweaty, and pumped by the amount of work they'd already achieved between the two of them. At this rate, Terrell's dump of a house would be leak-free before the

157

forecasted afternoon showers were to arrive. Dane was only too happy to help in exchange for the favor of an alibi. And it felt damned good to get his hands dirty.

Terrell turned and sat down on the gabled roof. "Take a break, man, we got time." He took two bottled waters out of the tool bucket. As soon as Dane sat down beside him, he handed one over.

They both drank. Looked at the rooftops before them, and the city beyond. Smog tinted the horizon, casting the distant high-rises in a dirty haze. It made Dane miss the clean air of Rosemont even more.

"She send you another photo?" Terrell asked.

He nodded beneath the shade of his ball cap. "Tosh has one hell of a shit storm coming." And that was despite the man's attempt to highjack the Sunday paper. When Dane first saw how watered down the front-page story was about the previous night's premier, his heart sank. The newspaper's owner, Gene, was a likeable guy, but easily manipulated by politics and greed.

Dane's morning took a turn for the better, though, when Leslie began sending him those pictures. The woman certainly had a knack for making him smile.

"You see, that's how I know you got some," Terrell said. "That look on your face tells me your rubber band has been unwound."

There were no denials, only a respective silence. His thoughts kept wandering to what he'd done with Leslie on the slopes of Whippoorwill Hill, but they were soon followed by a deep need to finish what he'd started. It was a serious problem that wouldn't go away. The image of her slender, naked body writhing in the moonlight haunted him. Her scent, her soft moans, her rose-tipped breasts heaving beneath his touch were all memories that would seep into his mind and cause his dick to rise. He already wanted her again, needed the taste of her to fill his mouth, to watch her come undone while he feasted on her body—unfinished business, thanks to their untimely interruption.

Great. Dane shifted against the fresh ache in his groin. "I was fine until last night," he said with a fair amount of chagrin. "Now I can't focus on what I should be focusing on, and I have to wonder what the hell I've gotten myself into."

"Nothing fucks with a man's priorities like a good woman." Terrell downed the rest of his water and threw the empty bottle back in the bucket. "In this case, I'm glad. You aren't such a pain in the ass to deal with this morning."

Dane could believe it. He was actually in a good mood for a change, and the physical labor filled him with a sense of accomplishment on top of his win from last night. "Are you going to start on that bathroom next?" he asked.

"You offering to help?"

He nodded. "I need the distraction."

A whistle came from down below, capturing their attention. On the sidewalk, two pretty Latina girls were staring, their hands shading their faces against the sun. "Whatcha doing up there, Sugar Free?" the tall slender one shouted in a thick accent. "Besides looking fine, that is."

Terrell blew out a breath that sounded an awful lot like angst. "Just patching my roof, Lucida."

"Why don't you come down here and introduce us to your friend?"

"Unless you're into cops, I'll save us all the

trouble."

"A cop?" The second, shorter woman reared her head back, her high ponytail brushing the back of her tight shorts. "Since when do you get cozy with the po-po, Terrell?"

Dane was wondering when he'd suddenly become a cop.

"I keep telling you, Valerie." Terrell lifted his arms in a show of defeat. "I'm an honest man now."

The woman laughed, an ornery sound that smacked of condescension. "I'll remember that next time I gotta tell Aniyah her daddy's in jail."

Lucida elbowed her. "Shut up, girl, don't be so mean."

Valerie rolled her dark eyes, and they resumed their walk. "Just cuz you want to fuck him don't mean I gotta fall for his bullshit."

Despite Valerie's surly mood, Lucida's gaze still showed spirit as she walked backward and cupped her hands around her mouth. "You and your cop friend better have shirts on when we come back," she shouted, "or I'll be needing some mouth-to-mouth!"

All Dane could do was sit there and blink. He knew Terrell had a couple of sons, but the man had never talked about a daughter, or of this Valerie with whom he apparently shared a kid.

Terrell's inked shoulders were tensed, his gaze trained on the women who continued down the sidewalk. "I ain't ever gonna shake it, man," he mumbled. "I'll always be a gangsta."

A pep talk was coming, but first Dane had to know. "Why haven't you ever mentioned her?" But before the last word was out, he knew exactly why. The look on

Terrell's face as he watched Valerie walk away said it all. He was in love with her.

Dane cleared his throat. "We both have work to do. It won't be easy, but as long as we keep looking toward what's important, we can't lose." He clapped his friend on the shoulder. "You'll shake it. I promise."

The ensuing silence was laden with doubt. Terrell finally nodded and looked down at his hands. "Sorry for playing the cop card."

"I'm surprised they bought it."

Terrell laughed. "Shit, please. You ain't ever gonna shed that skin. Only reason you survived the hoosegow is cuz you was *my* Road Dog."

Road Dog: best friend in prison, as well as his most dependable backup in a fight. No one believed the notorious Sugar Free would trust a lawman that much, and anyone who smelled a badge on Dane—which there had been a few—eventually were convinced otherwise. But Dane feared that the mentality had been slipping away for a while now, slowly but surely. "I'm one fuck-up away from going back," he said. "No different than you."

"You wanna go back so bad, keep crossing state lines." Terrell shot him a wide-eyed look that dared him to dispute such logic. "And if Leslie ain't around when you get out, there's always Lucida."

Leslie was the only reason Dane kept going back. The woman was deep in his soul, had burrowed there early on. "You're right." Dane cracked his neck and stretched his shoulders in an attempt to reset. "I'm done taking chances. From now on, I'm the model parolee."

****

A whisper of breath touched Leslie's skin, bringing

her out of a dream that had her body craving any kind of stimulation it could get. The last few days had been torture, knowing Dane wouldn't dare step foot back in Rosemont. They'd agreed to stay apart until the buzz died down just in case Mayor Tosh and his sheriff were planning to nail her with a trumped-up charge to draw him out. They already knew the mayor was capable of it and didn't want to test the waters with Devine.

But could Leslie wait that long? As much as her body ached for Dane, it was no wonder she'd removed her camisole at some point in the night, craving the sultry breeze from her open windows to touch her as he would. Groggy, her eyes still closed, she whispered, "Dane, what are you doing to me?"

She could feel him in the room with her. His essence was all over this house, because in a way it still belonged to him. It's where his heart was, which she could feel every time she walked through it.

She lowered a hand to her breast, stopping there to talk herself out of bringing herself to climax. Though her nerves were popping with sexual tension, she knew that making love to Dane would be that much more perfect if she didn't.

"Don't stop on my account."

Her eyes popped open. It had only been a whisper, but she knew the words had not been derived from fantasy this time. She sat up on a gasp, propping herself on her elbows and scouring the dark room for signs of him.

He stepped in from the swinging doorway, his broad shadow filling the void that had been left with her since Saturday night.

"Dane?" She began to rise from the bed. "What are

you doing here?"

He stopped her before she could put one foot on the floor. "Risking it all." In the dim glow of the security light outside her window, she could see his gaze skim the length of her body. "Just for the chance to see you this way."

His words caused a flutter deep in her belly. "Are—are you crazy?"

"Yes," he replied without hesitation. "Tell me you aren't just as crazy."

Oh yes, she knew exactly how he felt. The problem was if they were caught, *he'd* be the one going back to jail. An incredulous laugh escaped her throat. "Dane, you have to go."

"Your uncle isn't home, and no one else saw me sneak in here."

"How can you be sure of that?"

"Because I know. And this time I'm not leaving until I've had my fill of you."

The determination in his voice told her there was no use talking sense. Knowing he couldn't stay away only solidified her growing feelings for him, and once again she wondered if she weren't already in love with Dane. This definitely wasn't just about sex. He could have any woman he wanted without risking his freedom. "Promise me something," she whispered.

He touched her navel, gazing at it as if it were the eighth wonder of the world. "Anything."

"Don't get caught for me. I couldn't bear it."

"Then lay back and let me make love to you the way I should have the first time."

As he lowered his lips to her collarbone, Leslie thought her heart would beat out of her chest. The fact that he was here—answering her need to feel him in all the right places—told her just how much in tune they were with each other. Fully dressed in jeans and a black T-shirt, he seemed in no hurry to disrobe as he thoroughly hijacked her body, taking her to such heights she never thought possible.

Sometime later, they lay in bed skin-to-skin, simply enjoying the quiet after the storm. He played with her hair. She traced circles on his chest. The floor-length, gauzy curtains were in constant motion, lending the perfect setting to her mood. She sighed. "You should have called me. It would have given me the excuse I was looking for to get in the car and come to you."

He turned his lips into her hair. "I wanted to make love to you in my own bed."

She looked up at him. "This is your bed?"

"Mm-hmm."

No wonder she constantly felt him, his presence. "Why didn't you stay in the master bedroom?"

"It belonged to my parents. All the rooms are the same size, anyway."

He was right, except the master bedroom had direct access to the bath. "I guess they were all your rooms when you lived here by yourself."

"Pretty much. I used my parent's closet a lot. Kept my uniforms in there."

She would climb whole mountain ranges for a chance to see him in uniform. *His* uniform. "If you had a chance to become sheriff again, would you?"

He was silent for a while, his eyes unreadable in the dim light. Then he said, "I suppose it would depend on the climate."

But he didn't think the chance would ever present itself. He'd said as much to her once. "Now that I know you, it's hard to picture you as anything else."

His fingers grazed the length of her arm. "Honestly, Leslie…I'm not sure how well the badge would fit anymore."

It was sad that he thought so. She'd felt him in his office, too, the one Devine had yet to make her own. She could imagine the changes that had taken place inside him, though, having had to adjust his whole mindset in order to survive among the lawless. "Was what you went through in prison so horrible?" she asked him.

His chest jumped beneath her hand. "Words cannot describe."

"That was a stupid question."

"Nah, it's okay. Since I was police, they moved me around a lot or else I would have fared a lot worse."

"When did you and Terrell share a cell?"

"Potosi Correctional Center, second to the last stop for me. He got out before I was moved. I was happy for him but scared shitless for myself."

Her guts boiled at the mere thought of what he'd been forced to endure, all at the whim of one crooked politician. "Tosh will pay for what he did to you." She glanced up at him, studied his profile. "I was going to wait until I had something to show you, but…I got Gene Dennison to agree to print my article in tomorrow's *Independent*."

He reared back, gazed into her eyes with a small smile. "No shit?"

Her own smile appeared, sad as it was. "No shit. I told him that if he continued to allow the mayor to manipulate his paper, I'd sick Kyle Downing on him."

His smile faded a bit. "Your ex-husband?"

She shrugged a shoulder. "It's a legitimate worry, and the only thing that scared Gene worse than Mayor Tosh."

Not that she liked throwing Kyle's name around, but desperate times called for desperate measures. Of course she'd had to contact Kyle and warn him first. And he'd had questions, ones she wasn't willing to answer. Yet. The fact she'd found the courage to call him in the first place was an epiphany of sorts that took up much of her focus. It proved that she was no longer hung up on her losses. Even the sound of his voice failed to leave her with the same bloody wounds as before. No tears had been shed after the call since her resultant trips down memory lane lacked the drama.

"Kyle left *me*, you know," she said, sensing Dane's disquiet over the matter. "You aren't upset that I brought him into it, are you?"

"No." His reply was rough, but laden with truth. "I am sorry you were put in that position, though. I can imagine how hard it must have been."

She sighed. "Not really. All it did was prove how insignificant Kyle has become."

Dane's hand stilled. "Oh yeah? Why is that?"

"Because my mind is always occupied by a stubborn ass of a man who would risk it all for the chance to see me naked."

Dane curled his big body around her. Buried his answering growl against her neck in a rare, playful move that ended with them both laughing and gazing into each other's eyes. "Damn right I would," he murmured before lowering his mouth to hers. They shared a long, slow kiss that deepened until a new fire ignited between them.

And before Leslie knew it, he was taking her to the moon one more time.

****

Late Wednesday morning, Otter burst into the kitchen with his phone in one hand while he unbuttoned his blue uniform shirt with the other. Grinning like a fool, he held the phone out to Dane who was in the process of pouring his first cup of coffee. "Have you seen this?" Otter asked him. "Emergency town meeting *tonight.*"

On the screen was the online version of the Rosemont Independent, which featured a front-page article written by one Leslie Downing, investigative journalist extraordinaire. Dane replaced the coffee pot, his own smile a broad showing of teeth. "Yes, I've seen it. Pretty good, huh?"

"Pretty good? She'll have the whole town throwing rotten tomatoes at Tosh before he hits the podium."

Caleb poked his head out of the laundry room. "She got it published? Cool." He emerged in a fresh uniform and polished shoes. "I'm really happy for you, Mr. Chappell."

"Thanks, kid."

Dane was happy for himself, no matter how the town hall meeting went that night. Leslie's story was a masterpiece of truths, harsh realities, and brutal facts, along with interview segments from Clearwater, Iowa residents that had decided to stay. They were all but living off-grid, collecting rainwater for washing dishes and clothes, and trucking bottled water and food in from the city since there were no more local stores or shops to buy from. When he'd read the article, Dane was so proud of her, and so grateful for her willingness to help. Thankful for her sheer existence. Rosemont was her uncle's home, after all, and she was invested in more ways than she realized.

Just mentioning her name took him to places that were far more fun than this vendetta with Tosh. He glanced over at his son who removed a gallon of milk from the refrigerator and poured himself a glass. "You know," Dane began, "I've been thinking."

"Uh-oh." Otter swiped a slice of bacon from the plate on the counter and crunched loudly.

"I want to get a job. Find a place I can rent by the month and then maybe…"

"Maybe what?"

Buy a house. The thought had been circling his brain since he and Leslie had made love the first time. "I don't know, I feel like I've done my part for Rosemont. Now that the people are armed with the facts, it's time I start thinking for myself."

The crunching stopped. "You don't want the farm back?" Otter asked with wide-eyed shock.

"Of course I want the farm back." Dane just wasn't sure how many people he was willing to hurt in order to accomplish it. "But it'll be more than a year before I can legally step foot in Rosemont again, let alone move back there." He swiped a piece of bacon for himself, silently vowing to start eating better tomorrow. "I was thinking of using the land money to buy a house, something that would appreciate over time. Something I can sell if or when we get the opportunity to buy our land back."

The weight of skepticism hung heavily in the air.

Otter opened a cereal box and slowly began to pour its contents into a bowl. "I think that's the most you've said at once without mentioning your fight with Tosh," he said.

Dane opened his mouth to argue, but realized it was probably true. "It's sinking in that I'm forty-one years old and having to start over again." His talk with Terrell on the rooftop the other day had stuck with him. "I guess I'm not willing to give Tosh any more than that."

Otter half-turned, a look of revelation on his young face. "Is this about Leslie?"

Dane squinted his eyes. "What?"

"Not that I'm complaining, because I think she could be really good for you."

The kid had never been particularly vocal about Dane's past relationships, even the ones that were considered serious. Then again, Dane couldn't remember feeling this way about anyone else. "She's a remarkable woman," he admitted with thoughtful reverie.

"And you don't feel so alone anymore," Otter added.

Dane realized he'd been staring off in the distance. He cleared his thoughts. Washed the bacon down with a gulp of coffee that scalded the back of his throat. "I've never been alone," he wheezed. "I always had you."

The younger man chuckled. Clapped him on the back. "Damned lucky for that, aren't you?" By the time Dane recovered, Otter's grin had faded. "Are you going to tell her about the bunker?"

With that, the conversation went from awkward to worse. Dane's guilt over the lie had been eating at him since using the bunker last night as a means to access the house. That would have been the time to tell her it *was* still there, but his window of opportunity had been narrowed considerably the moment he'd gotten her panties off.

Then again, she did tell him that Claven would sell the land back if the bomb shelter didn't exist, and the chances of him actually finding it were slim to none. "Let's keep it buried for now," he replied. "If that's the only reason Claven wants our house, he doesn't belong there anyway."

Otter's look turned doubtful. "What if you and Leslie live there together? She'll be pissed when she finds out you lied to her."

Yes, but so many pieces would have to fall into place for that to happen. Dane was willing to risk it. "One thing at a time, kid. Right now I'm more worried about that town hall meeting tonight."

With a shrug, Otter wolfed down a bite of cereal. "I'll go."

Damn if he didn't hope his son would say that. But Dane had promised himself not to pressure Otter into doing anything he didn't want to do. "Are you sure?"

Otter nodded. "I want to."

Dane's chest swelled with pride, and he tamped down the urge to rip the cereal out of Otter's hands and bring him in for a full-on man hug. Luckily, Caleb chose that time to come out of the bathroom with a can of deodorant spray. "Hey, can someone smell me? I think this one's a little ripe."

Otter's spoon halted halfway to his mouth. He sent Dane a narrow look, prompting him to hold up a hand in oath. "I swear it wasn't me this time."

Chapter 13

Leslie sat in the back of the community center with her laptop and purse, prepared to take copious amounts of notes and nothing more. She didn't have enough skin in the game to stand up and ask questions, no claim to the community, or any real right to be there. Just a burning desire to help. After seeing her article in print that morning, she'd been overcome with a sense of accomplishment unlike any other. It proved to her that something *could* be done in order to reverse the damage that had begun the moment Tosh was elected. And she had no plans to quit before she saw the mayor unseated and Dane back in his sheriff's uniform where he belonged.

Just then, that very uniform filled her vision. Well...not the *same* uniform, but one just like it. Leslie's gaze moved upward, past the chunky utility belt, the pressed and pleated shirtwaist, and the shiny badge above Sheriff Devine's left boob. She sent up an awkward smile. "Hello."

The woman wasn't smiling as she lifted a foot and planted it on the chair beside Leslie's purse. Devine looked around. Leaned in on her elbow as if they were engaged in casual conversation. "That was some article you conned Gene into printing this morning."

It took fire to fight fire, and Leslie met the woman's gaze without fear or shame. "I guess he realized that the truth was more important than his bank account."

The woman's answering smile was bland. "You know he's using you."

Leslie knew which "he" she referred to and didn't bother with pretenses. "Would you believe me if I told you I'm not doing it for him?"

"Ha! It doesn't take a genius to know that you're sleeping together. Women are always throwing themselves at Chappell's feet, and I personally find it disgusting."

"I will agree that our tastes run in vastly different circles."

"Don't be a smartass." Devine leaned in closer, her slicked-back hair reflecting the halogen lights from overhead. "When this is all over and you finally see Dane Chappell for what he really is, you might be occupying your own jail cell." She removed her foot, stood tall, and straightened her uniform. "Those conjugal visits will be much harder to accomplish with both of you behind bars." Her smile appeared. And then she was gone.

"Bitch," Leslie muttered under her breath.

"What was that all about?"

She turned to behold Otter Chappell taking a seat on her other side. He was out of uniform this time, his street clothes and wind-rumpled hair making him appear much younger than the last time she'd seen him. For some reason, she was extremely surprised—and extremely glad—that he was there. "You're a sight for sore eyes."

The younger man chuckled. "Figured I could throw in my two cents, for what it's worth anyway."

Technically he'd never been a permanent resident of Rosemont, but Leslie guessed he was close enough. "You're here for your father, aren't you?"

A nod confirmed as much. "Same as you."

They smiled at each other, a united front for the good guys. "And for my uncle," she added. "He'll be here any minute."

Where was the old coot, anyway? Since he and Della had become a thing, she'd seen very little of him, though he did say he would be here tonight. From the size of the crowd already, the whole *town* would be here. It was a very good sign.

A few minutes later, Claven Gallagher did arrive. "Hey, String Bean."

"Uncle C." Mildly annoyed by his public use of that ridiculous nickname, Leslie moved her purse so he could sit down. "You remember Otter—uh, Oliver Chappell, don't you?"

"Of course I do." Claven and Oliver exchanged nods. "How's it going there, Chappell?"

Otter indicated the size of the crowd. "I'd say pretty good, thanks to your niece."

Claven let loose with a cackle. Patted her on the knee. "She's got her uses. Did wonders to that house you sold me."

"That's what I heard."

"Heard from who? Your dad?"

Leslie winced. Otter cleared his throat. "No, from the people in town. I still keep in touch with a few of them."

Like Maxi, Leslie thought, curious to see how the woman would react when she noticed her childhood crush in attendance. She decided to change the subject

173

before Uncle Claven inadvertently spilled more beans. "Where's Della?"

"Somewhere around here," Claven grumbled, casing the room for signs of her. "She isn't ready to be seen with me in public."

Leslie turned away just in time to hide her mirth. Otter looked ready to bust her, so she asked him, "Don't you work tonight?"

"No, I'm off," Oliver replied.

Which meant he'd have plenty of time to go home and fill Dane in on all the details of the meeting. "I saw Maxi on my way in. She's around here somewhere."

His gaze immediately flicked over the crowd. "We ran into each other outside. Looks like she's ready to pop any day now."

Leslie wondered again if he suspected he'd sired her first child. Or if he *knew* he had. "She said you two were pretty tight growing up," she added, watching him closely.

His eyes softened and a flush crept up his neck. "Yeah." He laughed a little and scoped out a fingernail that he began to pick at.

Fascinated by his response, or lack thereof, she was about to tiptoe deeper into the subject when the gavel pounded, filling the hall with the command for order. Everyone quieted. Those who couldn't find a seat had piled up along the walls and around the back. The city council members were all seated at the table up front. Mayor Tosh was there alongside an attractive, sandy-haired woman who was meticulously put together. His wife, Peggy, perhaps?

As Leslie scoped the couple out, the mayor's gaze locked on hers with the intensity of a thousand-yard stare. Her pulse quickened a bit, but she held it until he was the first to look away. The challenge sank in quickly, and she was more than ready to face him head-on if or when she had to. Or would he always send his sheriff to do the talking?

Feeling determined, Leslie opened her computer and brought up the notes she'd already started when she'd gotten there. Not that she'd had time to do much since folks kept introducing themselves and asking her more questions about her article. Twenty minutes into the meeting and those questions were repeated into the microphone that was set up toward the front. At first the folks lined up in the aisles, waiting for their turn to speak. But when voices were raised and the general tone became caustic, more and more people began shouting from where they sat. Leslie documented words like "fraud" and "underhanded" as the most cited among them. The council defended their actions, saying their vote had been made in accordance with the law, and that the majority had been agreeable up until now.

"Not Sheriff Chappell," someone shouted. "He was always against the idea, and I'm thinking now that he was right."

Mayor Tosh stood up and called the man out with a calm smile. "Mike Patterson, is that you? Come on up to the microphone and we'll talk about Mr. Chappell. Everyone move aside, please, and let Mike through."

It was almost as if the mayor had prepared for this. Leslie felt Otter stiffen beside her. They shared a look.

When Mike made it to the front, he leaned into the microphone.

"Before you begin," the mayor interrupted, his face an expression of personal anguish, "I want you to think about what kind of man your ex-sheriff is. For those of you who are younger and didn't know him as a youth, Peggy will attest that he was a troublemaker. Got himself into many scrapes from grade school on up to graduation. He also engaged in a lot of fistfights, and apparently he wore the badge of a lawman thinking he could continue on with that type of behavior." Tosh looked at the crowd, his eyes skimming the many faces for effect. "We can't trust a man like that to know what's best for our future, not when he can't even control his own."

Otter swore beneath his breath.

"I'm not condoning what the sheriff did to you, mayor," Mike said, his voice ringing loudly through the speakers. "But now I can see what got him so riled. You and the city council purposefully left us out of this deal. You snuck it in under the table and hid the truth until it was too late for us to back out. Well, I read in the paper this morning that it isn't too late. And in case you missed all those signs around town, a lot of us aim to stop Rydell from coming here."

Cheers went up along with a lot of clapping.

"Now, Mike—" The mayor called for the people to calm down and let him speak. When it was quiet enough, he said, "Mike, you can't make these types of decisions based on old footage taken *before* the new environmental laws were implemented. Rydell will be heavily monitored by the state *and* the EPA to ensure that Clearwater, Iowa, doesn't happen here."

"Doesn't matter, mayor. We no longer want to be a chicken town."

"Are you forgetting the revenue that will be brought in? All of you local business owners will see huge gains because of this plant. Property values will skyrocket."

The next man stepped up to the microphone. "Like the article this morning pointed out, we don't have the resources to support such a big operation," he said. "We'd have to build another water tower. Add more power lines. Your deal with Rydell didn't include them paying for any of it which means it'll come out of the taxpayers' pockets."

"It's just like any relationship, Virgil. We have to meet somewhere in the middle in order to grow."

"But our schools can't take more growth," a woman shouted from somewhere else in the room. "We're busting at the seems as it is, and I don't personally want our kids to have to sit in bigger class sizes than what they already have."

On and on they went. Leslie knew it was all stuff that had been mildly thrown around among the community, but the impact had been strengthened now that they knew Clearwater could happen to them. They'd seen the devastation with their own eyes. Visuals were good for that sort of thing, and now it was personal.

The gavel hit, calling for order. A female voice carried over the speakers, soft and pleading at first. Then it strengthened. "Everyone, please calm down. Let me speak!"

The crowd hushed. The woman beside Mayor Tosh had stood up and was clutching a hand-held microphone to her chest. Peggy Tosh had something to say.

"Now just about everyone in this town has known me all my life, or all of yours, whichever comes first.

You know I want the best for Rosemont. And when I first met Thurlow, I knew he was the man for me. He was caring. Thoughtful. An achiever and a natural born leader." She looked down at her husband and smiled warmly. "It's why I fell in love with him."

Tosh grasped her hand. "You left out the devastatingly handsome part," he said with an impish grin that earned him some laughs.

"Of course, darling," came her comedic reply, earning the two of them even more laughs. The mood calmed, and she went somber again. "My parents, Leland and Martha, who you all remember as devoted, lifelong activists for this community, trusted Thurlow to take care of their only daughter. And he has. More than I can say. And now I'm asking you—my friends and neighbors of Rosemont—to put that same trust in him. I promise he won't let you down."

It was such a heartfelt speech that Leslie's spirits plummeted. The tone had been effectively shifted.

Otter stood up then. "I would like to know exactly when my father became the bad guy." Heads turned, and the room filled with a low rush of sound. "Yes, he was a troublemaker when he was younger, but he grew up like the rest of us. He devoted his life to all of you from the time he was old enough to wear the uniform. Now, he always maintained that he wasn't the one who assaulted Mayor Tosh. Since when did you start doubting the man you *know* him to be over an outsider?"

"There was proof," someone said in a defensive tone. "Witnesses."

Otter was angry now, and he showed it in the fierce frown he'd inherited from his father. "The only witnesses were two criminals my father had arrested at one point, and the victim is a man with more to gain from this deal with Rydell than any of you."

"Watch it, son," said Mayor Tosh. "You're one breath away from a slander charge."

Leslie touched his arm. Five rows away, Maxi was turned in her seat, her visage wrought with emotion. When Otter met her gaze, he visibly cooled. Took a deep breath. "I'm asking you all to go back to your homes and think about it," he said to the crowded room. "Remember who my father was to you. Remember why you were here tonight."

And then he walked out, leaving Leslie with no choice but to watch him go. "I always liked him," she heard Della Hathaway say behind her.

With his gaze straight ahead, Claven smiled. "Turtle."

It almost sounded like an endearment. Leslie glanced back to see that Della's features were stiff and stoic as ever. "Love Bug," she muttered back.

****

When the town hall meeting was over, Thurlow and Peggy walked to their car hand-in-hand. The ride home from the community center was silent, the air a confusing mixture of angst and pride. The evening hadn't ended as he'd planned but would have been a complete disaster if not for his wife's outward show of support. Peggy had scared the hell out of him when she'd grabbed that microphone, but then warmed him with her tender words.

He parked the car in the garage and they both got out as the door came down behind them. When they entered the house, he watched her as she put her purse away and kicked off her high-heeled shoes. Indeed, he found a renewed appreciation for how well her bottom filled out those skirts she wore. He approached her from behind and put his hands on her shoulders. "Thank you for saying what you did in front of all those people."

She turned to him, her eyes as bright and beautiful as the day they'd met. "Why of course, Thurlow. We're a united front, remember?"

The tension eased out of him, and he could feel the faint stirrings of an erection coming on. "I am very glad to hear you say that." She was cooperating. Whatever had changed her tune, Thurlow could be grateful for it. "We'll accomplish great things together, Peggy. Both of us."

She began to unbutton her blouse, laughing a little on her way up the stairs. Thurlow followed her with a smile on his face and with big hopes of getting lucky tonight, but first he needed a trip to the medicine cabinet.

A few minutes later, he searched out the prescription bottle in question. Shook a tiny blue pill out into his palm and downed it with a glass of water. He then closed the medicine cabinet's door to see Peggy in the mirror, buttoning up the bodice of her favorite red dress.

"Oh, don't bother with that," she said in a jovial tone. "I'm going out."

His face froze. He turned around and walked out of the bathroom. "What do you mean? Where are you going?"

She slipped on a pair of silver heels and shook out her hair, moving as if she'd just found the secrets of youth. "Since infidelity is part of this contract of ours, I decided to embrace it."

Thurlow felt the blood surge to his neck, fearing that by the time it reached his dick he would be alone to deal with it. "Don't test me, Peggy."

She touched some perfume to the spots below her earlobes. "I don't plan to, Thurlow."

"I mean you aren't going anywhere tonight except for that bed."

"Or what?" Her gaze met his in the reflection of her vanity mirror. "You'll tell the people of Rosemont that I'm responsible for the death of Pastor Francis?"

"That's right," he snarled.

She laughed, a spooky sound that was laced with malice. "Don't forget I know a few things about you, too, mayor." Infused with her favorite scent, she approached him, an unspoken dare to stop her darkening her eyes. "Call 911. Get your butch sheriff over here to take care of that flaccid penis of yours. I'm going to Missouri." She brushed by him and headed toward the door. "And when I find Dane Chappell, I'm going to fuck his brains out."

****

"Great meeting tonight." Claven's neighbors, Howard Diedricksen and his wife, stopped by their booth on the way out of Cozy's diner. Many folks had come there for some post town-hall discussions over coffee and pie, including Leslie and Uncle Claven. "What Otter said sure made us think long and hard about what happened to Dane. It would be a darned shame if he really was innocent."

Annoyed, Leslie's smile of greeting cooled. "Too bad these doubts didn't come before his trial."

Howard's head fell in a show of understanding and

regret. "Tell him we said hello?"

With a nod, she watched the couple leave and wondered how many others had been tipped toward Dane's side that night. Hopefully enough to bring some truths out of the woodwork, or perhaps even evidence that would entice another investigation into Tosh's beating.

She couldn't help the small grin that appeared on her lips. "Something tells me Devine is on borrowed time."

Claven pushed his plate away. "You think so?"

"When the truth comes out, these people won't put up with a crooked sheriff."

"Nah, she's a pussycat," he observed over the rim of his coffee mug.

Since he'd managed to say it with a straight face, Leslie laughed. Then she sobered a little. "You're joking, right?"

His eyes twinkled in answer. "Anyone who wears John Wayne novelty socks can't be all bad."

The laugh was back, though she still wasn't sure he was joking. "I can honestly say I've never noticed her socks."

While Claven took their ticket up to the register, Leslie dug a tip out of her wallet and placed it on the table. She then drained her water glass before scooting out of the booth. It tasted extra sweet tonight, not because this particular battle with Tosh had been won, but because upon leaving the community center she had been bombarded with questions about Dane. The people wanted news, to know where he was staying, if he had a phone number, and did she think he'd want a chance to reconnect with the community.

Otter sure had left an impression. The interest in Sheriff Chappell was back. The people were restless, thirsty for the truth about what they now feared had been a horrible mistake. That alone was a bigger win than Leslie had anticipated.

She met her uncle by the door. He opened it for her and followed her into the parking lot. It was dark now, the streetlamps casting the few cars left in a stark light. They parted ways, Claven heading toward his old GMC, which was parked on the other side of the diner. Leslie's mind was still on earlier events, and she failed to see the man standing by her car until she almost reached it. With her keys in hand, she looked up—and froze.

No way would he dare show up here now. The man was crazy.

He smiled at her. "Baby."

Moving past her state of paralysis, Leslie looked around for signs that other folks may see him, too. "Kyle, what are you doing here?"

It had been three months since she'd seen him, long enough not to expect him to materialize out of thin air despite her recent phone call to him. But that was obviously why he'd decided to make the trip from Omaha. Her ex-husband stood a lanky six-foot-five, his relaxed stance countering the in-your-face way he had of looking at people. The way he was looking at her now.

"You can't make a phone call like that without expecting me to get curious," Kyle said. He lifted his weight off her car and closed some of the distance between them. His soft, light brown hair moved easily with the breeze. "It's good to see you, Leslie."

His olive-green eyes bore the look of an honest man, though she now knew it to be a lie. The excuses she'd made for him—citing her many faults as the reasons he'd left—circled her brain with fresh, painful clarity. "I didn't expect you to show up here."

Nor did she expect her pie to come back up so soon. Clearing the acid from her throat, she pointed her keys at her Camry. The doors unlocked with a flash of lights. "But I'm smart enough to know you won't leave until you've gotten what you came for, so let's get it over with."

The ensuing silence was interrupted by the growl of a familiar old truck passing by. Leslie closed her eyes. *Please don't let him notice.* But since there would be no mercy served from the heavens that night, a squeal of tires rent the air. Uncle Claven backed up the necessary few yards it took to enter their section of parking lot. His headlights swung around until she and Kyle were lit up like two actors on stage.

And it was about to become one hell of a production.

Chapter 14

With the engine still running, Claven got out and walked toward them, his gravelly steps spelling nothing but trouble for Kyle. The younger man produced a bland smile. "Uncle C, how are you?"

Claven stopped, hands on hips, his narrow-eyed scowl taking measure of the other. "Been real good, Slick. You?"

Kyle's gaze moved over to Leslie. "Just trying to sort some things out."

"Ya do it yet?"

"We've barely had a chance to say hello."

"Aw, dang." Claven raised both eyebrows at the man. "Guess that means you weren't quick enough."

Kyle's smile faded into a look of dull patience. "This is between Leslie and me."

"Let me put it to you this way." The old man shifted his weight. Rubbed his belly as he studied the ground. "If *I* don't kick your butt back to Omaha, her new boyfriend will. And you don't want to mess with him."

Leslie's head snapped up. "Uncle C—"

"He's an ex-con, you know. Real big guy who did time for beating a man half to death."

Her gaze took another quick sweep of the parking lot, searching for any locals who might be within hearing distance. "You don't know what you're talking about!'"

"The hell I don't. The walls are thin in that house, String Bean." His eyes took on a mean twinkle as they bore into Kyle. "Those two were going at it like rabbits the other night."

The pie was about to seriously come up now. "You weren't even home!" she hissed.

"I came home, not that you would notice. Didn't want to interrupt, so I snuck back out again."

Kyle's cool façade cracked. "You've never approved of our marriage, Claven, yet you condone her relationship with an ex-con?"

"She'd be better off with a can of pork-n-beans than you."

It had taken a whole ten seconds for their encounter to get out of hand. Leslie got between them, put her hand on Claven's chest and backed him up a step. "Kyle isn't here on any kind of romantic level, Uncle C. He's after a story."

Claven's scowl only deepened. "Well, he can't have that, either. It's *your* story."

"I'll handle it. Just please don't talk anymore."

"But—"

"Go home, Uncle C."

She'd put a growl in it, one that made her uncle flinch. Not that she cared how he treated Kyle, but he apparently didn't remember that Dane wasn't allowed inside the state let alone his house. The refresher would have to wait until later, though, when Kyle was out of earshot.

Claven's shoulders lost their starch. He peered around her and pointed a finger at her ex-husband. "Just remember he isn't welcome in my house." With a silent simmer, he turned back to his truck and got in. The door slammed. The tires spun and he backed out of there with as much attitude as the old truck could muster.

"Charming as ever," Kyle said behind her.

Leslie twirled around and pinned him with the same glare she'd granted her uncle. "Not a word about him, Kyle. He's protective, which is more than I could ever say for you."

He seemed to know when to clam up, at least. Leslie commended him for it as she circled around to the driver's side of her car. "Get in," she said. "I don't want to give the locals any more fat to chew."

Luckily no one else seemed to be around except for the few folks who still occupied the diner. With any luck, Uncle Claven's mouth didn't do too much damage. When they were safely ensconced in the privacy of her car, she started the engine and cranked up the A/C. Hot air blasted outward. Kyle fiddled with the seat to afford him more legroom.

"Don't get too comfortable," she said, willing her pulse to find a more normal rhythm.

Kyle trained his amused gaze on her. "So you're dating an ex-con, huh?"

"Let's keep this as non-personal as possible, shall we?"

"Leslie, just because we're divorced doesn't mean I don't care about you."

She rolled her eyes. "Oh, please. You wouldn't even be here if you hadn't smelled blood in the water."

"Look." He turned toward her. "I'm not here to step on your toes, just to offer some backup. I read your article online this morning. It was good enough to pique my interest. Hell, I even got here in time to make most of the town hall meeting."

Her shock was great, more because he'd bothered to come here rather than her inability to notice him in a crowded room. "You were at the meeting?"

He held up a hand. "To observe, that's all."

Since the man always had an agenda, she sent him a droll look. "I appreciate the sentiment, but I got this."

"Is *that* why you asked for my help?" he said smoothly.

"I didn't ask for your help, Kyle, just for the use of your name and reputation."

"Which got you a front page story."

He was right. She deserved this, but it had been so worth the cost. "And now you want to highjack it?"

There was a heavy pause, one that was meant to up the suspense. "I want to team up with you," he said finally. "Nail this Mayor Tosh to the wall."

With those words, the cost went sky-high. It would be a dream come true if the offer had come from anyone else. She closed her eyes and put her forehead against the steering wheel. "I don't think that would be a good idea."

"Why, because we were married once?"

"Honestly…no. I've made peace with our divorce."

She could feel him studying her profile. When she looked at him, he gave her the side-eye. "You're serious about this ex-con boyfriend of yours, aren't you?"

Leslie opened her mouth to reply, but nothing came out.

"Dane Chappell, right?"

Of course he'd know that. The fact he was here

meant he'd done plenty of digging into the early history of Rydell's move to Rosemont. Her shock turned to panic, and she pointed a finger at him. "Don't pull this reporter bullshit on me, Kyle."

"I'm just asking—"

"Dane asked for my help," she said, talking over him. "There is nothing illegal about that."

"There is if you're having sex with him in your uncle's house."

"Since when did you take anything my uncle says seriously?" she screeched.

He laughed at her look of utter horror, an indication that he'd only been teasing. "Come on, you need me and you know it. This little town has no chance against a giant like Rydell."

God, she hoped he was teasing. The fact that Dane had looked into Kyle first made her feel only a little bit better. "This town needs Dane as much as he needs it, so don't even think about throwing him to the wolves."

"Actually—" Kyle reached out and shifted the vents, which were just now starting to blow cold air "— I was hoping we could have a drink somewhere. You could fill me in on things, maybe even introduce me to Dane Chappell."

The horror was back in spades, so much that she couldn't hold back an incredulous, maniacal laugh. "That's, like, the worst idea to come out of an ex-husband's mouth in the history of worst ideas. Ever."

"Leslie, come on."

"No. N-O, no, not a chance in *hell*."

****

Dane entered Moonlights with a confusing mixture of jealousy and delight. Leslie had made the hour-long drive to see him, but it was in the company of a man he had no interest in meeting. When he'd taken her call, it was with hopes that she wanted to see him in lieu of the town hall meeting, and perhaps repeat what they'd done the other night. He wanted her again, and not because she was helping him. His thoughts of her were slowly drowning out his thoughts of Tosh. Of Rosemont. Of what he'd once viewed as top priority.

And the thought of Leslie spending time with her ex put such a sick feeling in his gut, he had to wonder if he might be in love with her.

He spotted them in the same booth they'd shared before. Leslie occupied the side Dane preferred, with her back to the wall. There was a head in front of her, higher than most, and with a boyish shape that smacked of metro-sexual. When he approached, her eyes brightened as they tracked his progress. She slid over, allowing him room. "Dane, this is Kyle Downing. Kyle, Dane.

Forgoing the urge to beat his chest, Dane reached across the table and shook hands. Kyle's fingers were long and lanky with no real strength in them but were plenty wet from his glass. Though obviously tall, the guy was puny and would be made short work of in prison. "Leslie tells me you were at the meeting tonight," he said. "Any particular reason?" *Other than wanting your wife back, June Bug?*

"I've covered a few environmental disasters in my career," Kyle replied with a touch of arrogance. "Leslie will tell you I've even taken on my fair share of crooked politicians."

"And?"

"I'm good at it."

"I've told him all about your reputation, Kyle," Leslie interjected in a flat tone. "He knows it's why Gene printed my article, so let's move past the résumé and get down to why we're here."

Kyle relaxed back in his seat and smiled at Dane, a cool guy used to getting his way. "If you're willing to sit down for an interview, I think I—" A quick glance at Leslie. "I think *we* can make this national."

There was something about this guy that Dane didn't like. Or trust. It wasn't just because he was Leslie's ex, either. "I don't want my life to go public. I just want it back."

"Sometimes you have to—"

Whatever he was about to say was cut off when Terrell came up to the table. His dark skin appeared darker against the low lighting and white chef's attire. He went right for Leslie, bending over them all to give her a kiss on the cheek. She beamed at him, a genuine, mega-watt smile that had Kyle doing a double take. "How are you, Sugar Free?" she asked him.

"Better now, Sunshine." He gave Kyle a brief once-over, then asked Dane, "Who's the June Bug?"

Dane struggled to hide his smile, relieved he wasn't the only one who pictured Kyle as a prison slave…if the man were to land in one of course. "Kyle Downing," he said. "Big reporter out of Omaha. Wants to interview me."

A dark eyebrow rose. "*Downing?*"

Kyle extended a hand, which Terrell took with exaggerated interest. "I'm Leslie's husband."

"*Ex* husband," both Dane and Leslie said at the same time.

"Sorry." Kyle sent them both a wolfish smile.

"Habit."

The ensuing silence was deafening until Terrell burst out laughing. He slid into the booth beside Kyle, forcing the man to move over. "Shit, I gotta stay for this."

While Kyle recovered from the intrusion of their newest guest, Dane peered over at Leslie and was delighted to see that she was amused. He relaxed back in his seat. Gave the reporter his measure from across the table. "No offense, Kyle, but I want Leslie. I trust her."

He let the meaning hang out there, to be taken any way the other man chose. Kyle took a long drink from what looked like a whiskey sour, clearly feeling the heat of any beta who'd just stumbled into a den of alpha males. "I understand." He cleared his throat. "You *should* trust her, she's a good girl."

Dane suddenly understood why Leslie had gotten so pissed off when he'd said as much before. "It's true," he agreed. Beneath the table, he took her hand and squeezed. She looked over at him, and he smiled into her eyes. "But she also knows when *not* to be."

Her pretty blush made it quite clear where her mind went with that. Dane continued, "Her instincts are spot-on, and she knows how to call bullshit when she hears it. I can probably thank you for that, Kyle."

Kyle's ears had already turned pink, and were on their way to a nice, fire engine red. "Look, the only reason I'm privy to this story is because she called me," he said. "There's no need to get territorial."

"Isn't there?"

"He could help you, Dane." Leslie's softly spoken words were effective in calming the storm. "I didn't ask him to come. But now that he's here, he could get the truth out much more efficiently than I can. He's exactly what you and Rosemont need."

And she was willing to sacrifice her chance at glory for the cause. Let the man who had broken her pride and her heart trample on it some more.

But Dane wasn't so willing. "Thanks, but no thanks." He took great satisfaction in watching the triumph drain from Kyle's visage. "We'll handle it on our own."

"What if I say Leslie's name will be all over the story?"

Dane reached up. Placed the words in the air for them all to see. "*No Rydell in Rosemont* by Kyle and Leslie Downing." When Terrell laughed again, Dane said, "I don't think so, Bub."

Kyle's chest jumped with a sardonic laugh. He drained his glass. "You're making a big mistake."

Ignoring him, Dane asked Leslie, "Did you drive him here?"

Her expression blank, she shook her head. "No, he followed me."

Good choice. It meant the arrogant turd could head straight back to Omaha. Having read Dane's mind, Terrell got out of the seat, giving Kyle a clear exit. When the man slowly slid out and was on his feet, he started digging into his back pocket.

"Drink's are on me," Terrell said with a smile. "Have a nice trip home."

Kyle gave Leslie one more long, heated look before he turned and left. Terrell watched him go, his shoulders shaking with leftover mirth. Then he looked back at Leslie and Dane. "As fun as that was, I better get back to the kitchen." He clasped Dane's hand in a manly farewell. "Always good to see you, Five-O. And take care of this lovely lady here, or I will."

"Fuck off, gangster," Dane replied smoothly.

Terrell laughed again, the sound following him through the kitchen's swinging door. Dane rubbed his face with his hands. Collected himself. "I feel like I've just come out of a bag of marbles," he said, the words muffled against his palms. He slapped them down on the table. Peered over at the woman beside him in an attempt to read her. "You okay?"

She swallowed. Looked down at her own hands and nodded. "Yeah."

But he didn't believe her. Guilt assailed him over the fact that he'd just shown a gross lack of consideration for her feelings. Cursing beneath his breath, he grabbed her hand and pulled her out of the booth. "Come with me."

It was late, the hour closing in on 11:00PM. When they left the lounge and crossed the parking lot, Dane steered her away from her Camry and marched her to the truck instead. He put her in the passenger seat, then circled around to get in the driver's side. When they were both closed in, all was quiet until he turned the key.

Engine noise infused the dark silence of the cab. Dane backed out, then left the parking lot while going over his apology speech in his mind. He didn't know where they were going until he spotted a quiet park on the right side of the road. The parking lot was empty with only one streetlamp by the entrance of the walking path, so he turned in and chose a spot as far out of the light as he could. With the truck's nose facing the park, he shut the engine off. Leaned an elbow against the windowsill. "Look, I'm sorry if I—"

"You know there is nothing stopping him from writing that story."

He could feel her studying him, and he kept his eyes trained forward. "Your ex-husband can write what he wants, but I don't want him quoting me."

"And if he gets it wrong?"

He rolled his head to meet her gaze. "You'll get it right."

She laughed a little, her eyes suspiciously glassy against the moonlight shining through the windshield. "I'm just so scared for you, Dane. For a man who takes so many chances, you're putting a lot of faith in me. I'm afraid it will be your biggest mistake."

He reached over. Grazed her cheek with the back of his hand. "Nothing about you is a mistake," he murmured.

A small breath left her lips, as if she'd been holding one. Her seatbelt retracted with a *zip* and then she was climbing onto his lap. Suddenly covered in woman, Dane found himself the recipient of a tempestuous kiss that scrambled his brains. His dick had already begun to harden, since just looking at her did that to him. She reached between them and cupped it with her hand, squeezing and rubbing him until he was drowned in madness. He somehow managed to find the button on the side of the seat, pushed it and moved them backward. With more room, he was able to tear at his fly. Reach under her skirt. He moved her panties aside, his fingers testing and invading. The two of them were a tangle of breath and need and sensation, rushing into a storm that demanded satisfaction. As they devoured each other's mouths, they made love in the driver's seat of Otter's truck until they came together with stunning force. It was an impromptu act that Dane refused to feel guilty about, even though he did it without a condom this time, something he'd only ever done once in his life. Nine months later, Otter was born.

Leslie lay boneless and panting against him for a moment, then she lifted up just enough to kiss him again. "You're a fool, Dane Chappell," she whispered against his lips. "And maddeningly irresistible."

He chuckled. Reached up and moved hair away from her face as they gazed into each other's eyes. "You're worth being foolish over," he replied, caressing her shoulders. "How else would we end up having sex in a public park?"

Laughing, she looked out the windows, completely unafraid of being seen through the tinted glass. "It's no Whippoorwill Hill, but it sure has its perks."

"Does this mean you aren't mad at me anymore?"

"I couldn't be mad at you."

"Give it time. I have a reputation to uphold, you know."

Her laughter at his joke faded until she was serious again. "Just don't ever lie to me. Okay?"

"Never." As soon as he said it, the bomb shelter came to mind, along with Otter's words of warning that he should tell her about it. The idea of getting his house back had compelled him to lie the first time. Now he didn't care where he lived as long as he had Leslie to warm his bed every night. "Actually...there *is* something I need to get off my chest."

"What?"

"When Otter sold—" His phone began to buzz on the dash. Dane reached out and grabbed it. Checked the screen. "It's Caleb." When he answered, there was a fair amount of angst in the younger man's voice.

"Mr. Chappell, there's a lady here looking for you," Caleb said. "She says she has something to give you."

"Who is it?"

"I don't know, she won't say. But she's wearing a super hot red dress."

****

After dropping Leslie back off at her car, Dane rushed home to find his driveway completely empty. According to Caleb, Otter left home shortly after Dane had, and borrowed Caleb's Prius to meet with some friends. Still, he expected to see the lady's car still there, whoever she was.

He parked the truck and went inside, opening the front door with a sense of caution, surprised to find it unlocked. The lights in the living room were on, but he was greeted with a complete and eerie silence. "Caleb?"

No answer. As he began to move through the duplex, he caught himself reaching for his hip holster only to be reminded that he would never wear one again. The training was still in him, though, and would probably always remain in the deepest fibers of his being.

"Caleb?"

He'd said it louder this time but was met with the same result. In the kitchen, he grabbed a filet knife. Turned the blade inward so that the blunt side was flush against his wrist and forearm. It was not his weapon of choice, but now that he was armed, he moved to the darker parts of the duplex. He peered inside the open door of the bathroom. Then through Otter's open bedroom door, flipping on lights as he went. Only Caleb's door was closed, and when Dane raised a knuckle and lightly knocked, his senses were on high alert. Someone was in there, and so far his repeated calls had yielded no response. Neither had his knock.

Dane quickly turned the knob and pushed the door open, shielding himself against the wall before proceeding with caution. When he reached for the light switch and got a good look inside, he noticed a body sprawled on top of the rumpled covers of the bed. It was Caleb, bare-naked, eyes closed, and mouth open. For a moment it looked as if the man were dead, and Dane felt that instant moment of panic when he'd found other crime scenes of people he'd known and protected over the years. The rush of adrenaline that followed kickstarted his heart into a full gallop and he rushed to the young deputy's side. Checked his pulse…which was still beating beneath his two fingers, thank God.

Caleb's chest rose and fell. He brought his hand up to his eyes and groaned, but it became quickly obvious that he was okay. Willing his heart to slow, Dane lowered his weapon. "What the hell happened to you?"

"She attacked me," Caleb groaned.

"She *attacked* you?" Now that he had time to absorb the full nature of Caleb's condition, Dane deduced that it was the kind of attack a young man like him wouldn't mind so much.

"Uh-huh. We were sitting on the couch waiting for you. She was asking a lot of questions, and I could tell she wanted you pretty bad, so I told her you were in a serious relationship. At first she seemed really disappointed, but the next thing I know she's all over me, kissing me, and pawing at my clothes. I tried for like a second to reason with her but...seriously, man, she was really hot and it's a miracle we made it to my bedroom."

It had all come out in a drunken rush, as if the man thought he was in trouble. If it weren't for the scare, Dane would be laughing. "Did you at least get her name?"

Caleb's eyes finally cracked open. "Nope."

"What did she look like?"

He raised his hands in the air and cupped them as if holding a pair of large, imaginary breasts. "Like this."

Dane rolled his eyes and grabbed a towel that was hanging from the back of a desk chair. Covered the man's junk with it since Caleb lacked the thought capacity to do so himself. "Did she say if she was coming back?"

He shook his head against the pillow. "No. But she told me to tell you that she was sorry it couldn't be you."

Chapter 15

By the time Peggy came home, Thurlow had been in bed for over an hour. Devine had taken care of that erection for him, but it hadn't been the same. Knowing his wife was looking to fuck his worst enemy had put a different spin on things, and Thurlow had been seeing red ever since. When he finally heard her climbing the stairs, he was ready to kill her.

She moved throughout the dark room without bothering to turn on a light, but he could see her silhouette against the window, and that her hair was a mess. She removed her dress. Stepped out of it and climbed into bed without putting her usual nightgown on. He also noted that there had been no panties to take off.

As soon as the smell of sex hit his nose, he knew what her game was. She'd done what she had threatened to do—fucked Dane Chappell's brains out. And she wanted him to know it, too.

His gaze bore into the back of her head. "How was he?" he sneered.

Her upper body moved with a sigh. "He was fantastic."

As the rage built, so did his desire to kill her *and* Chappell. His penis seemed to cooperate with his mood and began to harden once again. Since his lust for Peggy had died long ago, he could only chalk it up to an unadulterated need for supremacy. To show her that he was still the boss.

He lunged for her and they began a long, turbulent struggle. She screeched. Fought. Clawed at his face. But in the end, he was stronger, and soon had her in a position that was ripe for the taking. "You fucking whore," he raged against her hair.

"Let me go, Thurlow!"

Never. And after tonight, she would know better than to test him, because he was determined to leave her with a lasting reminder.

One that wouldn't allow her to sit for weeks.

****

The new washer and dryer would be arriving on Saturday, forcing Leslie and Claven to spend their entire Friday fixing the back porch. The biggest surprise came when Maxi brought over a pot of chili and offered up her husband's very capable hands. Their son, TJ, had brought his own workbench complete with a full set of plastic tools, a table saw, and wood pieces that snapped together.

Then several other folks offered to help, and they too brought their children and a dish of some kind. It became clear to Leslie that this had been planned, and her heart was thoroughly won over by the people of this small, Kansas town.

Big Trouble turned out to be a sweetheart. Leslie appreciated his help the most since he had the muscle *and* the knowhow when it came to installing floors. New support pillars were also installed that day, which were effective in propping the extended roof back up to its original state. If Leslie had known Claven was going to purchase the appliances so soon, she would have told him the truth about the bomb shelter, that it no longer existed. But maybe when Dane bought his house back, he could compensate for the washer and dryer since he would need them anyway. For now, she was enjoying the day too much to spoil it with unsavory reveals.

When the major work was done, the group of friends and neighbors sat down to big bowls of hot chili, vegetable dishes, a cool fruit salad that tamed the heat, and a whole host of desserts. It was a picnic in the sun filled with laughter, stories, and a four-year-old little boy who wanted to be a part of everything rather than play with the few other children that were there. In fact, TJ spent most of his meal in Claven's lap, for the two had become best buds at first sight.

Joy filled Leslie's heart that day, and the only thing that threatened her mood was the fact that Dane wasn't allowed to be a part of it. He of all people needed to be there, to have this chance to reconnect with the people who seemed to now want him back. Howard Diedricksen even told Leslie that a coalition was forming to keep Rydell from building their chicken plant. Protesters had mucked things up for the road crew that morning, and even the city council was starting to balk. Mayor Tosh was losing his support for the food giant's new build and would soon be faced with an ultimatum: make Rydell move somewhere else or kiss his mayoral seat goodbye come next election.

Leslie couldn't wait to tell Dane. After everything had been cleaned up and the last guest had left, she and Claven decided to apply one more coat of polyurethane to the new wood decking. They ran out of the stuff halfway through, so Claven hopped in his truck and drove to town to get one more can. To pass the time,

Leslie patched a few holes in the porch's enclosed screen. She was almost done when the sound of footsteps in the grass approached from around the house. Claven must have made it back in record time. She was about to scold him for speeding when she looked up and immediately saw that the new arrival was not her uncle.

It was Mayor Thurlow Tosh.

Her smile faded. She backed up a little when he climbed the porch steps and peered at her through the screen. His smooth face was a mask of polite regard. "Hello, Ms. Downing. I thought it was past time I stopped by and properly welcomed you and your uncle to the neighborhood."

His white-blond hair was aflame with vivid hues from the lowering sun. He would have been handsome in a clean-cut kind of way—if he weren't covered in political slime. Leslie's knowledge of the man kept her from falling for the old-school charm, but she decided to play it nice. For now. "Mayor. This is a surprise."

When she didn't invite him in, he smiled at the door handle. She could sense that he was considering his options. Wondering if he should come in anyway. So she decided to come to him and stand close so that he wouldn't feel the need.

Tosh's slow nod confirmed that the hint had been taken. "I can't help but feel that we've gotten off on the wrong foot," he said to her through the screen. "And we haven't even been properly introduced yet."

"I know who you are." Too tired for games, Leslie left it at that.

The light in his eyes changed. He leaned against the doorframe, a relaxed pose that showed he was in no mood for games, either. "I saw you at the meeting Wednesday night. I'd hoped to speak with you afterward, but my wife didn't feel well and wanted to get home. I'd really like the chance to speak with you now, in private, if you don't mind."

Not even if hell froze over. "My uncle is home," she lied. "Now isn't a good time."

A hint of anger flashed across his face and was quickly gone. "I saw him driving into town while I was on my way out here. We have a few minutes."

"I'm not inviting you in. If you want to talk, you can do it from there."

"There's no need to be afraid of me."

"Do I look like I'm afraid of you?"

His gaze raked down the length of her body then up again, lingering on her halter-top long enough to give Leslie the heebie-jeebies. "Okay then. I guess being from the city your hospitality only goes so far." His eyes met hers again, and this time they were flat-out burning. "I can appreciate that, especially since you'll be going back to Omaha soon."

She crossed her arms against the not-so-subtle hint to leave. "I might stay a while longer, just to see what happens with Rydell."

A laugh shook his chest, and his teeth flashed with a quick smile. "Why are you so interested? Oh, I know." He snapped his fingers. "You're Dane Chappell's cheerleader, aren't you?"

It was almost like he was mentioning a pet. "That's none of your business," she said with flat aplomb.

"I like a good romance as much as the next guy," he continued, "but you should know who Dane Chappell is before committing to a war you can't possibly win."

She lifted a brow. "War? Is that what this is?"

His voice lowered, along with the amused façade. "Rydell will happen. This town will prosper as a result, and no amount of bad publicity will change that."

"Then you shouldn't be worried about a little nobody like me. Certainly not enough to feel the need to come out here and confront me."

"I didn't come out here to confront you. I came to warn you." His expression hardened. "Leave Rosemont before you get in too deep with Chappell. He isn't worth going to jail over."

Though his words caused her hackles to rise, she masked it with a cool look of affront. "Funny, I told him the same thing about you."

"Ahhh… That was very good advice. I think even you get the idea he'll never be welcome back here. Not as long as I'm around."

Leslie remembered Howard's update from earlier. "I hear that may not be much longer if you don't back out of your deal with Rydell."

Tosh waved a hand, dismissing the notion. "The locals can gather, protest, put up as many signs as they want, but at this point nothing will stop Rydell from building in Rosemont. You and your entourage can try, just like Chappell tried when he filed those papers with the conservation agency. But it'll be the same story of too-little-too-late, and afterward I won't even *need* that mayoral seat." He winked at her with the arrogance of a confident man. "Because my next stop will be the Governor's mansion."

His mention of the conservation papers made Leslie's blood run cold. Tosh had known about them, probably even pulled some strings to make them disappear. Rage in its purest form took hold until all she wanted was to wipe that smirk off his face. "What if I told you another copy of those conservation papers exists, and that all Dane has to do is get them to the right lawyer?"

There was a small hitch in his expression. "I'd say you're lying."

He was absolutely right, but a snake like him needed to be rattled. He needed to walk away with doubts, and Leslie would be the one to plant them. "Why do you think I'm so confident that your days are numbered, mayor?" she said with the same lack of expression as before.

"He would have used those papers already," the man replied.

She shrugged a shoulder. "Not if he didn't know about them."

When Tosh's smirk finally disappeared, she quashed the urge to push more of his buttons. Knew when to quit, especially while she was ahead.

The mayor backed off the steps with a bland smile. "We both know he already violated his parole, probably multiple times. The next time, we'll arrest him." He turned and began to walk away, but then he stopped. Threw over his shoulder, "Oh, and please give him a message for me. Tell him that when he goes back to prison, I'll have him castrated for fucking my wife." His smile was mean. "I tend to lean toward the swifter justice of the old days."

Leslie watched him go with a potent mixture of fear and doubt. Tosh was a dangerous man, had just proven it in a very mild and effective manner. But something about that last threat didn't sit right with her. It wasn't the implication that Dane had slept with Tosh's wife, because she knew he wasn't the type.

It was a sense that Tosh *did* believe it.

****

Ready to light someone's ass on fire, Thurlow burst through the back door of his home and headed straight for his study. Once inside, it took a great deal of control not to slam the door. He picked up the phone, dialed a number. When the call was answered, he snarled, "You lying son-of-a-bitch. You switched sides, didn't you?"

There was a bored sigh on the other end of the line. "What are you talking about, mayor?"

"Dane Chappell. His girlfriend just told me he got his hands on another set of those conservation papers. And guess what? You're the only one who could have made that possible!"

"And you believed her?"

"That bitch was laughing on the inside! Yes, I believed her!"

"Look, my money's already spent. I can't afford to switch sides, same as you."

"Or you're taking a little extra from *him*," Thurlow snarled.

That last accusation was met with a thick silence. "You better watch what you say, Tosh," the man replied. "I don't like being called a liar."

Thurlow took a deep, calming breath. "You showed your hand a long time ago, Menendez. You've been holding those papers over my head so I won't expose you to the wrong people. But I guarantee if Chappell turns up with them, I'll be taking you down with me."

He disconnected the call, took a long look at the cordless phone in his hand, then promptly threw it at the bookshelves at the far end of his study. It struck an edge of the shelves and clattered to the floor in pieces.

"Who was that?"

Thurlow whirled around to discover Cecily Devine standing in his open doorway. "What the fuck are you doing here?" he barked.

"I came over at the invitation of your wife." She walked in and closed the door. Her crisp, black uniform was perfect as always. "For some reason, Peggy wants to be friends."

It was a ridiculous notion since Peggy knew he was having an affair with Devine. Unless this was about what happened the other night... Thurlow cursed and sat down heavily in his desk chair. "I wouldn't if I were you. She knows about us."

"Did you two have a fight?"

"None of your goddamned business."

The woman approached him in a slow, methodical manner that put his senses on high alert. She uncrossed her arms, placed her hands on his desk and leaned forward. "I have always admired you, Thurlow. You've proven repeatedly how much power you're capable of wielding, and I happen to find that sexy enough to put your cock in my mouth on a regular basis. But using brute force against a woman is a serious game-changer for me."

Thurlow silently cursed his wife for the bold move of ratting him out to Devine. "What did she tell you?"

"Nothing. But I have eyes, and if you're the reason she can't hardly move without flinching, you and I will be reassessing this amicable relationship of ours."

"I didn't do anything to her." Peggy's screams rolled through his head, reigniting the guilt that had been with him since the night he'd abused her. "And if she says I did, she's lying."

Devine studied his eyes for a good long time before she straightened. "Good. Then I won't expect to find her in worse shape the next time we decide to have tea together."

When she was gone, Thurlow scrubbed his face with his hands. Shit was falling apart left and right, and it was all because of a couple goddamned women. Should he believe Leslie Downing? Could he afford not to? Knowing that his own wife was turning on him, he had to be absolutely sure that Dane Chappell really didn't have the ammo needed to stop Rydell from moving to Rosemont.

****

"He's under the impression you slept with his wife," Leslie said over the phone. "Have you met with her recently?"

Dane stood outside the entrance to Moonlight's, having just finished his dinner with Terrell. The man had wanted an update on Leslie's husband, and the two of them had shared a few laughs at the prick's expense. Now he didn't feel like laughing. Because suddenly everything made perfect sense.

A juicy curse slipped out, gaining the attention of an elderly couple that was standing close by. He walked further out into the parking lot. "I haven't seen Peggy since I've been out of prison, but I think I know who has."

"Who?"

"I'll tell you later. Look, don't start any shit with Tosh. If he comes around again, call the Diedricksens and have them come over. In the meantime, keep all your doors and windows locked. Don't go into town alone."

"He can't do anything to me, Dane. He's a high-profile member of the community."

"That doesn't mean he won't hire an outsider to do it for him, Leslie, especially if he thinks you might have information about those papers."

Her answer was a heavy sigh. Dane felt like reaching through the phone and strangling her. What was she thinking, riling up a dangerous man like Tosh with lies that could very well get her killed? "Leslie?"

"What?"

"Did you hear me?"

"Yes, I heard you."

The line went dead, a clear indication that she didn't like his tone. Too fucking bad. He didn't like that he couldn't be there to protect her in case her mouth got her into trouble.

Ten minutes later, he walked into the duplex and caught Caleb getting out of the shower. The man had just returned home from work and was about to go out on a date. Dane pulled up the picture he'd found of Peggy Tosh on the Internet. Stuck his phone in Caleb's face. "Is this the woman you had sex with the other night?"

Caleb blinked. Zeroed in on the photo as well as the name beneath it. "Holy shit…"

Dane took that as a yes. "Fuck!" he yelled as he paced the hallway. "She told him it was me."

"Who—what—huh?"

"Peggy Tosh," he growled. "She came here with every intention of cheating on her husband with the one person he hates most. *Me.* But when you told her about my relationship with Leslie, she settled for you and lied about it." A maniacal laugh escaped. Dane ran a hand through his hair in abject fury. "Jesus-H-Christ!"

"Damn." With the towel wrapped around his waist, Caleb entered his room and sat down on the end of his bed. He looked absolutely crestfallen. "I'm sorry, Mr. Chappell, I didn't know. I should have kept it in my pants, but she was one determined lady."

And now they knew why. Dane feared it was because Peggy was retaliating against Thurlow for cheating, an affair she was only privy to because of him. He was the one, after all, who paid Terrell's brother to send her that graphic video. Thought he would shake up the household in his quest for revenge, a move that had come back to bite him in the ass. "I wonder if she knows what she's done," he murmured. "Or if she even knows what Tosh is capable of."

"You think he'll come after you again with some false charges?"

If that was all Tosh did, Dane could handle it. It was the other possibility that scared him most. "I think he put his crosshairs on someone else." He sent a troubled glance toward the younger man. "And if he hurts Leslie, I really will beat him within an inch of his life."

****

Leslie's eyes popped open as another rumble moved through her room. It was the plastic shopping bag hanging from the closet's handle, adding just enough noise to wake her up. Did that mean they were working on the road in the middle of the night again? It was a frustrating notion since every moment of construction meant they were inching toward Whippoorwill Hill.

In a dark mood, she sighed and rolled over. Punched the pillow beside her and tried to settle back into sleep. But her thoughts of Mayor Tosh continued to seep in, haunting her with the possible consequences of her actions. There were no existing copies of the conservation papers, but as long as he thought there were, he could very possibly send someone after her. Or Dane. God, she'd been stupid to put the idea in his head. He was smart enough to have come this far without slipping up. What made her think he'd do it now?

Dane was right. She *wasn't* thinking. It was a spur-of-the-moment thing that felt good at the time. Still, she hadn't liked being reprimanded by Dane. He'd sounded like the police, so distant and at the same time disappointed.

There was a scraping sound outside her window. She rolled over to look, wondering if Dane had decided to sneak back into Rosemont to talk things over. She was sprawled on top of the covers in her camisole and underwear, wondering if he'd be taking them off of her soon. Make up sex was the best sex, after all, and she wouldn't turn him away.

Sure enough, the window started to open. A leg came inside, soon followed by the rest of a darkly clad body. But when the man straightened, she knew instantly by the leaner and shorter stance that it wasn't Dane.

And he was coming at her with terrifying speed.

She opened her mouth to scream, but it was quickly covered by a gloved hand. Her intruder wore a ski mask, his eyes and mouth the only thing visible in the darkness. "Shhh, let's not get hasty," he whispered, his hot breath foul with stale smoke. "The old man is just across the hall, and if he comes in here, I'll have to shoot him." The shape of a gun appeared, clutched in the man's other hand. "Do we understand each other?"

Leslie nodded, her chest heaving, her head pounding with the blood that roared in her ears.

"Good. Now you're going to tell me all about those conservation papers you said your boyfriend has."

She shook her head. He uncovered her mouth long enough for an answer. "I lied," she gasped. "There are no papers."

"You're lying now."

"No! The only set Dane knew about was stolen before he could find them."

"Shhh, keep your voice down." The reminder came with another view of the gun. "Why did you tell the mayor there was another copy?"

She closed her eyes against the tears that threatened to come. "I was just trying to piss him off, I swear."

"That wasn't too smart, now, was it?"

She shook her head rapidly. "No."

"And what if I don't believe you?" The barrel of the gun came down, and the intruder grazed the cold, hard end of it across her nipple. "What then, Ms. Downing?"

Her body shuddered under the callous nature of the touch. "I'm telling you the truth. There is no other copy."

As he pondered her answer, he moved the barrel between her breasts and down the center of her belly. When he reached the bottom of her chemise, he wedged it up and mashed the gun against the bared middle of her gut. "If I find out you're lying," he whispered, "I won't come after you. I'll come after your uncle. So if those papers are real, now is the time to come clean."

"I've told you four times now that I was lying," she hissed between her teeth. "My answer won't change, so please just go."

He finally lifted his weapon, and more importantly took his finger off the trigger. "I was going to." His dark gaze raked over the length of her. "But looking at you, I can see why Chappell is so fascinated. A man can't help but wonder what you would feel like beneath him."

As the implication solidified in her gut, Leslie remembered Dane's words about soft parts. And now that the gun was no longer pointed in her direction...

With a surge of anger, she curled her fingers and jammed the heel of her hand into his nose, making his knees buckle. "It would feel about like that."

The intruder was now bent over and wheezing, though still clutching his firearm. Leslie took that opportunity to bound off the bed and run, but as soon as she passed through the door she heard a muffled curse, then the scraping of roof shingles. The man was already out the window, proving that he wasn't deadly enough to come after her in a rage. Still, the fear was fresh and turbulent within her. Swallowing it back, she shut and locked her window, careful to keep out of view. Then she put on her bathrobe and ran from her room to check all the other windows in the house.

Amid the racket, Claven popped his head out of his bedroom door. "What are you doing, String Bean?"

"I just heard another rumble and wanted to make sure all the windows are closed," she improvised, teary eyed. "Go back to bed."

When she'd checked all the ones downstairs, she grabbed her burner phone from a drawer in the kitchen and huddled down against the corner cabinets. With shaking hands, she began to dial Dane's number. But then she thought of the possibility that it was exactly what Tosh hoped she'd do. Dane would come running, and Tosh and his police force would be waiting for him.

So she dialed Terrell instead. He answered with a sleepy voice. "Who dis?"

"It's Leslie."

He must have heard the panic in her voice because his words became clear as a bell. "What's the matter?"

"A man just broke into the house. He threatened me." The tears were flowing freely now, and Leslie covered her mouth for a moment in an attempt to collect herself. "You don't have to come over." *Please come over.* "I just need to tell someone other than Dane. Mayor Tosh would expect him to come."

"Hang tight, Sunshine. I'm on my way."

Chapter 16

It was the longest hour and fifteen minutes of Leslie's life. She watched for Terrell through a small slit in the curtains at the front window, hoping like hell that Dane wasn't with him when he got there. She knew she was breaking the rules by telling Terrell about the intruder, but she didn't care. The man had connections that may trump anything a medium-sized smoker with a ski mask could manage. When he finally pulled into the drive, she turned on the porch light and opened the door as he topped the steps. He wore a hood over his head and kept his hands in his pockets, hiding the color of his skin as well as his identity from anyone who may be spying on them from the shadows. She pulled him inside, softly closed the door, and launched herself into his arms.

"Whoa, there." He hugged her only briefly, then held her back at arm's length. "Dressed like that, I ain't sure who I'm more afraid of. You or Dane."

She looked down at her thin bathrobe and could feel the heat rush to her face. Her curves were a little too emphasized by the porch light coming through the door's window. "I'm sorry," she whispered, crossing her arms over her chest. "I was too scared to go back up to my room to change."

Anger darkened his coffee-brown eyes. Following her lead, he kept his voice at a whisper. "Why didn't you call the police?"

"Because Tosh owns the police! Besides, they're probably watching us right now, thinking you might be Dane." He was a bulky, muscular man, after all. "I'd be careful when you leave here."

They moved deeper into the living room but were too restless to sit. "He knows I'm here, by the way," Terrell said.

Leslie didn't have to ask whom he meant. "You told Dane?"

"This way he knows things are getting handled."

He was right. For once that day, she'd made a good decision by calling Terrell first. "I don't know what to do. Uncle C is upstairs fast asleep, and he has no clue what's going on."

"Then you should tell him. At least he'll know to be cautious."

The thought made her shudder again. "He's sort of outrageous. I'm afraid he'll raise hell in town about it."

"So, let him."

The ensuing silence was thick with a warning that she needed to sort out her priorities. "You're right," she groaned finally. "It's better that he knows."

Terrell smoothed a hand over her hair. "I brought some guys to watch your house for the rest of the night. You'll never know they're around, and neither will anyone who's lookin'."

"What kind of guys?"

"The kind with lots of fire power."

The picture that entered Leslie's head was a scary one at best. "You mean like…*gangsters*?"

"Don't worry, they're loyal to me." His gaze cooled and his shoulders stiffened beneath the fabric of his hoodie. "Guess I'll never shed that skin."

Leslie felt instantly better despite the reputation of her rescuer. "We'll work on that later. For now, I'm *really* liking your skin." She held his face in her hands. "And I'm even more grateful that you're Dane's friend."

His smile appeared. "I'm your friend, too, Sunshine." With the tension effectively drained, he reached out and chucked her under the chin. "Don't ever forget it."

****

"He's wearing a hoody," Devine said through the phone. "I couldn't get a look at his face before he went inside, but he's big and muscular. I doubt it's Chappell, though, the walk is different. And he's shorter."

Thurlow looked at the phone as if she'd just told him to go to hell. "Well, you need to knock on that door and find out."

"What I *need*, mayor, is a reason to knock. Until I find one, I think I'll stay put."

"Devine, I order you—"

But the line had been disconnected. With shaking hands, Thurlow carefully placed his one remaining phone on his desk, determined not to throw it too. Earlier, when he'd called Menendez back to discuss a plan in a more calm and collective manner, the man had not only laughed in his face, he'd flat-out refused to get involved. He must have thought it through, though, because he'd texted a few hours later that there had been a home invasion at the old Chappell residence.

Yet no break-in had been reported—obviously because Leslie had called Dane instead of the police.

Brilliant.

Now, if there was the slightest chance that Devine would prove herself useful, she'd catch Chappell in the act of coming to Ms. Downing's rescue.

"I've got you this time, you rat bastard," Thurlow murmured under his breath. Then he downed the liquor in his glass…and waited.

****

The next morning, Leslie awoke to an uncharacteristic amount of sunshine streaming through the windows. Barely with it, she made a blind search for her phone to check the time and found that it was almost nine o'clock. A variety of sounds from the kitchen below alerted her to the fact that Uncle Claven was up and probably curious as to why she'd slept in four hours later than normal. The reasons invaded her thoughts with the ferocity of a Viking army, making her eyes pop open for the millionth time since her terrifying experience the previous night.

She retrieved her burner phone from beneath her pillow where she'd decided to keep it from now on when she slept. There were several text bubbles on the screen, one from Dane and one from Terrell. She checked Dane's first.

Dick—*Call me as soon as you wake up. We need to talk.*—

Boy, she could only guess what he wanted to talk about. Then she checked the one from Terrell.

Terrell—*A white sheriff chick pulled me over on way out of town. All is good.*—

It was followed by a thumb's-up emoticon that made her melt with relief. Leslie had already decided to go to the city that day, if for no other reason than to spend time with Dane outside the mayor's radar. But it was Saturday, and she'd have to wait until the washer and dryer arrived.

She speed-dialed Dane's number. He answered right away. "It's almost nine o'clock," was his greeting. "I take it you were finally able to get some sleep?"

There was a hard edge to his voice she'd never heard before. Unsure of her mood, or his for that matter, Leslie threw off the top sheet and stretched. Since the windows would be closed at night from now on, she was splurging in a glorious combination of sunshine and air conditioning. "Hi, yourself."

"Or you're still mad and decided to make me sweat."

She blinked lazily at the ceiling. "I'm not mad. You were right."

"I wish I weren't." His voice held a mixture of anger and regret. "I want you to tell me everything you remember about this guy, starting with what he said to you."

She did, at least to the best of her knowledge. With the ski mask and hushed voice, there wasn't a lot to report as far as his description went, but she relished in the tale of her heel-to-nose maneuver and said the guy would at least have a bruised face. Aside from that, much of her experience was a blur, especially when her attacker began fondling her with that gun. Her focus had been effectively shifted, so terrified she was that he would fire a bullet straight through her belly. The pressure he'd applied there even left a round, sharp-edged bruise. "Anyway, I called Terrell and that was that," she finished. "He said Sheriff Devine pulled him over when he left, which means Tosh *was* watching for you."

A moment of silence ensued, then Leslie heard a muffled bang that sounded suspiciously like damage. "Fuck," Dane mumbled, his restless footsteps coming through the phone. "I'm going to have to fix that."

She closed her eyes. "Don't beat up the house."

"I can't help it. It's not safe there for you anymore. I want you to pack your things and leave Rosemont."

Somehow, she expected him to say that. "And just where do you want me to go?"

"Back to Omaha."

That one was a surprise. If he'd said Kansas City, Leslie would leave in a heartbeat. Put her and Uncle Claven up in a room somewhere for a week, or a month, or however long it took…as long as she was close to Dane. She swallowed hard and tried to keep the disappointment out of her tone. "I'm not leaving my uncle in the middle of all this."

"Then take him with you."

If she were a weaker person, maybe. But since Tosh had made this personal, Leslie just couldn't bring herself to do that. Suddenly she was glad Dane hadn't suggested she move closer to him, because to leave Rosemont at all would be a mistake. "I'm too involved now, Dane, and I'm going to stay right here until this war is over." If she were honest with herself, she'd known it the moment Tosh backed down her porch steps with a threat in his countenance. "You should have seen the look on his face yesterday when I told him about those papers," she continued with feeling. "Yes, I did a stupid thing, but you know what? Tosh got stupid, too. So I'm going to spend this day searching the property for any evidence I can find on that intruder, because you know he sent him to terrorize me."

She could feel Dane's anger escalate as she waited for his answer. "You're a damned fool, Leslie," he said finally. "I wish I'd never pulled you in. We'd both be better off for it."

Instead of heat, his words carried a chill that went right down her spine. She ignored it, as well as the hurt he'd just inflicted. "I'm sorry you feel that way."

He expelled a breath that sounded like too much regret. "Look...don't search the grounds. You aren't trained and might contaminate evidence. Call the sheriff's department and ask for deputy Forester. He's a good kid. He'll come out there and have a look around."

"Okay." A recommendation like that finally told Leslie who Dane's contact was. She tried one more time to test his mood. To figure out where he was going with all this. "I was planning to come and see you today."

"Don't. If you insist on staying, we'll need to cool it for a while."

And now she was officially embarrassed. Before the tears could come, she replied, "Then I guess I'll see you when I see you."

Without waiting for a reply, she hung up. At this point there was no need for him to hear her get messy. All relationships were crap. Then again, Dane had never really indicated they had one.

She wiped at the lone tear that broke loose and got out of bed. After slipping on a pair of shorts, bra, and an airy blouse, she descended the stairs in a mood, following the sounds of whatever was going on in the kitchen. On the way, she mentally prepared for how she would explain the recent break-in to Uncle Claven.

Keep it watered down, stay cool, tell him not to worry.

Not that any of it would ensure a predictable response from the old man.

"Don't tell me you've decided to cook some...thing." Her words died off as she got a good look at the rattler of pots and pans.

Kyle twisted around just long enough to send her a smile before resuming his search of the open refrigerator. Even in jeans and a muscle shirt—which showed a severe lack of muscle compared to Dane—he exuded the arrogance of a licensed busybody. "Morning. Got any butter?" he asked, as casually as if he belonged there.

The amount of confusion that slammed into her overshadowed any anger she would normally have felt at such an intrusion. "Kyle—what are you doing here?"

"Making something to eat. I'm starving."

Her gaze quickly swept the room. "Does Uncle C know you're here?"

The man shrugged. "Haven't seen him. The front door was unlocked, so I let myself in."

Claven was probably out then, having breakfast at the diner. Since she was emotionally exhausted from her conversation with Dane, Leslie decided she wasn't ready for another fight. Not yet anyway. But she *was* hungry, and Kyle happened to make a mean veggie omelet. She shoved him aside, opened a compartment on the door of the fridge, and handed him the butter. "Make two."

He must have expected more of an argument because he regarded her with suspicion. "You aren't going to kick me out?"

She headed to a cupboard and pulled out two plates. "I'll need some protein first. You know, to build the energy for it."

The comment earned her a laugh. In truth, she didn't want to be alone. The fear of her attacker coming back would remain until he was caught. Kyle was a turd, but until Uncle Claven made it home, she welcomed the distraction. "I take it you'll be writing that article about Rydell," she said, leaning a hip against the counter as she watched him work.

"Yes," he confirmed, watching her in return. "But I'm here to call a truce. I really do want us to work together on this."

A part of her was relieved that he was being so stubborn. This way she could guarantee the town some positive results *and* keep an eye on the direction of Kyle's coverage. "Nothing negative about Dane. He's been through enough."

Kyle chopped scallions, the rapid rotation of the knife slowing only for a moment. "Are you in love with him?"

Yes, she thought. *Maybe. Madly.* Frustrated with herself and her lack of scruples where Dane was concerned, she sent Kyle a bland look. "I'll agree to work with you as long as we never go there."

He gave her a nod. "Deal." But he was watching her as if he could sense her troubled thoughts on the subject. And was enjoying it. "I just care about you, Leslie. That's all."

Miffed, she pulled open a drawer and got out some silverware. "My heart can take whatever comes next. Can't be any worse than what you did to it."

"If it makes you feel better, I have a lot of regrets where our marriage is concerned."

Leslie doubted those regrets would make it past the next temptress to cross his path. She decided to ignore that last statement altogether, mainly because she was over it and over Kyle. "I wrote a piece for the Sunday paper," she said instead. "I'm going into town this morning to give it to Gene, but if Tosh paid him more money, he'll fight me again."

"I'll go with you. Keep him honest."

Gene would likely crap his pants if Kyle Downing were to step foot in his paper. The thought appealed to Leslie, and she couldn't help but share a rare smile with her ex-husband. "I'd like that. But you should know…"

When she hesitated, his smile turned inquisitive. "What?"

"Things have ramped up a bit since you were last here." She chewed her lower lip. "It could be dangerous."

His eyes sparkled. "How dangerous?"

Leave it to Kyle to become excited by the prospect. Her desire to tell him everything came at her with the ring of a familiar tune. "Someone broke into my room last night and threatened me." When the spatula stilled in his hands, she rushed on so that he wouldn't have to pretend to be worried about her. "I'm going to call the police and have someone search the grounds, but I'm pretty sure the mayor sent him."

As the smell of sautéed mushrooms and onions wafted around them, the sounds of cooking escalated when Kyle resumed his use of the spatula. "Doesn't he own the police, too?"

Said as if he weren't surprised. Of course, Kyle

was accustomed to threats since he had been getting them throughout the length of his career. Leslie somehow felt calmed by his lack of drama about the whole thing. "Dane has one of the deputies on his side. A Deputy Forester."

"No." He shook his head. "We can't take the risk that he'll cover something up. I'll look around after we eat."

"But you aren't a cop."

He sent her dry look over his shoulder. "Fifteen years of investigative reporting, remember? I can spot a toothpick in a woodpile from forty yards away."

She hadn't thought of that. He *had* made a name for himself with his uncanny ability to dig up evidence. "Okay, but you better be quick. When Uncle C gets home, I can't guarantee he'll let you stick around."

The big moment came a few minutes later when the front door opened and slammed shut, followed by the sounds of labored breathing. Since Leslie hadn't heard Claven's truck pull up, she carried her plate guiltily to the doorway of the kitchen and peered into the living room. There was Claven, panting on the area rug wearing nothing but his jogging shorts and athletic shoes.

Kyle was right behind her—until he saw the raw condition of the old man. "Oh, God," he groaned through a mouthful of omelet, and backed promptly away from the view.

A wide-eyed, sweaty Claven pointed at the spot Kyle had occupied only a second ago. "Tell me," he huffed, "I didn't just see…that moronic ex of yours…in my house."

Beneath the copious amounts of white chest hair,

Claven's normally pasty skin was beet-red. Concerned, Leslie set her half-eaten omelet down on the dining room table and went to him. "You don't look so good, Uncle C." She felt his forehead. "You're overheated. Sit down and I'll get you some water."

"Don't…ignore me, young lady."

She rushed into the kitchen where she found Kyle staring out the window, hands flat on the counter and his plate of food in the sink. "I'm never going to un-see that," he said in a trance-like state.

"Lose your appetite?" She grabbed a glass from the drain board and reached for the jug of water. "If you expect to spend time here, you'll need a stronger constitution than that."

****

By the time Leslie pulled up to the police station, it was approaching noon. A whole hour had been spent with Kyle searching the yard for evidence while Leslie consoled Claven inside the house. The old man was fit to be tied, but easily distracted with news of their overnight break-in. His priorities had quickly changed, and he even failed to hurl insults at Kyle when the man had come inside with a plastic baggie. Inside it was a white cigarette butt that he'd found at the edge of the woods.

Luckily the washer and dryer had come early, freeing up Leslie's afternoon to spend in town. Kyle had accompanied her, and with the baggie in hand, they exited the Camry and marched through the police station's front doors. At her request, and with the threat of camping there until she got what she came for, Sheriff Devine appeared. The woman had a natural hard look about her, but at that moment she appeared rougher than sandpaper...as if she hadn't slept for a while.

"What's the matter, sheriff?" Leslie asked with attitude. "Up too late last night?" When the woman didn't answer, she held up the baggie. "You probably already know this, but I had a break-in. Whoever did it left this at the edge of the woods, probably because he didn't think anyone would bother to look."

Absent of makeup, Devine's eyes were smaller, more puffy than usual. It made Leslie wonder if more was going on than a lack of sleep. Without offering any sort of reply, the woman moved to take the bag, but Leslie held it out of reach. "We're keeping the evidence, sheriff. This is just a courtesy call."

"Oh?" Devine's chest jumped with a humorless laugh. "How so?"

"Tell your mayor that the next guy he sends over to scare me better not be such a slob. Things like this have a way of coming back on the person responsible." She jerked her head toward Kyle. "Especially now that he's involved."

Devine looked Kyle over. "Not that I'm confirming or denying anything, but...who the hell are you?"

"Kyle Downing," he replied in an equally bland manner. "Lead publisher of the Nebraska Tribune."

When the woman only blinked at him, Leslie gave her a patient smile. "Ask Gene Dennison. He'll fill you in."

****

As soon as the two unwelcome visitors left the department, Thurlow backtracked into Devine's office. Eavesdropping had its reward, but in this case all he wanted to do was give in to the rage and trash the entire place. Devine found him there, in her office with hands on hips and fantasizing about where he'd start.

"Don't even think about it." She slammed the door behind her. "Most of this stuff holds historical value."

His reply started with a low growl that ended in a roar. "That. Fucking. *Cunt!*"

Clearly unafraid, she approached him. "Why? Because she's on to you or because she brought her high-profile pet?"

"She's challenging me." And after Menendez's visit, she should be cowering inside her house. "Since an intruder didn't flush Chappell out, we need to go a step further. Bring his bitch girlfriend in for something, keep her in a cell for a while."

The creak of wood floors followed the sheriff as she circled around her desk, watching him carefully. "Bring her in for what?"

"Figure it out, Devine," he snarled, "or you'll be finding yourself another job. And get that fucking cigarette butt from her!"

****

Leslie and Kyle's next stop was the newspaper office. It was a hole in the wall joint that shared space with the local real-estate agency. Not for the first time since she'd been in Rosemont, Leslie felt powerful, as if electricity sluiced through her veins. The more she thought about her conversation with the mayor, and then the resultant attack by a mask-wearing smoker, the more pissed off she got. Gone was the frightened child who'd called Terrell while huddled on the kitchen floor. Today she was a woman who refused to be screwed with.

As soon as they entered the newspaper's front

door, she was confident that her latest article would appear in Sunday's edition of the Independent. Gene Dennison took one look at her, then at Kyle. His shoulders slumped. "You didn't have to physically bring him, Ms. Downing."

With her chin up, she said, "I hope you didn't take anymore money, Mr. Dennison."

Gene barked out a laugh. "Haven't you read the papers lately? The truth is where the money's at now."

Kyle set his laptop case down on the nearest workspace that had room for one. "Then what do you say we get to work?" He met Gene's incredulous stare. "The public already suspects you took bribes from the mayor. If they see that you're working with a reputable news team, you'll earn your credibility back. As an outsider, Leslie has already brought a lot to the table. I can provide the extra helping."

Her chest bursting with a euphoric sense of pride and accomplishment, Leslie beamed at Gene. "What do you say, Mr. Dennison?"

It took less thought than she'd expected. Gene threw a hand in the air, indicating a cluttered tabletop. "There's a desk under there somewhere. If you can find it, it's yours."

Chapter 17

Dane paced his living room wearing the dangerous mood of a caged animal. He'd been a complete prick to Leslie during their last conversation, and knew he deserved whatever attitude she decided to throw at him. But he was fucking scared now, and it was all because he'd involved an innocent woman in his affairs, and then had the gall to fall in love with her. Well all bets were off now. He needed her out of Rosemont and away from Tosh, no matter how mad she was at him. This wasn't about her hurt feelings…this was about her safety.

He was tempted to send Terrell back over there to pack her up and force her out, but he didn't feel right asking the man to fall on that kind of sword for him. Terrell had risked enough as it was.

Caleb was at work. Otter was asleep. The place was too quiet, leaving him alone to unravel in a growing heap of dread. His phone dinged, and he went to it. Checked the screen. There was a text from his contact, Deputy Forester.

Forester—*She never called the department but was here with some bigtime reporter.*—

Dane—*What happened?*—

Forester—*They flaunted some evidence in Devine's face and threatened the mayor. Not good.*—

Shit, she was determined to self-destruct with or

without him. *What did the reporter look like?* Dane texted back, knowing the answer before it came.

Forester—*Tall and lanky, hair like Jackson Browne.*—

Dane had to hand it to him. Kyle Downing was one determined motherfucker, even going so low as to use his ex-wife to get what he wanted. And now that Leslie was pissed at Dane, she was easy prey.

This was worse than he thought. Bringing a hotshot reporter into the mix would only make Tosh more desperate, like a cornered dog on steroids. And Kyle's arrogance could quite possibly get them both killed.

"Screw this." Dane grabbed the keys to Otter's truck, ignoring the voices in his head that told him this next trip to Rosemont might be his very last.

****

At almost 6:00PM a coffee appeared beneath Leslie's nose. She looked up at Kyle and took the paper cup he handed her with a huge thank you in her eyes. "My hero."

Kyle rested a hip on the edge of her desk, sipped from his own cup. "This reminds me of old times, you know. When you and I would work late for a big headline."

Yes, she'd thought plenty about those times since their split, and the recollections usually ended with an emotional breakdown. But this time… She smiled at the pleasure of knowing her suffering was over. "The people of Rosemont won't know what hit them." She turned back to her laptop. "Especially when all the major Topeka *and* Kansas City news crews show up at Tosh's doorstep in the morning."

Kyle nearly choked on his coffee. "I don't think

232

I've ever seen you so determined."

She shrugged. "You always did like a good leaker."

And that's exactly what they'd been spending the afternoon doing, leaking a whole host of corroborated claims to the major news networks: shady facts about the secret vote, witnessed accounts of the mayor exchanging envelopes with someone in a Rydell truck, exclusive interviews with anonymous city council members who were switching sides... Everyone was willing to talk now, and the calls had been pouring into the newspaper office since word got out that Leslie and Kyle were there. Even the notary who claimed to have stamped Dane's missing conservation papers had come out of the woodwork. The list of evidence against Thurlow Tosh was growing, forming the quintessential picture of a smooth-talking politician who was bought and paid for by the major food industry. The only thing missing was evidence that he'd lied about Dane being his attacker the night he was assaulted.

But Leslie was determined to nail him on that, too. Somehow. Some way. "All we need is that sit-down with Dane," she muttered almost to herself, "but it's probably better to save that for later, after Tosh's credibility has been thoroughly pulverized."

Kyle sat down at his own little cleared space and turned his chair to face her. "I'm really impressed with what you've done here. The whole town has started fighting back because of you."

"No, they're fighting back because of Dane."

He seemed annoyed by her lack of enthusiasm over such high-handed praise. "How so?"

"They want their old sheriff back," she explained.

"They know they screwed up by trusting the wrong man."

"You mean they feel guilty."

"A lot of them, yes. Now that they've been properly informed, they want what he wants—for Rosemont to stay the small, self-sustained bedroom community it always has been."

Kyle let her work for a few minutes, but she was keenly aware of his interest. As she expected, the quiet ended when he turned back to her and said, "Look…when you come back to Omaha, I want you to work for me again. As a journalist this time." When she returned his announcement with a blank stare, he threw her another hook. "If you can prove you have the chops to be an investigative reporter…"

She continued to blink at him over the screen of her laptop. "We were married for six years, and you never considered so much as a raise."

He gave a lame shrug. "I didn't want to show favoritism in the workplace."

Leslie took a long, angry drink from her coffee cup. It was an incredible offer, one that any copy editor with no degree would be a fool to turn down. And it was the second time that day someone had mentioned her going back to Omaha.

Her cell phone chimed with a text. She checked the screen and saw that it was from Claven. "Uncle C is wondering why I'm not home yet," she said aloud.

"Doesn't he know what you're trying to accomplish here?" Kyle asked as he tapped away at the keys.

"Yes, but it's past dinner time."

The tapping stopped, and Leslie looked up to see

her ex frowning at her. "That's such a small-town answer," he said, his voice tight and his hard stare an open challenge for her to rediscover her true passions. "It's great what you're doing for these people, Leslie, but don't forget where you really belong. Or what you really want."

****

When she pulled up to the farmhouse, Leslie grabbed the bag of food she'd picked up from the diner and hurried inside. Claven sat in his new recliner, glaring at her with the remote in his hand. Besides the muted television and the one lamp beside him, the house was dark and spookily quiet. "It's about time," the old man barked. "Almost thought I'd have to call 911 to get your attention."

"Don't be ridiculous." She passed by him on her way to the table and kissed his cheek. "If you were that lonely, you could have stopped by the newspaper office."

He made a production of getting out of his new chair, which he'd claimed was too deep the moment it left the furniture truck. "You've been with the moron all afternoon," he grumbled as he took his place at the table and opened the foam container she'd set on his placemat.

"We've been working with Gene Dennison. In fact, Kyle is still with him." She went to the kitchen, turned on the light and retrieved two cold sodas. When she turned back, a bottle on the counter caught her eye. It was the unopened, top shelf whiskey Dane had left in the basement. Uncle Claven must have been down there today, since she also noticed that the boxes of dried food packets were no longer stacked beside the porch entrance.

When she made it back to the table, Claven was unwrapping his packet of plasticware, his eyes still full of censure. "Don't forget you have a boyfriend," he said.

In the face of his surly mood, Leslie's mood remained light. "What's happening is a *good* thing, Uncle C. You'll see when you get the newspaper tomorrow."

"Does Kyle want you back?"

"No." In truth, Leslie wasn't quite sure what the man wanted, but at the moment her own hunger took top priority. She swallowed her first bite of spaghetti with closed eyes. "Mmm. I didn't know how hungry I was."

Watching her, Claven failed to touch his food. "I think he does want you back, otherwise he wouldn't be sniffing around here."

She shook her head, holding up a finger while she swilled from her soda can. "He did offer me a job, though."

"I knew it," Claven grumbled. "And you want to go back to Omaha."

No, she didn't. She wanted Dane. *And* the job in Omaha… "Regardless of whether or not I want to go back, me being here was never a permanent arrangement," she reminded him.

"It could be." He stabbed his spaghetti with a fork and shoved in his first bite.

Oh, lord. Leslie never suspected he'd want full-time company since he'd always been such a lone ranger. "What about Della? You two may want to live together some day."

He barked out a laugh. "Not in our lifetime. She treats me like some kind of dirty secret."

Yes, Leslie could tell. And it made her sad. "I'm sorry, Uncle C. Maybe she'll come around."

"I don't mind," he mumbled through a mouthful of garlic toast. "The sex is more exciting that way."

Before the unwelcome image could invade her brain, Leslie closed her eyes and pictured a blank screen. "Though I didn't really need to know that," she said, expelling a deep breath, "I will admit to being extremely curious about your past relationship with her."

"When we were kids?" He gave a casual shrug. "Hell, we barely spoke to each other."

Leslie's mouth fell open. "But you keep saying you were old friends."

His face warmed with a look of fond remembrance. "I worked nights at Pete's Garage during my senior year. I saw her there a lot."

Pete's garage… Leslie put down her fork. "The same place we were at the other night? With the white Oldsmobile?" The old man grunted an affirmative. She remembered Dane's story about an unsolved mystery, and couldn't help but wonder… "I heard that her father's *car* was there a lot around that time, when he was on the FBI's radar."

His brows drew down. "Who told you that?"

"Dane did. He also said the car was thought to be used in some interstate shipment thefts. You wouldn't happen to know anything about that, would you?"

A slow, gravelly chuckle shook his chest, and his focus shifted as if he were travelling back to a better time.

"Uncle C." Gob smacked, Leslie shoved her spaghetti aside and leaned forward with arms crossed over the table. "Did you help Della take her father's car out at night?"

His focus snapped back with comical speed. "I have no idea what you're talking about."

He was lying, and Leslie thought she knew why. A grin split her face. "The statute of limitations on those thefts would have run out a long time ago. You're safe."

"She was the most cunning thief I ever saw." The words burst out of him with enough enthusiasm to put color in his cheeks. "I knew what she was doing, and I wanted a piece of it. I wanted a piece of *her*. She was exciting and careless and so full of life. But for days our association never went past a secret pass of the keys."

The blue of his eyes both sparkled and burned. "Until one night I decided to wait for her to get back. When she did, she was all energized and messy, like she'd just been Mach 2 with the windows down. She handed the keys back to me. Her eyes were wild. Our fingers touched. Next thing I knew we were screwing like monkeys in the back seat of that car."

So their defiling of the white Oldsmobile had been a walk down memory lane for them. Leslie did the math. Grimaced. "Wasn't she fourteen at the time?"

"Fifteen," Claven corrected, stabbing a finger into the air. "And as I recall, *I* was the only virgin between us."

Disbelief had Leslie laughing in her seat. "It all makes sense now."

"What does?"

"You knew her secret. When you came back to

town, she was afraid you would expose her."

He waved away the notion. "I wouldn't know. We still don't talk much."

The rascally look on his face told her she should know why, making Leslie laugh some more. "You are a mess."

"I came back because of her." He dug into his dinner, appearing ravenous of a sudden. He continued his story with his mouth mostly full. "When the FBI left town, Della decided not to push her luck and she quit the running business. As a thank you for helping her escape the police, she gave me her good luck charm."

"The dashboard hula girl?" Leslie asked.

He nodded. "God, I treasured that thing. With every bump, her little hips would wiggle and remind me of those nights I spent with Della."

To associate such a sexy figurine with the little old lady who drove the short bus was still quite a stretch for Leslie. Each to his own, she supposed.

Claven turned the fork in his hand, his gaze distant again. "When I saw her at the bus station, a part of me thought it was fate."

"Maybe it was."

He shook his head. "Nah, turns out she drives the Manhattan route during summer break."

But in Leslie's mind that still counted as one hell of a coincidence. Or maybe she was just too much of a romantic.

"This place is good for us, String Bean." Claven's gaze told her his thoughts had taken the same path. "You and I both found love, almost from the start."

Before she could let that soak in, a noise below them drew her attention. A thump, or a scrape, coming from the basement. Her heart skipped a beat at the thought of another intruder in their home.

Deputy Forester came to mind, but Leslie knew he only worked the day shift, and she didn't have his private number. Calling the police was out. She stood up. "I'm going to check something, Uncle C. I'll be right back."

"It's probably your boyfriend."

So he'd heard the same noise... "Dane wouldn't risk it, not with Tosh watching for him."

The old man harrumphed over his bite of spaghetti before it went in. "Not much of a risk when you're invisible."

Leslie frowned. "Invisible?"

"I'll check the basement," he said through his mouthful before scooting his chair back. "You stay here."

But she couldn't let him go alone. "We'll team up."

She went to her purse and retrieved the stun gun she'd bought during her last trip to the city. Moved the switch to the on position. Prepared to fry the piss out of whatever boogeyman they may run into, she followed her uncle into the kitchen. Instead of heading to the porch, though, he went to the pantry and flung open the door. "Hand me that flashlight," he said, pointing to one on top of the refrigerator. She did. He reached down and threw aside the section of carpet on the floor, revealing the trap door underneath. Leslie watched in fascination as he opened it and shined the flashlight down into the dark abyss of the basement. Dust particles greeted them, quiet and ghostly.

Leslie peered down into the hole, her heart beating furiously with expectation. "Who's down there?" she yelled.

"I'm telling you it's your boyfriend," Claven said with a roll of the eyes. "No one can get past the lock I installed on the outside door, which means the only way in is through the underground bunker."

Her gaze flew upward, and she studied his profile. "There is no bunker," she murmured, forgetting that Uncle Claven hadn't yet been told. So much for breaking the news gently.

"Of course there is."

"Uncle C, I'm really sorry, but…Dane told me they took it out years ago."

Humor shined in his eyes. "That's what everyone thinks."

A bad feeling washed down the length of her body. "He wouldn't have lied to me. Maybe at first, but not after—"

"Don't get all offended, String Bean, he probably thought you wouldn't be able to keep it a secret."

But she didn't think that was it. Not at all. Even after they'd made love, he'd sworn the bunker no longer existed.

Because she'd told him Claven would sell the land back to him if it didn't.

That bad feeling turned into a deep dread that nearly buckled her knees. Swallowing hard, she looked back down into the hole, and in the circle of light she noticed that the dirt had been trampled regularly since she'd last used the trap door herself. "Dane?" she called in a shaky voice. "Did you lie to me?"

Footsteps sounded, then stopped just short of the light. There was a moment of silence, one that seemed to stretch for hours.

"Yes."

It was Dane's voice that rose up from the darkness. And with that one simple answer, her world fell apart.

****

The entry to the secret bunker was still open. Dane didn't bother closing it this time as he watched Leslie's slender figure drop down onto the dirt. Yeah, he was busted alright. Knew it the moment he passed through the bunker and saw all the changes that had taken place since the last time he'd used it. He had to hand it to Claven Gallagher, the man was no dummy. That he'd managed to find the new location of the hatch proved as much.

Leslie went right to the lightbulb overhead and pulled the string. Dane blinked against the sudden assault to his pupils but wasn't too blinded to notice the stun gun in her hand. Though he was wary of it, he knew she had every right to use it on him. Judging by the thunder in her eyes, she was thinking the same thing.

Her chest heaving, she said, "Show me."

Claven had lowered himself down and was coming up behind her. The man's look told him to duck and cover, and Dane knew the crush of true guilt for the first time since his younger days. "Cabinet," he said. "I uncovered it the first night you caught me in the basement."

She looked in that direction and he could tell when it computed. The lower doors of the cabinet were flung wide, as well as the back panel, showing that the space behind it went way beyond the stone wall. "Sonofabitch," she said with a laugh that hurt his heart.

Not bothering to look any further, she turned and

headed back toward the ladder. Dane knew by the wooden set of her shoulders, and the defeatist tone in her voice, that he was in deeper shit than he imagined. A part of him thought it was better this way, would give her the push she needed to leave town. The other part of him wanted to sink to his knees and beg her forgiveness.

As he watched her tromp up the steps, Claven's head reared back. "I thought you wanted to see it," he yelled after her. "There's a whole tunnel to the woods and everything!"

The old man sounded disappointed that he wouldn't be showing off his new digs—and Dane knew his chances of buying the land back were gone forever. The sense of loss wasn't nearly as crushing, though, as watching Leslie walk away from him in a manner that felt so…permanent.

"Let's go, Chappell." Claven waved him toward the ladder. "Might as well come up and have a drink."

"I don't think I'll be welcome," was his answer. But dammit, he still needed to talk to Leslie.

"A shot of that whiskey I found down here will loosen her right up. In fact, I think we could all use one. Or four." Claven chuckled at his own joke, then put a hand on Dane's shoulder in a show of sober camaraderie. "I, for one, appreciate the secrecy, Chappell. Don't know if Leslie told you this, but that bunker is the reason I bought the place. We'll have to talk about your habit of breaking in, though."

Habit? Had Leslie told him every time he'd broken in before? "It won't happen again."

"Damn right it won't. Don't particularly like coming home to all those hanky-panky sounds you two were making the other night."

Well, hell. Really feeling the need for that drink, Dane headed for the ladder. "I'll be lucky if Leslie doesn't sick the police on me this time."

When the two of them were back up on the ground floor, they found her staring out the kitchen window. "If you came here just to convince me to leave," she said without turning around, "it'll be a wasted trip."

The hurt and anger in her voice made Dane want to dig his eardrums out with a spoon. But he was doing this for her own good, and he had to remain vigilant. Turn off the crippling desire to beg her forgiveness. "That's exactly why I came."

"I told you before, it's personal now. Tosh made it that way, and you just made it the exact opposite."

"Leslie, I—"

"You lied to me when you swore you wouldn't. That makes whatever we had about as impersonal as it gets."

"I was going to tell you—"

"And I may have believed your sincerity if you had." She whirled around, a vision of flaxen-haired, righteous fury. "But it's too late for that. I want you to go."

She was mad. He got it, which was why he needed to remain calm. "Not until we've had our talk."

"Because you always get your way," she fired back. "No matter who you have to use."

"Because you feel the need to arm yourself in your own home." That calm slipped away, desperation slipping through the cracks as his gaze fell on the stun gun that was still in her grip. "I can't just sit by and wonder when the next paid thug will come through your window, Leslie."

"You said we should cool it for a while." A bitter laugh escaped her throat. "You got your wish. Tosh will no longer have any reason to believe I'm helping you because I'm not. I'm helping Rosemont."

"You're taking too many risks," he replied through gritted teeth.

"So are you."

"The difference is if I get caught, I can handle the consequences. What I can't handle is you getting hurt."

"I'm in love with you, Dane."

The admission seemed to surprise them both. While Dane searched for the right words, she bit her bottom lip and looked down at the floor. "Knowing what I went through with Kyle," she continued in a measured tone, "you just hurt me worse than anything Tosh or his thugs could ever do."

She was right. He deserved whatever she threw at him. And by all that was holy, he loved her too, but his love wasn't what she needed right now.

"Did you tell him your moron ex-husband wants you back?" Claven threw out from his place at the table where he continued to fork in mouthfuls of spaghetti. The man appeared to be completely unfazed by the drama that was now unfolding—the breakup that Dane both feared and hoped for.

Leslie threw her weapon down on the counter and stalked toward the old man. "Stay out of this, Uncle C."

With a flagrant display of rebellion, Claven shot Dane another burning look. "Chappell, you better change your tactic, or she'll be leaving the both of us."

"She isn't going anywhere," came a voice from the direction of the living room. When everyone went still, the familiar shape of Sheriff Devine entered the scene, her service pistol drawn. "In fact, I'd stay real still if I were you."

Chapter 18

The front door was standing wide open now, allowing in the orange-yellow skies of late evening. Mayor Thurlow Tosh followed the sheriff inside. Leslie watched them with a mixture of fear and anger, wondering if Dane had managed to make it back down to the basement where his getaway was all but secured. "You can't enter this house without a warrant," she told them with a haughty tilt of her chin.

"We heard you yell out Chappell's name," said Mayor Tosh, "which gave us plenty of probable cause."

Looking ready for a fight, Claven rose from his chair. "What you heard was my niece and I arguing. So back on out through that door before I'm forced to call my lawyer."

"Too late, Gallagher," Devine said. "We heard him in here." Then she aimed her pistol in the direction of the kitchen and yelled, "You have one shot, Chappell. Come out now or we take your friends in, too."

"I'm telling you—"

"I'm coming out!"

With horror-filled eyes, Leslie looked back at the pantry door and watched Dane come slowly into view. His hands were raised. He was turning himself in, and as soon as Devine got her cuffs on him, it would be too late.

But Dane wasn't watching Devine, he was

watching her. Must have read her mind because he said to her, "Don't move or say another word."

Just then, several deputies entered the home and Devine inched a bit closer. "As soon as you reach the dining room, Chappell, I need you to turn around and put your hands behind your head."

Before he turned around, Dane's gaze bore a hole through Tosh, who stood there with hands on hips and a burning look of triumph in his eyes. "They had no idea I was here," Dane said. "You can leave them out of it."

"We heard otherwise," Tosh replied. "In fact, I believe Mr. Gallagher even invited you up for a drink."

Claven's face was turning beet red again. His voice shook with anger. "My niece and I were trying to enjoy our dinner. What reason could you possibly have for approaching my house to begin with?"

"Just a courtesy call. To warn you that Chappell was spotted in the area."

"That's bull crap."

A weird kind of smile appeared on Tosh's lips. "We'll be needing you to show us where this bunker is, Mr. Gallagher, since he's been using it to get in."

When Claven's complexion went from red to purple, Leslie could only imagine the napalm-style explosion that was surely melting his brain. Since it was clear that Devine and Tosh had been eavesdropping for quite some time, she silently reviewed every part of their conversation, from the moment she walked in the door to the moment Tosh did. And there were many damning bits and pieces that might earn her and Claven more trouble.

By the time the old man disappeared with one of the deputies, Devine had Dane cuffed and on his knees while Tosh and his goons roamed around the place. The mayor appeared from the kitchen with the elegant bottle of whiskey in his hand. He was in the process of reading the tag when a smile appeared on his face. "I think Mr. Gallagher was on to something." He aimed that smile at Dane. "I feel like celebrating myself."

Tosh cracked the seal and removed the cap. Then he raised the bottle in salute, his eyes full of malice in the face of Dane's quiet rage. "To the whippoorwills," he said before taking a long, deep swig.

"You crooked bastard," Leslie raged. "Enjoy it while you can because your day is coming."

"Leslie, be quiet," Dane warned her. "Don't make this for nothing."

His own voice was so full of malice she could only comply. He'd just confirmed he was turning himself in to avoid trouble for her and Claven. It gave her even more reason to be pissed at him. Why couldn't he have just stayed away?

Tosh took another drink, not even trying to contain his elation as he capped the bottle and slipped it into the pocket of his suit coat. "See you in court, Chappell." He then turned to Devine. "I believe we have enough to bring Ms. Downing and Mr. Gallagher in as well."

"Don't do it, Tosh," Dane warned.

"They just aided a known parolee in breaking the law," Tosh replied with his signature arrogance. "They'll have their one phone call, same as you."

"You said you wouldn't arrest them if I cooperated, which I did."

"The sheriff said that, not me. She has no authority to make deals with you. Now, I think I'll go down and see what this bunker is all about." With hands in pockets, he strolled into the kitchen as if he owned the place.

****

Thurlow watched from his car as the three detainees were escorted into the police station in front of a sidewalk full of locals. There were a few shouts to Leslie to stay strong, but most of the people's voices were directed toward Dane.

"Look, it's Dane Chappell!"

"We have your back, Sheriff Chappell!" someone yelled.

"Dane! Dane, it's me, Veronica!" A woman was waving with both arms. "Call me!"

Damned women, always throwing themselves at Chappell's feet. Even Peggy, his own goddamned wife. He'd bet Chappell had fucked half the women in Rosemont, on duty and off, whether they were married or not. Disgust washed through him as he opened his car door and got out. He would stop this now. Stand at the top of the steps and address the lookie-loos in an effort to take those stars right out of their eyes. Halfway there, a drop of sweat trickled down the side of his brow, and it was then he noticed his entire forehead was sweaty. As the sun disappeared over the top of the bluff, he stood at the glass doors of the police station and held his hands in the air, calling for silence. It took some doing, but he finally quieted the growing crowd long enough to clear his throat.

But the dry feeling there wouldn't go away. His heart began to flutter. Thurlow tried again, but the clearing turned into a cough. Then another. His chest felt constricted all the sudden, and he rubbed a hand over the pain there.

"Better hurry and say something, mayor!" someone shouted. "Or we'll think you're full of shit!"

He tried to speak, but his air was gone. The only thing that came out was a gasp for help. His mouth went bone dry. His eyes popped.

And then Thurlow Tosh collapsed to the concrete.

****

Dane sat in the hot seat while Devine processed him, nurturing the kind of anger and humiliation that would likely follow him to the grave. But for now, he could only focus on Leslie. She was watching him, too, from where she was told to stand in front of the camera. It flashed, advertising the creation of her very own mug shot. As he watched his worst nightmare unfold, Claven was brought forward for his turn. It was all bullshit. The only reason they'd been brought in was to teach Dane a lesson.

Then they heard a commotion outside. Someone shouted from the front doors for help, and Devine went running. Deputy Forester took over, ushering them all into the part of the building with the jail cells in it. He guided Dane into one cell, and Leslie and Claven into the adjacent cell. "We'll finish your processing when we get to the bottom of whatever's going on outside," he told the three of them.

The young officer was the only one still loyal to Dane, enough to risk his career in his efforts to help him. Forester had been his contact since before he got out of prison, and he could be grateful that no one had figured it out yet. "Thank you, Steve."

When they were alone in their respective jail cells, Dane sat down on the cot and dared a look at Leslie. She was in the process of sitting, too, and would not look at him. He felt like absolute shit, having put her in this position. "For what it's worth," he said, "I'm sorry."

The only response he got was from Claven, who groused, "Not your fault, Chappell. Damn dirty politician."

"Devine is just as bad," Leslie mumbled.

While Claven paced out his anger, he sent her a look that said otherwise. "I told you she's clean. Just a bit misdirected is all."

Leslie's head reared back. "You were serious about that?"

"The John Wayne socks, remember?" Claven pointed at Dane. "Play your cards right, Chappell, and she can be a valuable ally. That Tosh character, though… He'll find out what a rotten bitch Karma can be, I guarantee it."

"Mayor Tosh just collapsed," Deputy Forester yelled through the door. "EMTs are on the way, but it'll be a while before we come back for you."

The man was gone as fast as he'd come, leaving a gaping silence behind him.

Claven turned to his stunned audience of two. "See? Told you."

****

Thurlow slowly came around to the sound of beeping. He was alone in a hospital room, the windows outside showing the blackest of night. A nurse came in and fiddled with a machine by the bed, which stopped the beeping. Then she looked at him and gave him a cross between a frown and a look of chagrin.

"You had a heart attack, mayor," she said simply. "I'll go tell the doctor you're awake." Then she looked up at someone he could now feel standing slightly behind his left side. "Visiting hours will be over in five minutes."

It must be Peggy. When the nurse left, Thurlow made an effort to look her way, but his heart nearly stopped again when a masculine voice filled his ear. "You stupid bastard."

Menendez. And Thurlow was completely at his mercy. The machine started beeping again.

"Always fucking shit up." The words were spoken so closely that Tosh could feel the man's breath on his face. Cold and ruthless. "I should have made sure you were dead that night I beat you within an inch of your life."

No…that couldn't have been Menendez. Chappell was the only one who'd hated him enough to want him dead. "That wasn't you," he managed with a raspy breath, hoping beyond hope he hadn't been wrong all this time.

But now it all made terrifying sense. Menendez had a brutal side, as evidenced by Leslie's accounts of her break-in. Thurlow hadn't meant for her to get hurt. There were other ways to rattle a person.

"Oh, it was me." Menendez's low, guttural laugh sent chills down Thurlow's spine. "And I enjoyed every moment of it. The only reason I stopped when I did is because I'm not a killer. At least not yet, anyway."

"Please don't…"

"I swear, Tosh, if Rydell pulls out of this deal because of your dumb ass, I'll still expect what I'm owed. Whether I have to take it from you…or your wife."

As Thurlow hyperventilated beneath the sheets,

Menendez straightened and walked out of the hospital room. If only he could tell someone...but he couldn't. To do so would incriminate himself. The whole world would know that he'd conspired to not only break laws, but to send an innocent man down a path of further ruination.

And he'd be the one wearing prison orange instead of Dane Chappell.

The nurse came back in to fiddle with the machine again. "You need to try and rest, mayor. Your heart has been through quite an ordeal.

No shit, Nightingale. He opened his mouth to speak, but in his exhaustive state, he could only croak out a few words. "My...wife..."

"Sorry, mayor, but Peggy hasn't come around yet. We put a call in to her when you were brought here."

The bitch wouldn't even come to see him. How was that for appearances? "Call her...again."

"We have. Five times." When he simply stared at her, the nurse gave him a look that said she sympathized more with the wife than with him. "Maybe she's just really, *really* busy."

****

Evening stretched into night. No one else was brought in, so the jail was quiet save for the throaty sounds of Claven's snores. Dane lay on the cot with his hands behind his head, staring at the ceiling. Leslie had refused to talk to him, and he was feeling pretty damned disgusted with himself, so he focused on other things. Like what it would take to get them out of there. Forester had fed them, but he said the sheriff had left the building for the night. No one else would leave until morning. Dane was saving his one phone call until then, too.

Leslie had already made hers, he knew, but it was a mystery as to whom she'd called—until the chamber doors opened and in walked Kyle.

Dane guessed he had his answer.

Leslie got up and went to the bars. They spoke for a bit in hushed whispers, stuff that Dane couldn't hear. He suspected Kyle was getting them out of there, which was good. She needed to be rescued, something he was helpless to do. Still, it pissed him off that the ex-husband was the one coming to her aid this time.

Before he left, Kyle threw Dane a hard glance. "I hope you're happy with yourself, Chappell."

"Oh, quit your posturing, you big putz." Having woken up at the sound of the opening door, Claven got to his feet and went to the bars. "And don't bother busting me out. I'm fine right here."

It was officially made clear to all that Claven would never allow himself to be indebted to a putz. Dane liked him more every day.

When Kyle was gone, Leslie stayed at the bars with her forehead resting against them. Claven came up behind her and gave both her shoulders a pat. "Well, String Bean, at least we can spend some quality time together."

With those words, she promptly burst into tears. Dane got up and went to the wall of bars that separated their cells. He could take her silence, but he couldn't take her tears. "Leslie, I'll do everything in my power to make sure your record stays clean. You can count on that."

She looked up at him with bloodshot eyes, but they were filled with more than just pain. They were filled with hostile amusement. "Oh, Sheriff Chappell, that ship sailed a long time ago."

Claven nodded. "What is this, the third time you've been arrested?"

She threw her uncle a dirty look. "Second. And as I recall, the first time was because of you."

"Oh. Right."

She turned those fiery eyes to Dane and slowly approached him. He knew he was about to get it, and thank God. He not only deserved her wrath, he needed it.

"You lied to me," she ground out.

He nodded once. "Yes."

"And you did it to get your house back."

"At first, yes."

"You didn't think Uncle C knew where that bunker was, let alone that he'd find it."

"No one was ever supposed to have known about it. My grandpa was too paranoid."

"That's why I admired him so much," Claven broke in. "And you, for keeping it such a well-guarded secret." His gaze went sideways. "Until tonight, anyway."

"I suppose now you're going back home with Kyle?" Dane asked Leslie, trying very hard to keep his anger in check. He had no right to her anymore, did he?

She let out a bitter laugh and backed away from the bars. "Why not? You'd be getting your wish. And as I recall, you told me to take my uncle with me, which would just happen to free up that house of yours, wouldn't it?"

"It was for your protection, Leslie." The reminder came with as much calm as he could manage.

"Someone attacked you in the middle of the night."

"For all I know, *you* could have sent him."

Her snarling reply landed like a sock in the jaw. Dane had to remember to let a breath out. "I know you're hurting right now but think long and hard about what you just said."

She sat down and put her face in her hands, the picture of pure misery. "I don't know what to think anymore."

"That—" he paused for the sake of composure "—right there, is worse than facing prison again."

But he couldn't blame her, could he? Maybe he'd just wanted so badly for her to believe in him that she would throw all doubts to the wind.

Claven paced, clearly uncomfortable amid such a tumultuous, lover's spat. He rubbed at his neck. "I really need that drink right now."

The chamber door opened again, but this time Sheriff Devine walked through it. She was coming to release Leslie and Claven, and it was about goddamned time. Dane stood there and waited, really needing a drink himself. The thought conjured the image of Tosh cracking open *his* bottle of top shelf whiskey, and contaminating it with his filthy, serpentine lips.

If there is a God, that son-of-a-bitch will choke on it.

Dane actually felt an iota of guilt seep in when he remembered that Tosh really was in the hospital. But the guilt dissipated quickly. Why not let his thoughts run wild? He was already going to Hell.

There was a clanking of keys against metal. Dane turned around to see Devine unlocking *his* cell door. He glanced over at the two occupants of the one beside him. "I thought you'd be coming for them," he said, his voice cold toward the woman who used to serve under him. Now she was his jailor. "Isn't that why Kyle Downing was here?"

"Actually," Leslie replied, her chin lifting a notch, "with the existing political climate, he said it would be better if we stayed overnight."

"You're joking."

She cocked an eyebrow at Devine. "Doesn't look very good for you, does it, sheriff? Especially when those headlines come out tomorrow."

"They'll probably share some space with the one about the city's mayor being hospitalized," the woman snapped. "Show some tact, Downing."

The words rolled through Dane's head as Devine cuffed him and led him out of his cell. But when they reached the hallway, instead of heading back toward the processing room, they took a right toward his office. *Her* office, he had to remind himself.

As soon as he entered it, nostalgia hit him between the eyes. The space was exactly as he'd left it. The books. Old leather chairs. The plaques and framed pictures ranging from sepia, to black-and-white, to color. Even the smell was the same. He knew it wasn't out of any kind of respect for him, but for the department. To change it would be like changing Rosemont's one hundred sixty-year-old history, when the first sheriff had graced these halls.

While Devine closed the door, she ordered him to sit. He preferred to stand, so she circled around the desk and faced off with him, her hand in constant repose against the butt of her service pistol. "What did you do to him?" she asked.

"To whom?"

"You know damned well *whom*. The man you beat to hell two years ago just suffered a major heart attack."

So it was as bad as that, huh? "Am I not showing enough remorse for you, sheriff?"

"Cut the shit. His heart was strong as a horse, up until the moment he came face-to-face with you again."

His detective brain also found that similarly odd, and he just couldn't shake the image of Tosh drinking from that bottle of whiskey. "Maybe he really did choke on it," he said under his breath.

Or there was another, more logical explanation. But, no, it couldn't be. It was simple craziness to even go there. To turn good people into bad over the only prospect that made sense…

Then he remembered the evidence that Leslie said Kyle had found beside the house. "I want to see Kyle Downing," he said.

"You only get one visitor, Dane, and I hear your son is on the way."

As the rage built inside, he repeated through his teeth, "I want Kyle Downing. He's probably still two doors down at the newspaper. Are you going to get him for me, or not?"

Her nostrils flared. When she opened her mouth, he knew it would be to deny his request, so he made a grand effort to put some respect in his voice. "Please, Cicely."

She stared at him for an intense span of time, her square jaw clenched tight. Then she picked up the phone and pushed a button. "Steve, go get Kyle Downing and bring him to the station."

Moments later, the man was ushered through the

office door. At first his expression was cool with a hint of confusion. But when he saw Dane standing in the corner, his eyes sparked with anger. "What the hell is this?"

"Leslie told me you found a cigarette butt close to the house," Dane said.

"Yeah."

"I want to see it."

Kyle's nostrils flared. "It's in Leslie's purse."

Dane turned to Devine. "Is that here?"

The woman blew out an impatient breath and got back on the phone. "Bring Ms. Downing's purse to my office," she snapped.

When the leather bag arrived, Kyle went for it, but Sheriff Devine stopped him. "*I'll* be handling the evidence."

Kyle was discernibly angry, his neck growing redder by the minute. "I'll just bet you will." He looked at Dane. "Nice going, Chappell, you just put that evidence in the wrong hands."

"Enough from you," Devine snapped. She searched the purse and immediately pulled out the clear plastic baggie.

Dane jerked his chin at the bag. "What brand?"

She squinted. Held it under the light of the desk lamp. "Rebel."

He kept his emotions in check, unwilling to blow it now by losing his temper. He turned to Kyle. "You can go now."

"I want that back," the newspaper man said. "It belongs to Leslie. We were going to send it out for analysis."

But as a movie reel of memories played through his

head, Dane already knew who'd left the cigarette butt.

Reko Menendez.

The epiphany was enough to put him that much closer to the boiling point, so any more talk from Kyle as if he and Leslie were a "we" again would push him way past it. "You've done enough, Downing." And his hard stare warned the guy not to test his boundaries. "Now get the fuck out."

He didn't need to elaborate any further. Kyle seemed to know it was because he was a breath away from getting punched. Hard. His tight smile said he knew why. "I'm going to make sure she comes back home with me," he said, bold in the presence of the sheriff. "If anything, to get her away from you."

When he was gone, Dane closed the door behind him. He looked back at Devine. "If you want to know who put Tosh in the hospital, you'll need to retrieve that bottle of whiskey he took from Claven's kitchen."

Chapter 19

The minutes dragged on like hours. Leslie sat. Then she paced. Then she laid down and stared at the ceiling for a while, wondering what the hell was happening with Dane. He'd been gone too long, and she began to think they'd already shipped him off to the county lockup. Did that mean if she saw him again it would be behind a bulletproof partition at some random penitentiary? Wherever they decided to secret him away because of the fact he was a policeman?

The mayor's words came up out of the darkness of her mind. *When he goes back to prison, I'll have him castrated for fucking my wife.*

A shiver of fear sluiced down her spine. What were Dane's chances of surviving prison again without Terrell there to have his back? Fresh tears welled up in her eyes, causing the dingy jail to blur into a sea of despair. It was pretty clear to her that Tosh wouldn't stop at the violent removal of Dane's genitals. He would have him killed.

Never before had she wished for a man to die. Now she prayed that Thurlow Tosh would end up in the hospital morgue before morning. The epiphany was in such stark contrast to her normally gentle nature that it struck home just how much in love with Dane she really was. And when she'd told him that, it wasn't to hear it in return, but the fact he didn't reciprocate stung just the same.

If he had, though, would it have made a difference?

As she pondered the question in her head, more clanking echoed throughout the chamber. The metal door opened again and in walked Otter decked out in full uniform. Leslie wiped her tears away, rose from the cot and met him at the bars. Her uncle was close behind her. "Have you been able to see him yet?" she asked.

Otter shook his head, his countenance dark with sorrow. "He's in Sheriff Devine's office. Steve assured me they won't take him to county without me seeing him first, though." He rammed his palm into the bars, and an angry curse burst out of his mouth. "I can't believe he let himself get caught doing something so stupid."

"It's my fault," Leslie said, feeling his anger as if it were her own. "We argued this morning and he wanted to smooth things over."

"What did you argue about?"

"He told me to go back to Omaha, and to take my uncle with me. Now that I know he lied about the bunker, it just feels more like he wants his house back."

Otter directed his anger toward her. "Are you kidding me right now? He sacrificed his freedom for you. He won't be getting his house back."

Feeling miserable, she put some distance between them. "I don't know what to believe, Otter."

"Leslie, he contacted a real-estate agent yesterday. He's been looking at two-bedroom houses in Jackson County, and he even applied for a job at a local roofing company. Believe me, he wasn't planning on coming back here, at least not anytime soon."

But none of that made sense. "Why did he continue

to lie to me, then? He had plenty of opportunities to come clean."

Otter threw his hands up in the air. "Okay, he lied about the bunker. So what?"

"Excuse me?" she fired back.

"Really, Leslie, what does it matter when his latest plan was to quit this war with Tosh and settle down with you?"

Shocked, she could only gape at him. "Is that what he said?"

"Not in so many words." The young officer paced with his thumbs hooked over his utility belt. He was clearly disgusted by her lack of faith. "But I could see the change in him. I knew he was healing, and it was all because of you."

When the chamber doors opened again, Otter turned and watched his father being escorted back to his cell.

"Kid." Dane held his wrists up and allowed the cuffs to be removed, though he never broke Otter's gaze. "You shouldn't have left during your shift like that."

Otter blew air through his lips. "Because you wouldn't have?"

When Dane's expression softened, Leslie knew he would have. But there was something that remained hardened in his eyes, as if he'd just gotten some bad news. "What's wrong?" Leslie asked him.

He must have sensed that she was ready to listen now because he walked straight to her and stared intently into her eyes. "I know you don't want to hear this again," he said, "but I need for you to get out of here."

She brought her fingertips to her brow and kneaded the tension there. "I told you I'm not leaving town until this is over."

"I'm talking about your jail cell. You have to call Terrell and tell him I need one more favor." When she lifted her gaze, he gave her a tentative smile. "Would it be a waste of breath to ask you to trust me?"

"Why can't I just call him for you?" Otter asked.

Dane's answer came with a fair amount of chagrin. "Son, as long as you're wearing that badge, you'll want no part in this."

****

The clank of a deadbolt woke Dane out of a restless sleep. He opened his eyes and rose as a group of men walked toward his cell. His mind was tired, and his eyes were scratchy. A drunken Walt Jenkins had been brought in shortly after Leslie and Claven were released, and had kept him up all night with a loud and looped version of *Friends In Low Places*, only stopping when he passed out sometime after midnight. Dane had used the ensuing silence not to sleep, but to think. To prepare what he'd say to Devine when she got the toxicology reports back on that whiskey bottle.

A deputy he didn't recognize opened his cell door. Four men were ushered inside. While Walt snored in the cell beside his, Dane looked the men over. They were supposed to be detainees, he assumed, but noted their lack of irons, their drilling eye contact, and more importantly the four pairs of steel-toed boots that were just brought within proximity of his person.

And he knew exactly why they were there.

He got to his feet. Blinked the sleep from his eyes, for his other senses were now on high alert.

"You boys behave, now," said the deputy, though he was looking right at Dane. "Breakfast is in twenty minutes…if you'll still want it."

A direct threat from Tosh himself. The man must have been busy making arrangements before his collapse. As soon as the deputy was gone, the tension inside his cell heightened to a degree that made him say a silent prayer. Dane flexed his hands. Braced himself. The first guy came at him with a fist, which he ducked easily and countered with a gut punch. The man folded, but others came at him with their fists. Dane took some hits, but his main objectives were to level the biggest one first, to avoid the steel-toed boots, and to make sure no one got behind him. The hits were hard, but his were harder, and before long two of the men were cooled on the floor.

The body blows, the sounds of pain, the impact of flesh against iron bars must have woken Walt because he began to shout for help, sounding an alarm that was sure to be ignored. Dane was distracted just long enough to be kicked from behind, and his legs went out from under him. He crashed to the concrete floor, tried to roll out of the way but then two men were on him, holding him down. A fist to the crotch ended his fight, taking the breath right out of him.

The sound of a switchblade broke through the haze of agony. Then the voice of his attacker. "Courtesy of your friendly neighborhood mayor."

His jeans were being yanked at, and he knew what his fate was to be since Leslie had given him Tosh's message before leaving her jail cell. They were going for his genitals.

Somehow he was able to cut through the intense

pain and began to fight again, but the other two men had come off the floor and were piling on.

"Hold his legs!" one of them shouted.

Walt begged for them to stop before calling out again for someone to come and help. It was the desperation in his voice that got to Dane. With a roar, he fought. Kicked. Summoned the kind of high-octane adrenaline needed to open the gates of Hell, which would let the demon in to rain hate down on all who dared mess with him. He was back in prison, fighting his way through yet another round of do-or-die. And he would die before allowing any prisoner to best him, because to lose this round would only mean a fate far worse than death.

With renewed strength, he broke an arm free and drove it into a soft throat. Gurgles filled the air as his fist then went into a mouthful of teeth, and he could feel the give beneath his knuckles. Blood was gushing, his hands warm and slick with it. There was a rattle as the broken teeth were spit onto the concrete.

"Fuck this," raged the biggest man. "I'm just gonna gut him."

The knife's blade flashed above him, but before it could come down, a pop and sizzle filled the air. The man broke into a violent tremor, his mouth and eyes wide before he dropped the knife and fell to the floor.

Behind him was Sheriff Devine, the Taser in her hand still tethered to the electrodes that had been buried in the knife-wielder's back. "Move away, gentlemen," she said. "Unless you want me to bring out the kind of weapon that shoots bullets."

They were all tired, bleeding, and breathing hard. None of them had the capacity to get to their feet, so they either rolled or crawled to the far end of the cell. Their compliance signaled the end of an event that was supposed to have yielded a much different result. But Dane *was* able to rise to his feet, and with enough residual rage to instill fear into the eyes of his assailants. "You fucked up," he told them, his voice rumbly with unspent testosterone, "letting a man like Tosh put you behind these bars."

One of them spat blood on the floor. "Like he did you?"

A bitter laugh tore through Dane's lips as he yanked his zipper back up to full closure. "The difference between us is I can hold my own when it counts. You four, however, are one transport away from getting it in the ass every time you strip."

"Rein it in, Chappell." Devine had just finished pulling the electrodes out of her target's back and was standing with her hand on the butt of her service pistol. She looked a little frightened herself. "Take some breaths. Your breakfast is waiting in my office."

Back in handcuffs, he preceded her down the hall and through his old office door. Devine closed it behind him and told him to sit. The savory smell of sausage and pancakes wafted from a Cozy's takeout container on her desk. Beside it was an orange juice, coffee, and a packet with plasticware and condiments. Despite the bruised ribs and bloody mouth, his stomach had been effectively woken up, and it grumbled loudly.

Devine opened her drawer. Took out more napkins. She put them on top of his carton of food. "Unless you need medical attention, that's the best I have."

With a shake of his head, he dipped the napkins in his glass of water and cleaned the blood off his face and beard. Then he opened the pancakes and dug in as if he hadn't eaten in a week.

Devine watched him devour the food. "You looked and acted like a real convict back there, Dane."

"You expected me to pretend my way through prison?"

A smirk. "I guess not. It just makes me wonder if there's any lawman left in you."

"And how much is left in you?" he asked her with a fixed gaze.

Her smirk disappeared. "Enough to save your ass."

He resumed his shoveling in of food. "Won't your boss be pissed?"

She looked away long enough to appear uncomfortable. "I suppose I deserve that. But I thought you'd want to know there were lethal levels of potassium found in the bottle of whiskey Tosh took from the house."

As he ate pancakes, his mind wandered down the timeline of when the bottle had been delivered. It was a damned miracle—and a blessing—Otter hadn't taken it for himself.

"I know it was meant for you." Devine shifted her gaze so that it drilled right through him. "And since you're the one who figured it out, I'm assuming you have an idea who poisoned that bottle."

He took a drink from his coffee cup. "I'm guessing the same man who nearly beat Tosh to death."

"I just saw what you're capable of, Dane. You're still saying it wasn't you?"

He paused before taking another bite. "I think if you still believed it, I wouldn't be eating pancakes in your office."

The doubt was most prevalent in her now. "Let's just say the last few days have raised some questions." She stood up and went to the window. "I'll be the first to admit that Tosh has gone off the rails a bit. Done some things I didn't know he was capable of."

Dane's chewing slowed. "Like paying four guys to cut my dick off?"

Her body moved with a slight shudder. "Unless you can convince them to testify, you won't prove that."

"What else has Tosh done?" he asked, sensing the woman needed to get a load off her chest.

Devine peered at him over her shoulder. "I think he physically hurt Peggy. And I'm pretty sure he's the one who sent that intruder to threaten your girlfriend."

Once he got over the shock of hearing about Peggy, he could only wonder what had taken Devine this long to figure it all out. "And *I'm* the one going to county," he said with a sardonic shake of his head.

A small laugh. She looked away and ran a shaky hand over her mouth. "I never called county."

Dane put his fork down. "What?"

"Before he collapsed, Thurlow asked me to keep you here for a few days."

The look of fear on her face made him laugh, a harsh sound that lacked humor. "And you still can't figure that one out?"

"If there's a chance he's behind that attack just now," she replied, "I want no part of him."

"Sounds like a step in the right direction," Dane conceded.

"Peggy is so damned scared of him now, she's had me over for tea three times." She released a long, uncomfortable sigh. "I'm pretty sure she knows he and I…you know."

"Have been intimate?" Extra-marital affairs weren't illegal but could look bad in court. Enough that Dane was surprised to hear the confession. "I know she does. She was pissed enough to make him think she and I slept together."

Her brows rose as she appeared to ponder that for a moment. "That explains why he wanted to cut your dick off. *Did* you sleep together?"

"Peggy and I were only ever friends, growing up and otherwise. I wouldn't use her that way just to stick it to her husband." And since Caleb didn't need to be pulled into his shit, Dane left the poor kid's name out of it.

Devine scrubbed her face with her hands. "This is all screwing with my head."

"Welcome to my world," he said deadpan before shoving the last bite into his mouth. God, he'd missed those pancakes.

Now that he was done eating, Devine sat back down and squared off with him. "Tell me who you think poisoned that bottle."

He considered his options while staring at the lukewarm coffee in his hand. "I'd rather not."

"Why?"

"Because I think he has something invaluable to me." Reko's advice about leverage meant he probably had some of his own. "If you arrest him, I'll never see it."

"What are you proposing I do?"

"Let me go," he said.

His suggestion was met with a stretch of stoic

silence. "You know I can't do that."

"Sheriff, if I have a shot at proving my innocence, I'm not above busting out of here." Dane leaned back and laced his fingers over his belly. "In fact, I know this place so well I could have done it already."

"Then why haven't you?" she asked him.

"Professional courtesy."

The corner of her mouth lifted. "I won't arm you."

"I wouldn't expect you to."

With a deep sigh, she stood up. Took a key off her utility belt and placed it on the desk. "I have to pee."

While she rounded the desk and headed for the door, Dane stared at the key, surprised that it had been that easy.

She turned the knob behind him, but paused long enough to say, "Don't make me regret this, Dane."

As soon as the door was closed, Dane sprang into action. First, he took the cuffs off with the key Devine had left, then he grabbed a ball cap off a display shelf, one he'd earned in the 2015 Police-vs-Firemen cook-off. "*My* hat," he mumbled under his breath, justifying the theft. The black rain slicker he grabbed from the coat rack, however, would have to be added to his tab. It was a little tight but made to fit over many layers. It would do.

He slipped into the hall, which was quiet and empty. Once he made it to the rear supply closet, he locked himself inside. Looked back at the only emergency exit door with the old sensor mechanism on the top. He went for the magnetic hook that still held a clipboard to the side of a metal cabinet. Chucking the clipboard, he peeled the thin, bendable magnet away from the back of the hook and headed for the door. He then reached up and slipped it between the two sensors so that when the door was opened, the top one would think it was still closed. Holding his breath, Dane tried it out. Nothing but sunshine and silence greeted him…and he smiled.

It was a good thing the department had spent their padded budget on a couple of new squad cars rather than the much-needed security upgrades he'd campaigned for. He made his way across the parking lot, avoiding the old security cameras that he knew were still there. Then he was on the sidewalk, just an average guy wearing a black rain slicker at eight in the morning. Since it was already warm, it wouldn't be long before someone found his attire odd, and he wondered if it would be best to steal a car. He'd need one to get where he needed to go.

The growl of a diesel engine approached, growing louder behind him. Dane pulled his cap down and hunkered as he walked, but whomever the driver was slowed to a crawl. Paced him.

Well, hell.

He took a peek only to be bombarded by a wall of yellow and tinted windows. Incredulous, he stopped. So did the short bus. The doors opened with a swish, and there was Della Hathaway, sitting behind the wheel looking straight ahead with her hands at the ten-and-two.

Unable to believe his luck, Dane looked left. Then right. Then he boarded the bus, which was thankfully empty. It wouldn't normally be on the road on a Sunday morning, yet was the safest, most unassuming mode of transport he could have hoped for. He settled into the front bench seat, diagonal from the driver who closed the doors and continued on down the road. "How did you know?" he asked Della.

"Let's call it intuition," she replied in her prim manner. "Where to?"

Intuition his ass. Someone must have known he'd be needing a ride. He gave Della the location of a crossroads closest to Reko's property, somewhere she could drop him off and turn around without being noticed. He stayed quiet and watchful as they made their way through town, but as soon as they swung onto the highway, he was able to shed the black slicker and breathe.

As he studied Della's profile, he couldn't help but ask. "Did you almost hit Claven Gallagher with this thing last week?"

Her chin lifted a notch. "There was no 'almost' about it. I knew exactly what I was doing."

Dane could only stare for an incredulous moment. "So you admit it?"

"Are you going to cite me, Sheriff Chappell?" she asked with a touch of dry humor.

The woman knew how to make a point. Dane shook his head and touched the tender spot beside his left eye where one of those solid punches had landed. "Della, this is the second time you've saved my ass. Even if I could be your sheriff again, as far as I'm concerned, this conversation never happened."

"That's very kind. I can at least assure you there were no children on this bus when Mr. Gallagher so carelessly placed himself in my path."

It took some doing not to laugh. "Remind me to never piss you off."

Since Reko lived outside of Rosemont, they were

on the highway for fifteen minutes before turning off. Another few miles down the road, she stopped at the crossroads in question. "Are you sure you don't want me to wait?"

Maybe she should since there was no assurance that Terrell was able to come through, or that he'd even gotten his message.

Before descending the steps, he turned around. Hesitated. "Go back to Rosemont, Della."

She cocked a brow. "Are you sure?"

"If all goes according to plan, I'll have a ride. If not, it'll be a moot point."

Her eyes softened, and for the first time since knowing Della Hathaway, Dane thought he saw a hint of fondness in her countenance. "Then you better have planned well," she replied. "Because I have a feeling Rosemont will be needing their old sheriff back."

If all the stars in the universe aligned just right, perhaps it could happen. But Dane couldn't afford to hope. Just focus on the next few moments, one roadblock at a time. "Thanks again, Della." He went down the first step. Turned back. "And give Claven Gallagher a chance. Life is too short to waste on appearances."

Chapter 20

When Thurlow came to, he was surprised to see the light of day. Hear the voices. Taste the rancid saliva in his mouth. It was probably because every time he went to sleep, he never expected to wake up again. Menendez was out there, screwing with his mind in order to instill the worst kind of fear in him.

And Thurlow knew that when a man was after you, being stuck in a hospital was no better than being stuck in prison.

As soon as he opened his eyes, the muffled voices cleared. He was able to identify one of them as his wife's, who must have finally broken away from her busy teatime schedule to come and visit. He turned his head and saw Peggy standing by the doorway, talking to a doctor, and looking as if she'd been there all night in her rumpled sweater and low ponytail. Her face was tired, devoid of makeup. Tears were in her eyes, which she dabbed at while she spoke about chest pains and shortness of breath. Thurlow quickly realized she was describing his symptoms on the police station steps before he'd collapsed.

The doctor left. When she noticed him watching her, she gave him a wobbly smile and came to his side. Took his hand in her own. "You're awake. I'm so glad."

"Are you?" he croaked.

Her eyes softened, and in them he thought he saw the old Peggy—the one who'd worshiped him in college. "This experience has opened my eyes, Thurlow." She swiped a well-used tissue across her nose, the redness there a clear indication of true suffering. "I realized how much you mean to me."

A voice inside warned him about the last time she'd played the dutiful, loving wife. "Then what took you…so long to…get here?" he said between breaths.

She closed her eyes. Brought his hand up to her lips. "I went to church and did a lot of praying. I asked for guidance. I begged for mercy on your soul and on mine. And you know what?" Her voice had become a whisper. She opened her eyes and produced a teary smile. "He answered me, Thurlow. He showed me that it isn't too late for us, that our wedding vows are not to be treated like some disposable thing."

Wedding vows? Mercy? Was he still asleep and dreaming? "You aren't upset with me anymore?"

She kissed his hand again. "No, Thurlow. I've let go of the past. From this day forward, I will stand up for you, I'll stand with you, and I will honor and cherish you as long as we both shall live."

That would be good. If she was willing to let bygones be bygones, he would do his best to forgive her for sleeping with Chappell. Chappell, on the other hand, could rot in Hell. Sure, the man may have been innocent in his near-death beating, but he had become the worst of enemies over time. There would truly never be enough room in this world for them both.

At nine o'clock, Cecily walked into his hospital room. He'd already eaten breakfast, been up and down the hallway for a few laps, and had even showered, all with the help of his loving and dutiful wife. Peggy had only just now left to visit the cafeteria, and he was wary of their newfound peace being disrupted were she to come back and find that his lover had come calling. "Make it quick," he told the sheriff.

"I see you're feeling better." With hands on hips, Devine circled his bed. "It even looks like you could go home soon."

Yes, he was certainly ready to get out of there. Let Peggy take care of him instead of the hospital staff, who treated him like a leper. It seemed everyone had turned on him since the town hall meeting. "Give me an update on Chappell," he said. "You didn't send him to county, did you?"

"No."

"Good. I want a chance to *see* him in my jail before I send him back to prison."

Devine went to the end of the bed and leaned against the rail on those thick arms of hers. "Really, Thurlow?" She fixed him with a stale expression he couldn't quite assess. "Or were you expecting him to be assaulted by the four drifters I arrested this morning?"

Her delivery told him to proceed with caution. "Drifters? What are you talking about?"

"I caught them breaking open the change machines at the car wash. To my surprise, they never tried to run or resist arrest. They just let me and Deputy Miller bring them all in without so much as lawyering up."

"I take it by your line of questioning they assaulted Chappell." It took a monumental effort not to cackle with glee.

"They tried." She nodded before straightening and strutting toward the window with her thumbs hooked in her gun belt. "One had a switchblade that somehow made it through the metal detectors and the body search. They told Dane they were going to make him less of a man, but he didn't go down as easily as they'd hoped."

As long as he went down, Thurlow didn't give a damn how long it took. But he asked anyway, for appearances if nothing else. "What happened?"

"He fought them off long enough for me to get there and stop it."

A rush of angst popped Thurlow's bubble. Damned Miller. The young deputy was a recruit he'd brought in to pull off this deal. Devine had always been cooperative with him for the most part, but he always sensed there was a limit with her. Miller had no limits and was supposed to ensure there were no interruptions while Chappell received his punishment.

"I was forced to move Dane to a safer location," Devine went on. "And en route, he escaped."

The earth tilted so that Thurlow had to grip the bed sheets. "He *what?*"

She approached his bed again and made herself comfortable on the edge of it. "He escaped, Thurlow."

"That's impossible!"

"You're forgetting he served nineteen months in a maximum-security prison. He learned a thing or two, including how to defend himself against a mob."

"You almost sound as if *you're* defending him." But she wouldn't do that, not with the milestones they'd achieved together after running that motherfucker out of town.

"Now, now." She patted his hand before getting back to her feet. "You know I would only defend him if he were truly an innocent man." Her footsteps clopped along the vinyl flooring as she made her way toward the door. "By the way, you were poisoned by that bottle of whiskey you took from his house. Thought you'd want to know."

He really was going to have a heart attack. "Poisoned?"

"Yep." She stopped just before dropping out of sight. Gave him a dry smirk. "Next time you pay someone to lay a trap, try not to fall into it."

With that parting shot, she walked out of his room. "Devine!" he yelled. "Goddammit, get your ass back in here!"

Peggy came in with a sparkling water in hand. "What was that all about?"

She didn't look upset that Devine had just left his private hospital room. Maybe she really had let go of the past. "She was here to tell me I'd been poisoned," he said, his own voice sounding far off.

"What?" Peggy put the water on his bedside table, her eyes wide with shock. "How?"

"By a bottle of whiskey I took from Chappell's house." Thurlow rubbed a hand over the day-old stubble covering his jaw. "First he tried to kill me with his fists and now with poison."

He was referring to Menendez, though he found no fault in letting Peggy believe he was talking about Dane Chappell. And he'd continue to let everyone believe it. Perhaps this was a blessing in disguise, a way to pin Chappell with the longer sentence he deserved. Thurlow's mind began to work, conjuring ways to make it look like the man had manipulated him into drinking from a bottle he'd poisoned...

****

Amid the climbing heat of the late morning sun, Dane walked up to the edge of Reko's property and headed toward the water meter. The grass was disturbed there, some of it loose and piled over a mound of fresh dirt. He dug at it, and about three inches down found a metal lock box. There was no need for a key since the box was unlocked. Inside was a fully loaded Glock 22 with three extra magazines, a prepaid cellphone, a bundle of cash, and keys to a car that was waiting for him in an undisclosed location.

Thank you, Sugar Free.

He stuffed the magazines in his socks, the phone in his pocket, and the firearm in the back of his waistband before moving on to the house. Since it was Sunday, there was a good chance Reko was home, and hopefully still living single. Just in case, the plan was to draw him outside and away from the house for this particular heart-to-heart. He opened the cellphone. Dialed a number.

"Hello?"

It was Reko. He was home, meaning half this battle was already over. Dane spoke in a higher, more nasally pitch. "Yeah, uh, this is Mark from the Clearwater County water department. I'm at your meter here, and the readings indicate you got a possible leak. I was wondering if someone can come out and help me look for puddles."

A disgruntled sound was heard. "Okay. I'll be right out."

"Thank you."

Two minutes later, the garage door opened. A huge German shepherd came bounding out from beneath it, soon followed by a man holding a soda can in one hand and a cigarette in the other.

Reko wore swim trunks and a muscle shirt. Not a big man, but he was plenty fit as well as a martial arts aficionado—good enough that Dane would be avoiding another fight if he could help it, especially since his face and ribs hadn't stopped complaining about the last one.

Reko's black hair was thick on top and shaved on the sides. His big nose, pockmarked complexion, and weekend scruff went well with the steely eyes that could either bore a hole through a man or gleam with rascally humor. Women either loved or hated the guy, probably because he kicked off dates with a direct avowal to never marry. He at least never had kids, none that he or Dane knew of. In fact, Dane didn't know Reko well enough to make good assumptions, so the plan was to find out what he was capable of—and where he was the night Leslie was attacked.

Since he obviously wasn't with the water department, Dane knew his time in hiding was up. So, he just stood by the meter and waved his arms, inviting the man to take a good look and do as he would. The dog came barking. Seemed friendly enough as he sniffed then licked his hand, but Dane knew that one command from Reko would get his throat ripped out. He'd have to tread carefully, as unwilling as he was to shoot a dog in self-defense.

As Reko approached, the shepherd took off toward the back yard with his nose to the ground.

"Dane?" Reko's gait slowed. His eyes widened. "Holy shit, is that you?" He put his cigarette in his mouth, and they clasped hands.

"I know." Dane noticed above all else the bruise beneath Reko's right eye. Chances were it had come from Leslie, but he pushed his rage aside and put on a convincing smile. "I'm prettier than the last time you saw me."

"You look like horse shit, even with the beard." Reko gave an incredulous chuckle, his expression bright with welcome. "Come on, let's get away from the road." He looked over his shoulder before guiding him toward the side yard, a shifty sweep of his eyes that gave away his nerves. As they walked, he asked, "What happened to you? I heard you were in jail again."

"I sort of slipped out."

"Before or after that happened?" He pointed to the cuts and bruises.

"After. Tosh hired some men to rough me up." He indicated the man's shiner. "What's your story?"

"Sparring accident." Reko blew out a breath. "God, that Tosh is something else. Most crooked politician around. Don't know what Peggy ever saw in him."

Dane stopped in front of a brand-new shop that had been erected since he was there last—the time he was invited to stop by and talk about the conservation easement that would prevent Rydell from building on Dane's land. "New man cave?" he asked.

Reko smiled. "Come on, let's get out of the heat."

They entered thc lofty shop, which was loaded with high-end tool cabinets and a workspace for his taxidermy projects. Mostly fish and small game, and mostly critters that had been brought to him already dead. Dane also noted the sleek new fishing boat parked inside, the ceilings tall enough to accommodate the boat's standing shelter and high antennas. "Whoa.

Nice." He caught the beer that was thrown at him. Opened it with a spray of foam.

Reko opened his. "Yeah, she's alright."

"Looks like you've come into some money."

Squinting his eyes against the smoke, Reko took a drag and flicked ashes. "My uncle died. Left me a part of his estate."

Dane swallowed his first, cold, glorious mouthful of beer and exhaled loudly. "Nah." He met Reko's gaze with an air of amusement. "This has Mayor Tosh's stink all over it."

Damn. He hadn't meant to show that particular hand so soon, but Dane never was one to beat around the bush. He soaked in his friend's reaction. Noted the practiced look of confusion, the denial forming in Reko's brain. Before he could utter the words, though, Dane held up a hand. "Don't bother. I know he bought you."

All amusement vanished from the man's countenance and was quickly replaced by anger. "Why would I help that asshole?" he growled.

Dane shrugged. "I don't know. You tell me."

A sardonic laugh escaped. Reko took one more long pull, burning the last few centimeters of tobacco close to the filter. He blew the smoke out slowly. "Is that why you came to my house? To accuse me of selling out to him?"

"Oh, I think you did more than sell out. I think you're the one who beat him up. Helped him get rid of me. Lost those easement papers so Rydell could build on my land."

"You're fucking crazy." Anger radiated from Reko's stance, his voice, and the hard set of his shoulders. "I'm the one who made that easement possible in the first place."

Dane had never seen the man angry, but he also had a feeling there was a lot to Reko Menendez that he hadn't seen. Perhaps was about to, because he wouldn't back down or leave without getting what he came for. "Yes, the easement was your idea. And Tosh would see that as a good reason to make you switch sides."

Reko stamped out his cigarette, those steely eyes drilling right through him. "You have a lot of balls, man. After all I've done for you."

"What did you do for me that Tosh's money hasn't *undone?*"

"Fuck you!"

"Did you think you were doing me a favor by sending a poisoned bottle of whiskey to my house along with those copies of the signed papers? Did you think I'd be better off dead than in prison?" Dane had to laugh at that one. "Well…you were sort of right, anyway. I spent half my time behind bars wishing some rank con would end my misery. But I had too much of a reason to live. Besides my son, there was one other thing keeping my nose above water. Do you know what that was?"

Reko only glared.

Dane smiled. "Revenge."

"I never blamed you for beating Tosh," Reko snarled. "But I won't let you pin it on me. You'll need proof to do that."

When he'd made the connection, Dane knew this wouldn't be an easy task. Had prepared himself for the denials and the demand for proof. What he hadn't prepared for, though, was the hurt that was seeping into his very bones at that moment. Almost as if it was just hitting him how much he'd liked and trusted his so-called friend. Dane left the nearly full can of beer on one of the workshop benches, no longer in any mood to test his luck. He went over to the fishing boat. Inspected the dual outboard motors as if he gave a crap how much horsepower they yielded. "Did you even wonder what led me to your doorstep in the first place?" he finally asked.

"Yeah-yeah, you think the whiskey I gave you was poisoned," Reko replied. "Which is bullshit. Not only did I send that to you unopened, but I also planned to drink it with you."

"Then why didn't you take it when you stole the copies it came with?"

A juicy curse escaped. "I didn't do that, either!" Whatever he was going to add, he stopped himself. Took a breath. "Like I said, you're going to have to find some kind of proof before you point fingers at innocent people."

"I think it's pointed in the right direction. That's enough for me."

A dangerous calm settled over the man. "Well, I'll do you one more favor, Dane, which is more than a rotten friend like you deserves. I'll let you get a good head start before I call the police."

The threat was issued in a syrupy smooth voice that warned Dane to run. "I probably am headed back to prison, Reko," he said, barely containing his own wrath. "Because without your confession or Tosh's, I'll never be able to prove it was you who put the fists to him. And we both know he isn't about to incriminate himself. But I'm not leaving empty handed. I want that copy of my conservation easement."

"What makes you think I have one?"

"Your big advice about leverage. I do believe there is no love lost between you and Tosh, which tells me he has something on you. In turn, you would have armed yourself with whatever you could, and what better ammo than the means to stop Rydell?"

By now Reko was pacing, laughing, shaking his head. "Good luck finding it, man, because it doesn't exist."

And Dane was reaching the end of his rope. "I took your advice, Reko. I've come with some leverage of my own." He picked up the mashed cigarette butt from the ashtray. "You left one of these on Claven Gallagher's property when you broke into his house Friday night."

Some of the spark in Reko's eyes faded. "I'm not the only one who smokes those."

"You're right. But all I have to do is get Leslie Downing in front of you. She'll identify your shape. Your voice." He pointed. "Even that shiner she gave you." The more Dane spoke, the more pissed off he got. And he knew by the way Reko's breathing picked up that all of his assumptions had been dead on. "I'm the only one who knows, Reko. Just give me the papers along with your word that you'll stay away from her, and all of this will go away."

Reko's tough, ugly nose flared with anger. Dane could sense he wanted to say more, but instead he silently went to one of the tool chests, unlocked a drawer and slid it open. He unlocked another compartment. Took out an envelope and walked it over to Dane without getting too close.

Dane accepted the envelope. Tore at the flap.

Removed the documents inside. When they were unfolded, the sight of them almost brought tears to his eyes.

Because he wasn't holding the copies. He was holding the originals.

Dane folded them back up and stuffed them in the breast pocket of his bloodstained shirt. The desire to burn everything down around them both was prominent enough to make him take a few deep breaths. Yes, Reko would pay, not only for helping Tosh but for the fear he'd put in Leslie's eyes. But there was a time and place for everything, especially when it came to revenge.

"I'll need your word, Reko." He'd managed it with enough calm to keep things on a cool level. "You won't go near Leslie again."

"As long as you keep *your* word, I'll keep mine."

Clever answer. It rang with enough of a threat to convey how dangerous Reko Menendez had become. Some of the anger died and was replaced by a small shred of sympathy. "Tosh really did a number on you, didn't he?"

The man continued to stare silent and wide-eyed at the ground, just one iota away from losing his shit.

Dane took that as a good time to go. Headed for the door. "Looks like we'll always have that in common, at least."

Chapter 21

The doctors threatened to hold him for one more day, so a paranoid Thurlow had left against medical advice. They forced him to sign an AMA—a document that would absolve them of blame if he were to fall over dead. But they didn't know how easy it would be for Menendez or Chappell to kill him when he was tethered to an IV pole, did they? No, he was better off at home with all the security and the officers he planned to have posted inside and outside his home.

After a quick stop at Cozy's, Peggy got behind the wheel and handed him the plastic bag containing his first good meal in days. Once she got him settled in bed, he ate like a king while imbibing in two glasses of his favorite cranberry lemonade. After he popped some pills, he began to fall asleep in front of a soothing rerun of his favorite TV show. Before his eyes closed, his cellphone rang. Having been pulled out of the promise of a drug-induced coma, he answered the phone groggy. "Tosh."

"Guess who came to see me today?"

It was Menendez. Tosh was really starting to hate that last name, since he would much rather see the full-length version on a headstone. Too tired to be intimidated, Thurlow grunted, "The Virgin Mary."

"Nope. Dane Chappell."

That woke him up a bit. "How did you handle it?"

"I didn't incriminate you, if that's what you mean."

Thurlow let his head sink back down to the pillow. "Good."

"Yeah. That's real good, Tosh, because you have other problems."

"Look, I'm recovering from a major heart attack. Can we do this later?"

"Sure, sure. If you live that long. You see, Dane told me something interesting today. It was about a bottle of whiskey that you took from his house. The very same one I sent him with those papers."

"I didn't incriminate you either, Menendez, so don't worry about it." And this conversation was already getting old, especially when Thurlow just wanted to sleep. He decided to end the call, his thumb hovering over the red button when Menendez's distant reply came through the speaker.

"I'm not worried. But you should be."

Cursing himself, his slow thumbs, and his curiosity, Thurlow put the phone back to his ear. "Why is that?"

"It took me a while to figure out, but I finally remembered where that bottle originally came from."

Thurlow rubbed at his eyes. "Where, Menendez?"

"From you."

Disgust laced his voice. "Pardon me?"

"It was your gift to me for my cooperation. And as a big ole' 'fuck you' I re-gifted it to Dane along with a copy of those easement papers. Told him we'd drink it together next time I was over at his place."

"That's impossible," Thurlow sneered. "I wouldn't try to kill you. I *needed* you."

A low chuckle came over the line. "That, my

friend, is where this becomes your problem."

The man hung up, leaving him with more questions than answers. "I never sent Menendez a bottle of whiskey," he mumbled out loud to the blacked out phone in his hand.

"No, Thurlow," Peggy said from their bedroom doorway. "I did."

His gaze flew to hers and he could sense that the woman was eager to share some secrets. "You sent poisoned whiskey to the man we were trying to recruit?"

"The man *you* were trying to recruit," she reminded him with a spooky look of serenity on her face. "At least that's what everyone will remember."

"Peggy, I—"

"Because they will never know how truly incompetent you are." A small laugh chimed from her mouth. "They'll never know that you couldn't negotiate your way around a used car salesman let alone a giant like Rydell. You don't have the charisma or the balls."

"What are you saying? I made that deal happen."

"No, Darling, *I* made it happen. *I* met with the VIPs of Rydell when you failed to secure a deal. *I* convinced Reko to destroy the conservation papers Dane filed—something I very much regret doing."

"You? But why would Menendez—"

"Because Reko Menendez does what *I* say, not what you say." She approached the bed and sat down beside him, bent over real close so that her breath touched his lips. "And he does it because he loves me."

Horror of the worst sort flooded through him, fighting for space among the confusion. "Are you sleeping with him?"

Her lips curved with a soft smile. "Oh, we do a bit more than that."

"You two-faced bitch." It was a pitiful attempt at outrage without the energy behind it. "You've been cheating on me this whole time."

"Reko hates you almost as much as I do," she continued as if he hadn't spoken. "Especially when I told him about all those years you've been blackmailing me into remaining your wife. We both wanted you gone. But when he beat the life out of you that night, you actually thought it was Dane." She sat up, straightened her spine, and her pretty smile was replaced by a look of loathing. "You should have died. Instead you ruined a good man's life."

"But...I really thought Chappell was the one..."

"You were wrong. You're always wrong."

Menendez had always desired Peggy, made it no secret with his wanting looks and flirtatious manner. The man was even so bold once as to ask him how his wife was in bed. "If you love Reko so much, why did you try to poison him?"

"I never said I love him." She bit her lower lip. Cocked her head. "Just like I haven't loved you for a very, *very* long time."

Suddenly feeling like a rabbit trapped in a snare, Thurlow watched her reach over and grab his empty glass of tea. She looked at the wet glass, turning it in her hand.

"Reko is a fantastic lover, but he's too unpredictable. After he made Dane's conservation papers disappear, I couldn't allow him the time to change his mind. So I sent him a *special* bottle of his favorite whiskey. From you, of course, thanking him for his continued support. It was supposed to be a foolproof plan to kill two birds with one stone, because he would be dead, and you would be linked to his poisoning."

As her confession unraveled, Thurlow felt true dread seep into his bones. Menendez's latest warning hit home with frightening clarity as she tucked the glass in the pocket of her cardigan—a curious move that spelled nothing but trouble for him. "Peggy, no…"

"But I'll take my opportunities where I can get them. Like I did with Reverend McCabe."

Thurlow's heart was pounding now. "You said that was an accident."

She squinted her eyes as one would when pondering an answer. "I *may* have killed him on purpose."

Pounding and pounding.

"He thought he could use me, too," she continued. "Multiple times. He took the young, popular sixteen-year-old daughter of the wealthiest family in his congregation and forced her to perform sex acts on him. His death wasn't planned, though, more like an act of impulse. When I saw the ravine coming up, I unfastened his seatbelt and grabbed the wheel, steering his car straight into it. I guess I wasn't really thinking of my own safety at the time." She cocked her head as she stared off into space. "Men are cruel, aren't they? At least the ones I attract, anyway." She smiled down at him again. "I've decided I have no more use for them, unless of course it's on *my* terms. So don't fight it, Thurlow. I put another dose of potassium in your lemonade, enough to put you out soon."

"You can't do that," he gasped, struggling to catch

his breath.

"Why not? The doctors won't think a thing of it. Your heart was already weakened by your first dose, and you did leave the hospital against medical advice."

"No!" He tried to rise, but he was panicking now, and she was holding him down with that freakish look of serenity she'd mastered so well. "Don't do this Peggy," he begged. "Call Cecily. Tell her to bring the defibrillator from the department. I won't breathe a word, I promise!" His heart was beginning to flutter madly now, his chest and arms on fire until he lay there gasping.

"It's okay, Thurlow. Thanks to Dane I've learned what's good for my hometown. It will be a much better place without you or Rydell in it." She covered his mouth with hers, stealing the last of his breath with a long, slow kiss.

****

The news came one week after Mayor Thurlow Tosh's death. Rydell was pulling out of Rosemont, taking its promise of economic growth and development with it. New evidence had turned up that would halt construction of their access road and tie it up in court beyond what was financially acceptable. The evidence? A conservation easement that had been filed with Fish and Wildlife *before* the state had granted eminent domain to the county of Summit. Though Rydell had the resources to fight it, they also knew it was just easier to go somewhere else, especially in the face of the recent backlash from town locals. They had other offers to consider, ones from bigger towns that were struggling financially and were better equipped to handle the bump in population.

When Dane reached the bottom of the article, he folded the paper back up and set it neatly on the table. The sense of elation he expected to feel was notably absent, probably because of the anger and loss he'd been consumed with over the last nine days on the run.

Not that he'd done much running.

When the door to the garage opened, he leaned forward and laced his fingers over the tabletop. Peggy Tosh entered her kitchen while in the process of removing her hat. The moment she spied him, she gasped and stopped dead in her tracks. Though she failed to say anything, Dane could see the fear, the confusion, and even a spark of excitement in her pale blue eyes. "Peggy," he greeted, his gaze assessing her appearance. "Been a while."

"Dane." She swallowed hard, the movement visible beneath the high neck of her black dress. "I almost didn't recognize you."

"That's funny since according to you we slept together a couple weeks ago."

His blunt assessment made her flinch, but Dane felt no sympathy for the fragile-looking woman before him—at least not until he was able to get a more in-depth reading on her. "That particular stunt put innocent people in your husband's crosshairs."

There was a tremble in Peggy's hands when she placed her hat and purse on the table and sat down across from him. "It was a foolish thing to do."

The words were barely audible, the regret in them ringing with sincerity. Dane had a feeling she'd been weighing many of her actions since Thurlow's death. How many he wondered? "Aren't you going to ask me what I'm doing here?"

"No."

Because she already knew. Something told him Peggy Tosh knew a lot of things, and that beneath the mild façade lurked a shrewd, determined woman with a lot of regrets. Dane felt a dry laugh develop in his chest. "You don't even seem surprised to see me."

Her eyes came up, and she smiled a little. "Because you always were attuned with the people in your town. It was one of your most admirable qualities as sheriff.

"So how did I miss you?"

She shrugged. "I'm harmless."

His gaze held hers for a good long while. "Maybe. Maybe not."

Her smile faltering, she got up and headed for the kitchen. "Thurlow victimized a lot of people. I was even planning to leave him, and I won't deny that I was relieved when he died."

"Did you kill him?"

"Of course not. You know what happened."

"He drank from a tainted bottle of whiskey." What Dane hadn't been able to figure out until now was who had tainted it. "I'm willing to leave it at that if you tell me one thing."

She opened a cabinet and retrieved two glasses. "Not that I'm guilty of anything, but what would you like to know?"

He watched her open the fridge and remove a pitcher filled with pinkish liquid. "Why did I find an empty container of potassium chloride in your neighbor's trash bin?"

"My guess is because he's a veterinarian."

"Charlie doesn't practice out of his home."

"But he does make house calls." She filled the

glasses with ice then emptied the contents of the pitcher into them. They rattled as she walked them over to the table. Slid one in his direction.

He thanked her. "Cranberry lemonade?"

"Yes, how did you know?"

"It was your husband's favorite, right?"

"Yes, it was."

He raised the glass to his lips, and at the same time she took a sip from hers. Dane allowed a tiny bit into his mouth. Swished it over his tongue. "That is tart."

"Thurlow had a fetish for all things tart," she replied.

Dane almost laughed. Almost. "Then I'm sure it went down a lot smoother for him than it will for me." He pushed the glass away.

"You don't like it?"

"I'm sure it's fine, Peggy. I'm just not willing to test my theory."

"What theory?"

"That lemons and cranberries are strong enough to hide the taste of potassium."

Her gaze flickered to his glass. "I wouldn't know."

"What was your relationship with Reko Menendez?" he asked with the rapidity of a seasoned interrogator. Noted the deepening of her breaths.

"I didn't have one," she answered, maintaining her casual tone.

"That potassium-laced whiskey came from this house, Peggy. And Thurlow wouldn't have drunk from a bottle he'd potentially poisoned."

"What makes you think it came from this house?"

"I saw Reko's confusion when I accused him of trying to poison me. It was genuine enough for me to get curious, so I hung back and observed a little from the sidelines. First thing he did was make a phone call to your husband. It was a pretty telling phone call."

A fine sheen of sweat developed on her upper lip. "I don't know anything about that."

"How about Reko's suicide?" Dane sat back again, making himself comfortable and garnering some kind of satisfaction in knowing that his cop instincts weren't completely dead yet. "Did you know about that?"

"Suicide?" Peggy's gaze had dulled a bit.

"It happened a few days ago, right after Rydell announced they were pulling out."

"You sure are privy to a lot of things for a man on the run."

Dane was wondering when the threats would start dripping from her mouth. She'd held out longer than he predicted. "I've had a few reasons to stay close."

"And here you are, taking a hell of a chance that I won't turn you in."

"You won't."

She barked out a laugh before taking another long pull from her glass. "I always did admire your confidence, Dane."

"We both have secrets, Peggy, ones that neither of us can afford to get out. I admired you when we were kids. Always thought you were a good person, and I know firsthand what Thurlow's influence could do to good people. I just want to leave here knowing that his influence was buried with him."

With those words, the air between them changed. Dane meant what he said, knew that Peggy Tosh held her own special brand of influence over the people of Rosemont. All he wanted was a little peace for a change, and she was the key to making it happen.

Her pretty features relaxed, and her pale cheeks returned to their rosy hue. "Yes, his influence was buried with him. He may have left his mark, but I'll make it my life's mission to reverse the harm he's caused this town…and the people in it." She twirled her glass, ice clinking as she held his gaze. "Especially you, Dane."

As long as she reversed the harm within a timely manner, he was all for it. He was tired of running, but he would only turn himself in when those assault charges went away. Feeling good about their talk, Dane got to his feet and headed toward the door.

"Dane?" When he turned back, she said, "I didn't kill Reko. I've never touched a gun in my life. But I'm glad he's gone."

Dane was, too. He'd taken so many chances in order to hang back and keep an eye on the man for the few days he'd been alive. And he was inclined to believe Peggy, could tell by her tone that she was in a place of absolute honesty—also because she *didn't* deny killing Thurlow. When he was free, Dane planned to investigate the possibility further, whether it was as Rosemont's sheriff or as a free-lance PI kind of thing. A woman capable of murder was a woman to be feared. Not trusted.

Even if she did do a great service to mankind.

But if she didn't kill Reko, who did? The martial arts aficionado wasn't the type to commit suicide. Or was he? As his detective brain began the process of ticking through the possibilities, Dane stopped. Took a breath. The detective brain could be a huge pain in the ass sometimes, especially when it collided with instinct.

And his instinct told him—at least in this case—to let sleeping dogs lie.

Chapter 22

Two months later:

Leslie returned the sleeping infant to his mother's arms, a careful transfer that tugged at her heartstrings. He was three and a half weeks old, warm, cuddly, and so much the spitting image of Big Trouble that there was absolutely no doubt who had sired him.

Maxi rolled her new son over her shoulder in the way of a seasoned mother. She smiled. "He won't break, you know."

They stood in the Dillard family's driveway, Leslie having been loathe to give up the little bundle until she absolutely had to. "Give me enough time and I'll find a way."

Now that her hands were free, she quickly reached for her door handle to tamp down the maternal urges that were settling over her psyche. She swung the door of her Camry wide, waved to Trouble Junior who waved back from his solid perch atop Big Trouble's shoulders.

Definitely Otter's kid. Definitely Dane's grandson.

Definitely none of her business. Big Trouble obviously loved TJ like his own, and the four of them were as close to perfect as any family could be. Some things played out the way they did for a reason. Choices were made. Blessings were cultivated to their fullest potential, and in Leslie's book it was just another win for humanity.

As she drove away, she wondered if she would ever see Maxi and her beautiful family again. This brief visit had been jam-packed with feels, and she was slammed with the realization of just how much she'd missed her new friends. The picturesque town of Rosemont was now blanketed with colorful red, orange, and gold leaves, and she couldn't help but long for the sight of it covered with snow. But without Dane, it would never feel like home.

Weeks had gone by since she'd left, and only a few locals were still whining about Rydell's exodus. Most were relieved, though, having found peace with their small, quiet, bedroom community. It may not be much in the way of prosperity, but it was comfortable. Quiet.

And the air was simply remarkable. Having pulled into her uncle's driveway, Leslie got out of her car and breathed it in deep. She'd never get the same air quality in Omaha. The city was…well, a city. That meant smog, car exhaust, and thousands of people stuffed into every square mile. There were parts of it that she loved, too, and had been back long enough to call Omaha home again.

But there was something special about Rosemont that had burrowed under her skin. The people. The land. Movie night in the park.

And the sound of the whippoorwills on the hillside where she and Dane had first made love. From the day he disappeared till the day she finally left, she'd visited that hill often, wondering what he was doing. Where was he? When would he come back, if ever? Otter had been quiet, and he was her only link to Dane. He wouldn't say if he'd ever heard from his father since

Dane was officially a wanted fugitive. Otter was probably still pissed at her for the accusations she'd made against him, and after what he'd told her, Leslie was a little pissed at herself. Would she ever get the chance to tell Dane she'd forgiven him? That she loved him and believed in him and wanted nothing more than to hold him in her arms again?

If he was still on the run after all this time, probably not. If he was free and hadn't bothered to contact her…probably not. Every time she thought about it, she went for a bottle and corkscrew, so she took that journalism job Kyle offered her which was working out better than even *she* expected. She finally had her life back, even a new apartment that she shared with a pet turtle named Short Bus. He was the only pet she could have that didn't require a lot of care; a necessity due to the demands of her job. And since her memories weren't quite enough, Short Bus acted as her daily, physical link to Rosemont.

She supposed she'd left some of her things at Claven's house as an excuse to revisit. Her uncle was still mad at her for going back to Kyle even though she'd assured him theirs was strictly a professional relationship. Besides, Claven was so wrapped up in *his* relationship with Della that he never seemed to have time for even one phone call.

Not one.

With her heart in her throat, Leslie climbed the front porch steps of her uncle's house. Knocked. When there was no answer, she used her key. It still worked and she was thankful that he wasn't ticked off enough to change the locks on her. "Uncle C," she called out. "I'm here."

The place was eerily quiet. In fact, it still didn't look completely lived in. "Uncle C!" she called again.

The kitchen door creaked open. When she peeked her head in that way, Claven was reaching for a pair of dirty work gloves on the counter. He froze. They stared at each other for a moment, long enough to make Leslie wonder if he would kick her out. "I—I told you I'd be coming today to pick up the rest of my things."

He grinned then, a Claven grin that usually made the family nervous. "String Beeeeean," he crooned, then held his arms out to her.

Oh, thank God! Leslie went to him and hugged him tight. Was surprised at how much she'd missed him, so much in fact that she was beginning to tear up. "I thought you were mad at me."

"As long as you didn't bring the putz with you."

She laughed through her emotion, which was seriously beginning to get messy. She backed away, but not quite enough to let him go. "I told you Kyle and I aren't a couple. We only work together."

Claven reached behind him and plucked a tissue from the box on the counter. Handed it to her. "That's how it started the last time."

Last time she wasn't hopelessly in love with another man. "Give me a little credit, will you?" She followed him outside, wiping her eyes and nose. Why was she such a damned mess all the sudden? When she saw the old GMC in the back yard, its bed half full of boxes and tarps, she stopped. Frowned. "Isn't that all of your survival gear?"

"Yep."

"Why are you moving it out?"

"Because I sold the house."

Shocked, Leslie could only stare at him. "What? Why?"

Ammo cans were stacked by the basement door, waiting to be loaded. He retrieved a couple and handed them to her. "Now that God and everyone knows about the bunker, I don't want it anymore."

"So, you're letting it go, just like that?" The least he could do was wait until Otter or even Dane could buy it back. As she helped shove the cans into the bed of the truck, a spark of anger lit within her chest. Maybe Otter was right—her uncle never deserved to live there after all. He didn't love it like Dane did.

She looked up at the gabled roof, the whitewashed siding, and the old, drafty windows. Who was she kidding? He didn't love it like *she* did. "Where will you go?"

"Della and I bought a '67 Winnebago. We'll be going everywhere." Claven handed her a cardboard box and quirked his eyebrows. "She'll drive, of course."

She put the box on the tailgate and pushed it forward. "So you'll be living on the road?"

"She convinced me that the future isn't underground. It's straight ahead, going Mach 2 with the windows down."

Leslie rolled her eyes. "Oh, lordy."

"Besides, our rig is old enough to survive an EMP attack. If America shuts down, we'll be headed to NORAD."

She thought about that. "Do they let civilians into NORAD?"

"They'll let *me* in," he mumbled.

Though he'd said it under his breath, Leslie heard and stopped dead in her tracks. The man was crazy, always had been—the certifiable kind of crazy that families wished they could sweep under the rug. And the weeks Leslie had spent with him here in Rosemont, she'd been treated to more than a few of his eccentricities. But when she thought about it…he'd always been right.

Right about Della.

Right about the bunker.

Right about Sheriff Devine and her socks.

Before entering the basement, Leslie gave a tentative look up at the sky, hoping like hell he wasn't right about *everything.*

She sat down on the basement steps and watched him gather more things. "Uncle C…I wish you would have told me you were selling the house. I might have been interested in buying it."

"What for? You live in Omaha."

Her gaze assessed the now exposed entrance to a not-so-secret bunker. "I don't know, it's sort of…special to me, I guess."

"You did put a lot of work into it." Claven was scoping out a box full of brown packets. "Want some of these? Can't fit them all in the Winnebago." When she wrinkled her nose, he waved one in the air. "Beef stroganoff and a cookie."

"No thanks." Nothing of the dehydrated variety had ever appealed to Leslie. "And it isn't just the work I put into this place, Uncle C. I don't know, it—it wouldn't be right letting anyone else live here. They won't respect it like I do, or like…"

He set the box on top of two more just like it and paused. Looked at her with that rascally sparkle in his eye. "Like who?"

"I don't know, I—" Her shoulders became heavy with the effort to keep things positive. "I was hoping Otter would be able to buy it back some day."

"Why not Dane?"

Just the sound of his name made her heart hurt. She looked down at her hands, fighting yet another wave of sadness. They'd had such a short time together, yet they'd managed to stuff more emotion, more happiness, more fulfillment into those few days than she and Kyle had in nine years. And all she could do was wish for the chance to turn back time and part with Dane on better terms. Anything would have been more tolerable than leaving him in that jail cell with the impression she no longer wanted him. "You know why, Uncle C. He's on the run, and at this rate he'll never be coming back."

"That's funny." Claven's voice was laden with humor. "I thought he *was* back."

As the words settled into place, Leslie blinked up at him. "Huh?"

"He's going to move in as soon as I move out."

She slowly got to her feet, her heart beginning to tap dance inside her chest. Surely someone would have *told* her… "*Dane* bought this place back?"

With a chuckle, Claven moved toward the bunker's entrance. "Yep."

He disappeared for a moment. By the time he re-emerged with an armful of blankets, Leslie was ready to strangle him for leaving her with such a colossal hook. "How is that possible, Uncle C? Did he turn himself in?"

"He was set free last month."

Which could only mean one thing. A sense of pure joy put a smile on her face. "They found proof he didn't assault Thurlow Tosh?"

"Peggy Tosh found it, with the help of the sheriff." He glanced up at her. "Peggy is the interim mayor now, you know."

Yes, she did know that part. The town seemed agreeable with it, not that Leslie had much of an opinion. She'd never met the mayor's wife, just knew that the woman sucked at choosing husbands. The two of them had that in common at least.

Perhaps Peggy Tosh would make better choices as mayor, as it appeared she was already doing.

"Anyway," Claven continued, "turns out Tosh was assaulted by some guy he'd been conspiring with all along. A guy named Mendoza? Martinez? Something like that. Police couldn't arrest him, though, because he'd already blown his brains out by then."

"Oh, my God..." So much had happened in the short time she'd been away. "Why didn't anyone *tell* me?"

Claven rested an elbow on the stack of boxes beside him and peered at her through his glasses. "I thought Kyle told you. He was here asking questions."

Seriously? Why did that even surprise her? "That pig."

"I told you." Claven cackled and waved his finger at her. "He's a slick bastard, and he doesn't want to lose you to a guy he hates."

"He wrote a follow-up piece about Rydell, but he never mentioned Dane." Which was easy to do since Dane had opted to stay out of the headlines before. And, in true Kyle fashion, he'd left her name off the piece, too. Leslie was good with it. Knew that the glory had already been gleaned from Rydell-vs-Rosemont.

Any news to be had following Mayor Tosh's death was considered scraps from that point on.

But the possibility she could see Dane again rose above the top of all that, making her boosted career and life changes in Omaha seem very, very far away. "D—does that mean he's back in Rosemont?" she asked in a small voice.

"No, he still lives in the city." Claven cocked an eyebrow. "But he's here today."

"Today?" Her whole body was abuzz with nerves now. "Why?"

"Because I told him you were coming."

The nerves turned into a potent mixture of excitement and relief. Uncle Claven had officially become her favorite person in the whole, wide, crazy world. Well…second favorite. "Where is he?" It was all she could do to keep her composure.

"Don't know, but he said you'd know where to find him if you were of a mind to."

Leslie backed up the steps with a dumb smile on her face. "I'll, um…I'll be back in a little while, okay Uncle C?"

He winked at her. "Take your time, String Bean."

She got in her car and left skid marks on the asphalt. By the time she pulled up to the base of Whippoorwill Hill, her heart felt like it was exploding. She slammed the car door and ran up the grassy slope, refusing to give her mind time to come up with reasons to take it slow. But when she came around the side of the hill and into the open pasture where she and Dane had made love, there was no sign of him anywhere. As the doubts began to seep in, she turned into the chilled October wind, her skirt and hair billowing around her.

Could he have meant another place? Her old bedroom maybe? Was he in there wondering where she was or if she even wanted to see him? "Dane!" she shouted, the desperate sound of his name carrying over acres of grass.

Her eyes continued their frantic search until a movement to her left had her whirling around. Out of breath for so many reasons, Leslie could only stand there and stare at the most glorious sight she'd been treated to in months. He was coming toward her with a cowboy hat in his hands, wearing a denim jacket and boots. Even clean-shaven and with a new haircut, Dane Chappell was still the poster boy of rugged masculinity—so beautiful that Leslie couldn't move.

"Sorry, I was, uh…visiting some old relatives," he explained, his rich voice settling over her like a potent aphrodisiac. When he stopped in front of her, his gaze scoured her face with wary caution. "I was beginning to think you wouldn't come."

Her blood was racing, her lungs incapable of holding enough air to breathe. As she struggled to find the right words, she put a hand over her heart. "I came here every day after you left, Dane," she finally managed. "I was hoping you'd text or call or even sneak up behind me. I didn't care as long as I knew you were okay. But I didn't get squat, not a single peep from you." She pointed at him. "*You're* the one who's late. Not me."

His eyes gave away a brief flash of relief before they masked over with sorrow. "I couldn't risk contacting you until it was over. Hell, I wasn't sure you'd want me to."

"That didn't stop you before."

"I didn't know I was in love with you before."

Her chest expanded until she thought it would burst. The angst of the last few months drifted away with the chilly breeze. Though the world was quite literally lifting from her shoulders, her breathing had yet to slow. "Is it really over?" she asked him.

With a curious look on his face, he reached into his back pocket and pulled a plastic bag out of it. "I've been hanging on to this like you told me to."

Her gaze darted down to what he held. "Is that a cookie?"

"It's *our* cookie. I was saving it for the next time we saw each other. I'll eat it if you want me to, but…" he looked at the bag. Made a face. "I *really* don't want to."

Her smile broadened. "I don't blame you. I'm sure it's pretty gross by now."

His humor faded and his voice grew husky. "If it's all the same to you, I'd rather have it bronzed."

The heat in his eyes curled her toes. Unable to stand the distance a second longer, she drifted into his arms where he enveloped her in the most wonderful sense of strength, warmth and protection she'd ever known. He lifted her off the ground, and then she was being kissed so deeply that she forgot about their surroundings altogether.

"I love you, Leslie," he murmured against her lips, the declaration making this moment as perfect as it could be.

"I love you, too, Dane," she whispered back.

He lifted his head just enough to gaze intently into her eyes. "Then leave Omaha. Come back to Rosemont and spend the rest of your life with me."

Oh God, the tears were coming now. "I can't think of anything I'd rather do."

As if surprised, he searched her eyes. "You won't mind leaving your dream job?"

"I can freelance from anywhere."

"Oh, yeah?" A broad smile appeared, setting off a pair of dimples that only deepened the rugged planes of his face.

Leslie couldn't help but trace one of them with a fingertip. "I've built up a nice résumé since August. It starts with a compelling story about a big chicken plant, a crooked mayor, and a small, Kansas community that decided to stand up against both."

His smile broadened. "Sounds like the start of a pretty good outcome for that small, Kansas community."

"But there was one very important element missing." She ran her hands through his wavy hair. "The man who made it all possible. A man who wasn't afraid to take chances in order to stand up for his community, but who refused to give a single, stinking interview."

When her expression went flat, Dane chuckled. "If all goes well, you might be hearing more from him." He looked up and out over the horizon, toward the small spread of buildings and homes in the distance. "They want me to run for sheriff again. Devine won't be throwing her hat in this time."

If that were true, it would mean Leslie was getting everything she could possibly ever want. Through her joy, however, she wondered if it was what *Dane* truly wanted. "You weren't sure you could ever go back there."

Her reminder did little to change the aura of peace that now surrounded him. "I can do anything as long as you're with me."

Good answer. "Then it's already a done deal, Sheriff Chappell," she replied, her heart pounding with happiness against the beat of his own.

Smiling into each other's eyes, they kissed again, a long, deep, pairing of souls that never really grew apart.

No matter how great the distance.

A word about the author…

Jules Parker is a longtime lover of action movies, fast cars, and good books. She picked up her first romance novel at the age of 12 and has been crafting white-knuckle love stories ever since. Having published 10 novels under the name J.A. Dennam, she took a short break to focus on health and family, and is returning with a fresh set of ways to deliciously torture her characters. Her favorite thing is to immerse herself within the creative confines of her she-shack, though she is also known to ride motorcycles and cuddle chickens. Learn more at www.JulesParker.com.

www.ingramcontent.com/pod-product-compliance
Lightning Source LLC
Chambersburg PA
CBHW072103020726
47501CB00003B/697